THE ANGELS OF EVERNOW

BOOK FIVE - THE KINGDOMS OF EVERNOW

HEIDI CATHERINE

SEQUEL HOUSE

For Granny - I wish you could see this

BEFORE THE EVERNOW

The Queen stood on the highest balcony of her lighthouse, her mood mirroring the anger of the sea below.

"Where's my treasure?" she called into the wind as it whipped at her hair, tangling the long strands into her eyes and mouth. She clawed them away with her jewel-encrusted fingernails.

The King was taking too long. He normally visited her far earlier than this. And it was a special day, too. He'd promised her a treasure. Her greatest treasure yet. Taken from deep in the mines and brought to her lighthouse for her to keep forever.

And now the sun was almost at its highest point in the sky and still, there was no sign of the King's boat. Sometimes he didn't visit her when the sea was too rough or if he was on a treasure hunt, but that excuse would be unacceptable today. She needed her treasure and each moment she waited was a moment too long. How dare he keep her waiting like this!

"You're a liar!" she called, gripping the railing with such force that her knuckles turned white. Perhaps he wasn't coming at all.

Letting go with one hand, she reached into her pocket and took out a large purple amethyst. It glowed now, just as it had when the King had first given it to her. Later, the stone had given her a vision of a daughter with her same red hair and fair skin. A daughter she was to name Angel. A daughter who'd be her greatest treasure of all.

The Queen had kept the amethyst with her always, waiting for the day her Angel would be born.

But there'd been no daughter. There'd been no sons either. Her belly had remained as void as her arms. This was when she'd moved to the lighthouse. If she couldn't have her daughter, then she didn't want anybody, her husband included.

Now, she was too old to carry a child, yet the amethyst continued to lie to her, just like the man who gave it to her and it glowed brighter than ever, her vision of a daughter the clearest she'd had yet. But what use was a daughter who lived in her head?

On the King's most recent visit, he'd told her he'd found her an Angel. He just needed to have her cleaned up so that she sparkled and shone like the treasure she was. Maybe that's what the stone had been trying to tell her?

But he must have lied. Otherwise, he'd be here by now. He wouldn't have left her hanging like this. He knew how long she'd already waited.

"You're a liar! Everyone lies!" The wind took her words and swept them out to sea. She imagined them twirling in the currents and plummeting into the cold water, being churned up by the waves.

"And you're the biggest liar of them all." She looked down at the amethyst, still clutched tightly in her fingers.

She held out her hand over the railing, deciding if she didn't see the King's boat by the time the sun began its descent, she was going to drop the amethyst into the sea. That would be one less liar to poison her with hope.

She waited. The wind blew. The waves crashed. The sun rose to the highest point in the sky. Her grip on the amethyst weakened.

"Where's my treasure?" she cried, but still a boat didn't appear. "I want my Angel."

The sun dipped a fraction and she threw back her arm and flung the amethyst into the air. It spun as it tumbled, catching the light and sending purple sparks through the air until the greedy ocean opened its jaws and swallowed her most prized treasure along with all her hope for a daughter.

"Noooo!" she screamed, regret piercing her in the gut like she'd been shot with a fire-burning arrow. She'd been foolish! Her treasure was gone and her fear of the water would keep her from ever finding it again.

She leaned over the railing and reached toward the sea as if she could summon her treasure back from the water. But it was gone.

She reached out further and her head spun with the grief of what she'd done. As the world whirled around her, it felt almost as if she'd crashed to the ground along with the amethyst itself.

Then it appeared. Not the crystal, but the King's boat, fighting the waves as the oarsmen struggled to keep pushing forward.

He was coming! She squinted as the boat got closer, clutching at her thumping heart to see a mane of red hair flying in the wind. There was a young girl seated next to the King. A girl who looked just like the Angel in her vision.

The amethyst hadn't lied to her after all. Nor had her husband.

She turned back to the lighthouse and ran for the stairs.

Her husband had brought her a daughter! Her greatest treasure of all.

Her Angel had arrived at last.

ANGEL

THE BEFORE

*A*ngel kicked her way through the freezing water, her lungs screaming for air.

She broke the surface, took in a deep breath and blinked away the saltiness of the water, looking up at the lighthouse looming above. It was old and dull from the outside, a necessity in these harsh conditions. But on the inside, it couldn't be more of a contrast. Every surface was covered in treasures of all colors and sizes. Moonstone and onyx and peridot and sunstone. Jade and quartz and agate and tiger eye. They lined the ceilings, the banisters, the walls, and the floor. They were embedded in the chairs, the tables, the beds, and the window frames. There were millions of treasures and Angel was certain she knew every single one of them. For that lighthouse had been her home for the past ten years. Although, home was a generous word, as really it was her prison.

The woman standing on the balcony waved to her—Mother, although that was also a generous word as really, she was her captor.

"Did you find it?" called Mother, the shrillness of her voice bouncing off the water, her red hair flying in all directions.

Angel shook her head, sending water droplets flying from her own red hair and back into the body of water from where they'd come. Everything returned to the ocean eventually. Even the lighthouse would get old one day and crumble into the sea, taking its treasures with it. She only hoped she'd live long enough to see it.

"Look again!" screeched Mother, holding her hair back from her face. "You have to find it!"

Angel tried to steady the shaking of her body as she took in a deep breath and plunged back under the water to look for what Mother called her lost treasure. It was so dark and she'd been scared the first few times she'd been forced to put her head under. But now she almost enjoyed it. It was quiet down there with only the fish for company. The fish didn't screech at her like Mother did.

Every day, no matter the weather, Angel was sent into the depths to search for a giant purple amethyst Mother had thrown from the balcony to punish it for lying to her. Only, it hadn't been lying at all. The daughter it promised had arrived only moments after the amethyst had sunk beneath the surface. Angel shuddered to remember that day. She wasn't sure what was worse—fossicking for treasures alongside the other children in the mines or living with the Queen pretending she was her daughter.

Angel pushed her way through the water, swimming down to the clump of rocks near the base of the lighthouse, even though she'd only just looked here. How did Mother expect her to find the amethyst after so many years? It would've been swept away in a current by now, not sitting there waiting for her to pick it up.

She knew all these rocks by feel and as she ran her hands over them now, it was like saying hello to old friends. Just as her breath was about to run out, she plunged her hand into a small space between two large rocks, half expecting a fish to bite her fingertips. But instead of an angry fish, she brushed over something smooth. Something that definitely didn't belong under the ocean. She'd never felt anything like this down here before and it wasn't just the texture of its surface. It was the way it sent tingles down her body from her fingertips to her toes.

Desperate to investigate, but even more desperate for air, she pushed off the rocks to head to the surface, gulped in a large lungful of air and went straight back down.

A warm wave rushed through her body as she made contact with the smooth surface once again. This couldn't possibly be the amethyst, could it? She was sure she'd looked in this very spot a hundred times before.

She pulled at the object, trying to dislodge it, but it was stuck tight, so instead, she ran her fingers over it. It was exactly the right size for the amethyst Mother had described.

With her fingers still on the smooth surface of the stone, she closed her eyes and the image of a man with golden hair filled her mind. He had a kind face, handsome and strong. He looked brave and smart...and lonely. There was something about him that made her certain he needed her as much as she needed him.

A sharp ache in her chest brought her back to reality. She wanted to stay down here, basking in the warmth of her golden-haired prince but her lungs wouldn't let her. She needed air, which meant she needed to push back up. If only she could take the amethyst with her. But maybe this was for the best. Nothing was hers in the lighthouse. Down here everything was hers. It was the only place Mother would never find it. Mother never left the light-house, let alone went into the water. She had a daughter to do that for her.

The amethyst may not have lied to Mother, but Angel was going to. Because there was no way Mother was getting her hands on her stone. She shouldn't have thrown it away if she wanted to keep it.

The treasure was Angel's now.

Breaking through the surface again, Angel gasped in a great gulp of air and coughed.

Mother was leaning over the railing, her eyes wide.

"Have you got it this time?" Her eagle eyes examined Angel for any evidence of having found her treasure.

"Didn't find it," called Angel, pulling herself onto the rocks, her wet clothing turning to ice in the blasting wind.

Mother went back inside, the door slamming in the wind behind her, echoing around their tiny island.

Angel grabbed for the blanket she'd left on the rocks and wrapped herself in it, trying to remember the spark of excitement she'd felt at finding the amethyst. But memories didn't keep you warm. Only real life did that.

One day, her golden haired prince was going to come for her and they were going to run far away from her fake home and her fake mother.

Because her memories may not keep her warm, but they were still important. Memories were what made her who she was. And this was how Angel knew she wasn't really Angel at all. She was Princess Lily of Forte Cadence, daughter of Queen Rose and Prince Jeremiah and no matter how many times Mother called her Angel, she was never—not ever—going to forget who she really was.

RAPHAEL

THE BEFORE

*R*aphael tied the blindfold around Grimm's face only a little more tightly than was necessary.

"Ouch!" Grimm stepped away and tripped over a stick on the forest floor. "Here, let me do it."

"I need to make sure you can't see," said Raphael, running a hand through his white blond hair. "Don't cheat."

"I'm not going to cheat!"

Raphael watched as Grimm removed the blindfold and re-tied it. They'd known each for almost two decades now. Not that Grimm looked anything like he did as a child. Back then, he'd been scrawny and scared. These days he was burly and brave. Although, his fascination with the apothecary Raphael was in charge of had never changed.

"Is this okay, Uncle Raphael?" Grimm grinned from beneath the blindfold.

"I've told you a million times I'm not your uncle." Raphael shook his head and broke into a smile.

Grimm was the nephew of his sister's husband, King Ari. It was a relationship that made Grimm royal, but it didn't make them related. The idea of him being his best friend's uncle was ludicrous.

"You're scowling at me, aren't you?" asked Grimm. "I can tell."

"I'm actually smiling."

"Told you I couldn't see a thing. Now, let's get this started. I'm hungry!"

Raphael reached into his pocket for a small bottle filled with what he hoped would be his most important elixir yet.

"Hold out your hands," he said.

Grimm did as he was told and Raphael tipped the elixir into Grimm's palms. Having done this before, Grimm knew what to do and rubbed his hands together as he drew in the scent.

"Doesn't smell any different to the last one," he said.

Raphael rolled his eyes. "That's because I tweaked it. I didn't reinvent the whole thing. Now, spin around twelve times."

"Twelve! Last time it was only ten."

"Stop complaining, Your Majesty," teased Raphael.

"Sorry, Uncle."

Grimm turned in a circle, counting as he went, his feet getting wobbly after the eighth turn. Raphael walked slowly around him in the opposite direction. It was important Grimm didn't know which direction the apothecary was located.

"Twelve." Grimm came to a stop and tried to steady himself as he drew in the scent on his hands again.

Raphael stood quietly behind him, waiting to see in which direction he'd set off.

Grimm sniffed at the air, turning his head from left to right, before taking off in exactly the right direction for the apothecary.

Raphael punched the air. It was working! Grimm had never been so certain of which direction to go before.

"Stop!" called Raphael, just as Grimm walked into a tree. "Sorry!"

"Would you just hold my arm, for goodness sake?" Grimm rubbed his forehead and cursed.

"But I don't want to accidentally lead you. I need to know you can find your way on your own."

"You'll be finding your way on your own in a moment." Grimm held out his arm and Raphael took hold of his elbow.

He needed Grimm's help with this. He'd just have to be careful not to influence his direction.

"Smell the elixir again," said Raphael.

"That love potion you make me had better be good." Grimm scowled and set off again, walking a little faster now that he had the reassurance of Raphael's hand.

"I never said I was going to make you a love potion. I've told you before that you can't force love. One day you'll find a woman able to put up with someone as annoying as you without any need for a magic potion." Raphael steered Grimm gently away from a tree, careful to set him back in the direction he'd been heading.

"That was my one condition if I helped you with this stupid homing elixir!" Grimm complained. "You can't back out."

Raphael sighed, not wanting to argue about this right now. Maybe he'd tinker with some kind of love potion for Grimm when he got back to the apothecary. It couldn't be too difficult. Just as long as it was one that enhanced genuine feelings of love and not one that manufactured feelings. Their kingdom had experienced enough damage at the hands of such an elixir before and it had nearly cost Raphael his life.

Grimm continued in the direction of the apothecary and with each step they took, Raphael felt his heart beat just that little bit faster. It was working!

But no sooner than he'd congratulated himself for perfecting the elixir, Grimm turned, then continued in the wrong direction. Damn it! Something still wasn't quite right.

"I've stuffed it up, haven't I?" asked Grimm.

"How did you know?"

"By the way you just huffed!" Grimm tore off his blindfold.

"I didn't huff."

"There was a definite huff. A distinct exhaling of air."

Raphael sighed again and caught himself.

"See! Like that," said Grimm.

"Okay, okay! I huffed. It doesn't matter, anyway. You did turn. What happened? Why did you turn? Can you explain it to me?"

"I'm not sure. I started out certain that I was going the right way, but then, I don't know, all of a sudden, I lost the scent. I doubted myself and made a turn I shouldn't have."

"You doubted yourself. Interesting...Maybe we need more bergamot."

"Let's get back to the apothecary," said Grimm. "That's enough today. I'm starving."

Raphael nodded. That was fair enough. Grimm was a good sport helping him out. The least he could do was let the poor guy eat.

"You can't save everyone, Raph." Grimm patted him on the back as they walked. "Don't look so disappointed."

"I know," he said, thinking of all the children who'd vanished right from under their parents' noses, including Princess Lily of Forte Cadence. Nobody was safe. "But I have to try something! Jazz is never going to let my poor nephews leave the palace for fear they'll disappear."

"Nobody's going to take those little horrors away from Jasmine," said Grimm, laughing. "They'd return them in five minutes flat. Especially Clary!"

"Leave Clary alone." Raphael laughed, although he knew Grimm loved those three boys as much as he did. They were spirited, that was all, mainly due to the fact their mother watched over them like a hawk. It wasn't natural to keep young boys so cooped up. They wanted to run in the fields and climb trees and throw rocks at each other. Their father, King Ari, wasn't much better, hovering around them—the brooding hen to Jasmine's hawk.

This was why the homing elixir was so important. He had to find a way to protect the children so the next child who was taken would be able to find their way home. Jasmine wanted him to invent one that would tell them where Princess Lily was, but that seemed impossible. She'd been gone for too long now. Besides, there was only one of her.

He needed to protect the many children within his reach, not chase after one missing girl. Just because she was a Princess, it didn't make her any more important than an ordinary child. Both their mothers would miss them equally.

"Food!" said Grimm, when the apothecary came into sight.

"This is why you could never be an Alchemist," said Raphael. "You'd eat all your ingredients before you could make a single elixir."

"Harsh!" Grimm laughed. "But probably true."

Surrounded by lush gardens bursting with colorful flowers and fruit, the apothecary was a stark contrast to the dark forest. Raphael was certain he could find his way back here from anywhere in the world, with or without an elixir. This garden was a part of him, just as he felt like he was part of it.

"You go on to the house." Raphael pointed to the small home he'd lived in all his life. "There's plenty of food in the kitchen. Come and find me in my workshop when you're done."

"You want anything?" Grimm quickened his pace. "You could look like me if only you ate a bit more."

Raphael shook his head, laughing, not at all keen to swap his lean frame with Grimm's rounded belly. "I'm fine, thanks."

The friends parted and Raphael went to the apothecary, smiling as he passed the women working in the garden. They smiled back, with genuine love in their eyes for their Alchemist.

That was how his life was. He was surrounded by love, yet he sometimes felt like the loneliest man in the kingdom. Because when he saw Jasmine with her King, he couldn't help but wish for the same kind of relationship for himself. Someone special he could love, who would love him in return. Not because he was her Alchemist, but because he was the one who set her heart alight.

Perhaps Grimm's love potion idea wasn't so foolish after all. At any rate, it might keep him quiet for a while.

He went to his workshop and studied his shelves, removing several small bottles and setting them down on his bench.

He picked up his favorite mixing dish and added a few drops of neroli, then some rose and ylang-ylang. Taking a sniff, he watched the oils mingle with each other on the dish. It wasn't quite right. He went and got some lavender, adding that to the mix, and on a whim, he reached to the back of his shelf for some oil of the lily flower, quietly thanking the missing princess for reminding him of this rarely used fragrance.

Taking a small spoon, he stirred the oil, breathing in the fragrance as he went. It was beautiful. One of his most delicate elixirs yet.

Closing his eyes, he leaned over the bench and drew in more of the scent.

Then it hit him. Not the scent but an image in his mind so clear it was impossible to ignore.

A girl with long red hair was calling to him. She was wearing a pale blue dress and sitting on the sandy floor of an ocean, the raging sea above her and a purple crystal glowed in her hands. Her hair was floating in all directions and desperation leeched out of her eyes. She was so sad, so beautiful, so... clear. And as vivid as she was to him, somehow, he knew he was just as vivid to her. Almost like she could see him, standing in his workshop staring into a dish.

She reached out to him and the dish dropped from his hands and clattered to the ground, spilling the elixir on the floor and filling his workshop with what was unmistakably the scent of a Princess who needed his help. Because there was no doubt in his mind that his vision had been one of Princess Lily, almost as if his earlier thoughts of her had somehow conjured her into his workshop.

He reminded himself of all the other children who needed his help and instead of believing in his heart that this was where his focus should be, for the first time a slither of doubt crept in.

"Lily," he said, aloud, testing her name on his lips. "Lily."

LILY

THE BEFORE

*L*ily brushed her hair, being careful the brush didn't catch on any of the numerous knots she'd acquired while diving under the ocean. She had the same long red hair as Mother, which was no doubt why Father had selected her to be their daughter.

But apart from their hair, she really didn't look even a bit like Mother. Mother was short and rail-thin. Lily was tall and lined with fine muscle from her swimming and chores. Mother had a long pointed nose and Lily's was…normal. Mother's eyes were the palest of blue—almost translucent. Lily's eyes were dark. Mother's skin was white like the foam on the ocean. Lily's skin had been kissed by the sun and glowed like the golden calcite stones set into the window frame in the kitchen. Once Mother's hair turned gray, there'd be no similarity between them left. And that was exactly what Lily hoped for.

"I want my treasure back," Mother whimpered.

"We'll find it one day." Lily removed another knot from her hair. "Would you like me to brush your hair? It might make you feel better."

"Don't touch me! You know I don't like to be touched." Mother's voice turned hard. Her moods switched more frequently than the tides of the ocean and with far less warning.

"I'm sorry, Mother." Lily continued to brush her own hair, hoping the tide would drag them into less treacherous waters.

"I'm ready for my bedtime story now, Angel."

Lily returned the brush to its place on Mother's curved dressing table, remembering a time when her real mother had told her stories as she'd fallen asleep. If she ever managed to get back to her, she was certain her mother wouldn't ask Lily to make up any stories. Her fake mother didn't seem to know if she wanted to be the mother or the child and oscillated between the two roles with as much ease as her moods.

Mother lay down on top of her circular bed, which had been shaped to fit snugly into the curved wall of the lighthouse. Most of the furniture was the same, having been custom-built for a Queen who refused to live anywhere else. The room itself was decorated mainly in blue quartz to calm Mother's nerves, although the color gave off a rather cool effect. Lily preferred the red jasper stones that lined the walls of her own bedchamber.

She went to the window and closed the shutters, then sat down on the quartz-lined chair next to the bed, deciding which story she'd tell Mother tonight. Sometimes she made up her stories and other times she recited the stories her mother had told her as a child. Her mother's favorite was the story of a girl with long hair locked in a tower, a story that Lily could certainly relate to, but her own favorite was the story of another girl who was desperate to escape.

"Once upon a time, there was a beautiful girl named Ella. She lived with her mother and father in a faraway kingdom..." Lily paused, pushing away thoughts of the time she'd also lived like this.

"Go on, Angel." Mother's eyes were wide and eager to hear a story she knew by heart.

"But sadly, one day Ella's mother died and her father remarried a young widow. They lived happily together until the day Ella's father also died and she was left in the care of her stepmother."

"I like this bit." Mother's eyes twinkled.

"Almost immediately, the stepmother started bossing Ella around and making her do the chores in the house, all the time complaining and moaning about how she was doing them wrong."

Lily paused and looked at Mother as she always did in this part of the story, wondering if maybe she'd recognize herself in this sad tale. She never lifted a finger in this lighthouse, making Lily do everything for her.

"What a horrible person," said Mother. "Poor Ella!"

Resisting the urge to roll her eyes, Lily continued. "One day, there was a ball at the palace and all the young ladies in the kingdom were invited as the Prince was looking for a bride. He was a handsome Prince, with golden hair that shone like moonbeams and eyes the color of the sky."

"The Prince has black hair!" Mother crossed her arms and pouted. "He's always had black hair."

"He has golden hair now," said Lily. "And fair skin and sad eyes and a tall, lean frame."

"You can't change the Prince." Mother's pout deepened.

"This is how he's always looked." Lily did her best to smile in a reassuring manner. "I just didn't realize it until now."

"Go on then, Angel! Get on with it." Mother didn't like it when her pauses stretched out. "But the Prince really does have black hair."

"Ella desperately wanted to go to the party, but her stepmother wouldn't let her, afraid that if she left the house, she'd never come back and who'd mend her dresses and sweep her floor and cook her meals if that happened? So, Ella stayed in her small room in the attic and looked out at the palace from her window."

"Then the Fairy Godmother came!" Mother clapped her hands and sat up on her bed.

"That's right," said Lily. "Ella heard a noise in her room and when she turned around there was a Fairy Godmother standing there, holding a wand with a purple amethyst on the tip."

"My lost treasure," said Mother, looking toward the window, as if a Fairy Godmother really had her amethyst instead of it lying between some rocks on the ocean floor.

"The Fairy Godmother waved her wand and a puff of smoke filled the attic. When it cleared and Ella looked down, she was wearing a beautiful dress and a pair of slippers made from crystal that the Fairy Godmother said would fit only her feet."

"What kind of crystal?" asked Mother, even though she already knew.

"Leumarian seeded crystal to reawaken her spirit," said Lily.

"Rare." Mother shook her head, with a greedy look in her eyes. "I only have a dozen of them. I need more."

"The Fairy Godmother told Ella she must return by the time the moon reached the highest point in the sky, otherwise her dress would turn to soot and her slippers would become stuck to her feet. Then she waved her wand again and Ella found herself flying out her window directly to the palace. She was set down outside the ballroom and went immediately inside without looking back once."

"Then the Prince saw her!" Mother held her breath, waiting.

"That's right. He saw Ella and fell immediately in love. They danced and danced and Ella was so happy, until she caught sight of the moon dangerously high in the sky. She dashed from the ballroom and into the garden to take off her slippers. The first one came off easily, but the second was stuck fast. She ran behind a tree just as her dress turned to soot, leaving her cold, dirty, and naked, wearing only one slipper."

"Poor Ella!" Mother looked genuinely sad for her as she shook her head.

"Yes, poor Ella had no choice but to pick up a fallen branch to cover herself, accidentally dropping her slipper in the process."

"Her leumarian slipper," corrected Mother.

"That's right." Sometimes Lily thought Mother knew the details of this story better than she did.

"Go on," urged Mother.

"Hearing the Prince calling for her, she ran all the way home hoping nobody saw her."

"She must go back for the slipper!" Mother raked at her hair. "She should never have left it."

"She did go back," said Lily. "Early the next morning, she snuck out of the house and went back to the palace hoping to find a way into the garden. Although the slippers had been comfortable when she'd worn them as a pair, it was difficult to walk wearing just one of them."

"The slippers are a pair." Mother's voice was wistful. "They belong together."

"Ella was surprised to find a long line of women queuing at the palace gates. She joined the queue, hoping to sneak inside. But as she got close to the front, she gasped to see the guards were holding her missing slipper! The guards were asking each of the women to try it on, but no matter how much they tried, they couldn't get it to fit. A few of the women noticed Ella wearing the matching slipper and they pushed her to the front of the line, where she eased her foot into the shoe. The slippers sparkled to be back on her feet, together once more."

"Did they shine with bright light?" asked Mother.

"They sparkled," said Lily, wishing Mother would listen more carefully. Every time she told this story, Mother would ask this question and Lily was determined not to change it from how her mother had told it to her.

"The slippers sparkled and Ella found her one true love." Mother smiled, looking toward the window, as if her own true love was coming for her.

"That's right. So, the guards called for the Prince and he came running from the palace and swept Ella into his arms. They got married and lived happily ever after. And not once did Ella check to see what became of her awful stepmother, who'd been right about not wanting to let her out of the house, because she never went back."

"And what happened to the Fairy Godmother?" asked Mother.

Lily's eyebrows shot up. She'd never asked this question before.

"She went far away to rescue someone else who needed her help."

Mother's face fell at this answer, as a flash of anger crossed her eyes. "Who's she helping?"

"I don't know. Somebody who needs her, just like Ella did." Lily hoped this answer was good enough. How did Mother expect her to know what happened to a made-up character in a story?

"But who?" pressed Mother, her voice rising in pitch. "Who is she helping?"

"Someone who needs her," said Lily again. "Some poor girl trapped somewhere who's made to do chores and treated like a servant, never allowed to leave her house."

Mother winced and Lily shrank back, knowing she'd pushed things too far.

"The balcony," said Mother pointing to a double set of doors. "You're to sleep on the balcony tonight, Angel. I don't want to see your face."

"No, Mother, please," begged Lily. The last time she'd been forced to sleep out there she'd almost frozen to death. Perhaps this time she would. And how could the golden-haired prince save her if she was already dead? "It was only a story. I don't know what happens afterward!"

"Out! Out! Out!" Mother shrieked and for the first time, Lily wondered what punishment could she give her that was worse than how she currently lived? Now that she'd seen the face of her prince, she didn't want to live by Mother's rules. Or her punishments. She had a destiny that didn't involve telling stories to a selfish woman who'd lost her mind.

"No." Lily crossed her arms and stared down at Mother.

"What did you say?" Mother stood up and crossed her arms in return.

"I said *no*." She stretched out the word to make sure her meaning was clear. "You sleep out there if you like."

Lily left the room before another word could be spoken.

"Angel!" called Mother. "You'll be sorry for this. Angel! Come back here."

But just like Ella in the story, Lily went straight to her room and closed the door without looking back once.

If only there was somewhere further she could run. If only the Fairy Godmother could hear her cries.

GABRIELLE

THE BEFORE

Gabrielle sat at her table, peeling her orange with careful precision so as not to waste a single segment of this delicious fruit. Once, there'd been a time in her life when food like this was a luxury. But that was back when she'd been locked in a cell accused of being a witch.

She wasn't a witch. Or maybe she was and just thought of herself using a different name. She supposed, she was old and gray with a crooked back and missing teeth and she did see the future. Did that make her a witch? Queen Rose's mother, Aurelia, had called her an angel. That sounded so much better than a witch.

Many years ago, she'd had a vision of an army who could whisper for Forte Cadence and make their wishes come true. She'd told Aurelia about her vision, who'd told her husband. But instead of wishing for food for the people, King Virtus had made selfish wishes. He hadn't counted on three things, though.

Rose. Jeremiah. And Micah.

Three incredible human beings who overthrew the King and restored health to the people. Now Rose was Queen, with Jeremiah her Prince. And his sister, Micah, lived in the Valley of the Blessed with her husband, Tallis, not far from Gabrielle's small but comfortable home.

She slid a piece of orange into her mouth and smiled. Life would be perfect, just as it was meant to be, if it weren't for one thing. Princess Lily had vanished, an event that not even Gabrielle had foreseen. She was so upset with herself she'd left the palace and moved to the Valley. What use was a seer who could no longer see?

It'd been years since Gabrielle's eyes had turned blind, but the loss of her visions was more recent, having vanished upon the King's death, almost as if the universe had decided she no longer needed them.

It was quiet in her head now and she almost wished to be back in the dungeon underneath the palace with her visions to keep her company. *Almost.*

She heard her front door open and a set of familiar footsteps approaching.

"Hello, Micah," she said, a clear image of what she thought Micah looked like imprinted in her brain.

"How do you always know it's me?" Micah sat down in the chair next to Gabrielle.

"Would you like some of my orange?" asked Gabrielle, having already heard Micah bite into a piece.

"Nothing gets past you." Micah laughed.

"How's that handsome husband of yours?" asked Gabrielle.

"How do you know he's handsome?"

"Do you always answer a question with a question?" Gabrielle smiled. "He has a kind voice. That makes him handsome to me."

"He'll be over later with some more food for you from the palace."

"I told you he was kind." Gabrielle may have left the palace but she was still well looked after. She never wanted for anything, not that she needed very much.

"Yeah, and just for the record he's handsome, too," said Micah.

"Kind faces are always handsome faces." Gabrielle reached for Micah's hand. "So what brings you here to visit an old woman like me?"

Micah encased her hand in the warmth of her grasp. "I need to talk to you about something."

Gabrielle waited for her to continue. "Yes, my child."

"Your visions. I know you said you haven't had one for years, but... what were they like when you did have them?"

Now, this was unexpected.

"I can only describe them as dreams I had while I was awake. I quite liked them, especially when they were good visions. It felt like I could see again. Why do you ask?"

"I had a dream last night," said Micah. "It was while I was asleep, which doesn't sound so unusual, but I've never had a dream this clear before. It was about Lily. She was underneath the water with her hair floating out like some kind of crown. She looked so sad and scared. Like she was reaching out for me to help her. Do you think it could mean something?"

"It's hard to know," said Gabrielle, truthfully. "Only you can answer that, my sweet girl. Do you think it means something?"

"I don't know. I mean, Lily would be seventeen by now. Everyone said she looked like me." Micah was tapping her feet on the floor, never able to sit still. "Maybe I'm dreaming of myself, but why would I dream of myself under the water? We live nowhere near the ocean. Do you think she's still alive? Could she really be out there somewhere?"

"I wish I knew." Gabrielle sighed, deciding she'd happily go back to the dungeon if it could somehow have prevented that poor child being snatched away. Her disappearance had tainted so many lives.

"Oh, Gabrielle, I miss Lily so much." Micah grabbed at her hand more tightly now. "Do you think it could be her? I want it to be her. But, am I just seeing what I want to see?"

"I know you miss her." Gabrielle moved a little closer. "Maybe it would help if you had a child of your own?"

"What's the point if they only get taken away?" Micah sounded angry now. This wasn't a subject Gabrielle should have raised. Not everyone had a say in whether or not they were blessed with a child.

"Forgive me," said Gabrielle, but Micah didn't seem to hear.

"I want to go and look for her, only Tallis says it isn't a good idea. But I know how to look after myself. I did it for years when Jeremiah first went to the palace as a Whisperer. I can do it again. I'm older now and stronger."

"You're very strong," said Gabrielle, fully aware of her own weakness. She wasn't long for this world now. Soon it would be time to move onto another place, whatever that was. "But where would you look for her?"

"Feldspar."

Gabrielle's heart picked up a strong beat and she sat back in her chair, letting go of Micah's hand. "You can't go there! It's the one kingdom not in the alliance."

"That's why I'm certain she's there. She can't possibly be anywhere else. We've already looked. Feldspar is surrounded by water. It must be the place I saw in my dream."

"But you may never come back. Micah." If only she had her visions, she'd be able to advise her properly. It was so frustrating not knowing the outcome of such a big decision.

"Have you had a vision about this?" asked Micah.

"No, it's just a fact. Nobody comes back from Feldspar. They never have."

"And the Whisperers weren't supposed to be able to break free either, remember? Jeremiah would still be walking silently through the palace with his head shaved bald if I didn't come to break him out."

Gabrielle nodded, unable to argue with this. Micah had indeed rescued her brother at the time he needed her most.

"I would've gone years ago, except Jeremiah begged me not to endanger myself again. But this dream… Maybe that's what it's telling me? Maybe I'm meant to go. It has to be better than sitting here wondering. Rose was such a wonderful Queen before this happened. The best ruler we've ever had. But ever since Lily's disappearance, she's been… distracted. It won't take long before we're all back to where we started and I can't let that happen!"

"Hush, child." Gabrielle didn't wish to hear a word against Rose, even if it was true. Both Rose and Jeremiah had lost some of the fight in them the day their daughter had vanished. But Micah hadn't. She was as feisty and determined as ever. Perhaps her going after Lily wasn't such a bad idea. If only they could be certain of her safety.

"Is there anyone else you know of who has visions like yours?" asked Micah.

"Not in this kingdom," said Gabrielle, answering as honestly as she could.

"Then where?" asked Micah, picking up on what Gabrielle had left out.

"The Alchemist in Wintergreen is known to have visions," she said.

"Jeremiah met him at the royal wedding in Wintergreen," said Micah, pushing back her chair. "He said he was a good man."

"But I didn't say you should—"

"Thank you!" Micah stooped to kiss Gabrielle on the cheek and rushed off the same way she always did. That woman didn't seem to know how to walk.

She just hoped Micah would get her answers from the Alchemist. Answers that she herself had been unable to give.

She stood up from the table and went to her bed, overwhelmed with fatigue. That conversation had taken more out of her than it should've.

Her bones creaked as she lay down and pulled a blanket over herself.

It was only then that she was hit with a vision so strong it knocked the breath from her lungs. She saw a girl with long red hair sitting on the bottom of the ocean. This was Micah's dream. But was she only imagining what Micah had described or was this a vision of her own? The girl held a purple stone in her hands and her dark eyes were imploring Gabrielle to help her.

"Princess Lily!" gasped Gabrielle, no doubt that this was a real vision of her own. Her imagination had never been as vivid as this.

Gabrielle drew in a deep breath, watching as the vision faded, surprised to see it replaced with a new vision of a lighthouse, standing alone in the middle of an angry ocean. The stone structure was shaking, with large cracks opening up down its sides.

"Watch out!" Gabrielle called to Princess Lily beneath the water, despite knowing she couldn't hear her.

The lighthouse shook more violently now as parts of it broke away and tumbled into the ocean, sending water shooting into the air. If Lily was under there, she'd be killed for sure. Micah hadn't mentioned this part of the vision, which must mean she hadn't seen it.

Then the entire structure fell. Slowly at first, gathering speed as it collapsed in on itself, the greedy water below opening its jaws and swallowing the lighthouse like a hungry beast, leaving nothing but the angry sea in its place.

It was Micah who Gabrielle called for now, shouting her name over and over inside her empty house until her voice was hoarse. She needed to warn her. That lighthouse was destined to crash into the ocean, taking down anyone who was near it. Micah may have been given the vision of Lily needing her help, but she didn't know that soon it would be too late.

"Micah!" she called again. "You must hurry!"

Gabrielle clutched at her chest, unable to fill her lungs with air.

Had her visions been restored to her right as her life was about to be taken? Please, let her stay alive long enough to warn Micah of the lighthouse's impending doom. No time could be wasted. If Micah wanted to rescue her niece then she had to do it now.

Gabrielle closed her eyes, fighting the realization that her own time was up. She'd reached the end of her own journey and it was time now for her soul to fly into the sky to join her own loved ones. There was one soul in particular who'd been waiting a very long time and she couldn't wait to be by his side once more.

Her heartbeat slowed.

Slowed some more.

Before the heavens could claim her, she decided to try to do one last thing. She brought Micah to her mind. Not her face, as she'd never set eyes on her, but her spirit. She concentrated on Micah, sending her strength and power. If she succeeded, she'd also send her the power Gabrielle had thought she'd lost. The power to see things that couldn't be seen. Perhaps then, Micah would know how quickly she needed to act.

Gabrielle's heart beat its very last beat, then stopped.

The woman who'd once been called an angel was a real angel now. Her soul was free, and at last her eyes could see.

LILY

THE BEFORE

*L*ily rubbed at the fluorite stones that lined the banister of the curved stairwell in the lighthouse, enjoying the way they sparkled at the attention. There were pink stones, green, purple, and blue arranged in an order so random that it looked planned. Fluorite stones were known to draw away negative energy and cleanse the mind, although as Lily polished them, her mind felt far from cleansed.

Over the years, Mother had taught Lily about the benefits of all the stones in the lighthouse and Lily often wondered if because she was the one to polish them, if she was also the one who derived the most benefit from them. It did seem that was the case. She felt stronger than she ever had. She'd stood up to Mother and refused to sleep on the balcony, and apart from Mother calling out after her and giving her the silent treatment for a few days, there'd been no significant fallout.

She'd spotted Father's small boat riding over the waves not long ago, which meant he was due to arrive soon. This was why she'd decided to clean the stairwell. Sometimes, she waited outside for him, perching herself on one of the sharp rocks that surrounded the lighthouse, but not today. The wind was too cold and the rain too persistent. But so devoted was Father to his Queen that he'd braved the elements anyway. Or perhaps he didn't want to create a storm inside the lighthouse with his absence.

It wasn't only the Queen who was disappointed when Father failed to visit, it was Lily too, not because she especially liked his company, but because he was the only other person she had contact with apart from Mother. Sometimes he brought snippets of news from Feldspar or the other kingdoms themselves and she'd hang on his words and turn them over in her mind later.

The giant iron door at the bottom of the stairwell swung open and she saw a servant stand back and allow the King to enter.

"Angel!" Father smiled up at her. He was a tall man, with thinning black hair and a bushy beard that did its best to balance out what was missing from his head.

"Hello, Father." Normally, she'd run down the stairs to him, but not today. It was about time he saw her life for what it was, so she continued to rub at the banisters, each stone winking at her one by one with her touch.

"I have more treasures for you." Father climbed the stairs, holding up a cloth bag for her to see. "A beautiful new apophyllite amongst them."

"Great!" She grinned at him. "I was running out of treasures to clean."

"You'll never run out of treasures," said Father, missing the sarcasm in her voice.

"Wonderful." Lily continued to rub at the fluorite stones, wondering if any of them had been dug out of the earth with her own hands. It was very possible given the number of years she'd spent as a Fossicker, mining for treasures, before she'd been brought here. Of course, back in those days, she hadn't known the names of the crystals or what powers they possessed.

"What do you see when you look at these treasures?" asked Father, reaching the landing and noticing her concentration.

Her stomach pulled tight. How could she tell him that when she looked at the crystals, she saw the children who'd fossicked for them? Children with dirty faces and empty stomachs who'd been taken from their parents' arms and forced into small tunnels underneath the earth.

"I see beauty," she said, getting as close to the truth as she dared. The children had been beautiful.

"Like mother, like daughter." Father shook his head and laughed.

Lily tried to hide her grimace. There was so much wrong with what he'd just said.

"Shall we go and find your mother?" he asked.

"She'll be angry if I don't finish my chores." Lily wanted to be very clear that she wasn't polishing these stones by choice and the frown that crossed the King's brow told her that her message had hit home.

"Mother loves you, Angel."

"I'm her greatest treasure." She smiled at Father hoping it would be enough to placate him.

"Where is she today?" he asked.

"The kitchen," she replied, wondering why he didn't just look for her himself. There weren't too many places she could be.

"Please join us," he said. "You know I like it when the three of us spend time together as a family."

He turned away and she poked out her tongue at his back.

They weren't a family. They never would be, no matter how long they kept her prisoner. It saddened her that she'd lived in this light-house longer than she'd lived with her real parents in Forte Cadence.

She scrubbed at another fluorite stone, delaying having to go to the kitchen.

The stone shone brightly, reminding her of the light that'd caught her attention at the royal wedding in the desert. She'd wandered away and the closer she got, the more the light had pulled her. She could hear people calling her name but somehow her feet couldn't stop moving. She'd kept walking toward the light, drawn to it like it was the only thing that mattered.

Her parents had called her name over and over, yet she never turned around. It wasn't until she'd walked into a man dressed in black that she'd realized her mistake. She'd tried to scream, but he'd held a hand over her mouth. She'd tried to struggle but he'd pinned her tightly to his chest.

It'd been so hot and she was so thirsty and tired that in the end, she'd just collapsed against the vile man's body and allowed him to carry her far from her family, far from the desert and far from any place she'd ever called home. She should've fought harder. Maybe if she'd know what was to become of her, she would have. But it was too late for regrets now.

She'd never found out what the light was, despite the other Fossickers telling her similar stories of being lured away from their families by a light that seemed to call their name.

"Angel!" called Mother. "Where are you?"

"I'm cleaning the staircase," she replied, unsure if she should be happy that her silent treatment seemed to have ended.

Mother appeared at the top of the stairs. "Your father is here!"

"I know, Mother," said Lily. "We spoke already."

"Don't be so rude. You can finish cleaning later. You might do a better job of it after a rest. Look at all those spots you missed!"

Lily tucked her cleaning cloth into her pocket and went to the kitchen. Father was sitting at the table with Mother standing beside him, waiting for her to make them some tea. This was the real reason they'd wanted her to join them. They might burn their royal fingers making it themselves.

But instead of going to the stove, Lily pulled out a chair and sat down, smiling at them from across the table.

"Tea, Angel," said Mother, although Lily wasn't sure why she bothered. She never drank her tea anyway.

"Oh, no, thank you, Mother," said Lily, deliberately misunderstanding. "I had one earlier."

"This is what I mean," screeched Mother, pacing across the room. "You're out of control. More like a devil than an angel."

Lily noticed that Father didn't seem at all surprised by this outburst. Had Mother already told him about her apparently bad behavior?

"It's his fault." Mother pointed at Father. "He's never here."

Suppressing a laugh, Lily looked at Father.

"What are you laughing at?" Father flushed such a deep shade of pink that she almost felt sorry for him.

"Nothing," said Lily, turning back to Mother. "It's not his fault I'm like this. I'll try harder to be the daughter you ordered."

"Oh, my darling Queen." Father hung his head in his hands. "How can I give you peace?"

Lily shook her head at this poor man who was the leader of his kingdom and a slave to his heart. His love for his wife was a driving force that he had no control over. And in her strange way, she loved him in return. They were the two broken parts of a misshapen whole.

"You can't bring Mother any peace," said Lily.

"See!" Mother strode back to the table. "See!"

"You must look after your mother." Father scowled at Lily. "She needs you."

"True. My mother does need me," said Lily, thinking of her beautiful mother with hair of spun silk.

"That's better," said Father, blind to what she meant by her words. Had he forgotten that she'd had a mother before he'd brought her here? Did the life he'd severed her from mean so little to him that he thought it no longer existed?

"And you still haven't found my amethyst!" Mother wept, yet Father remained in his chair, her hatred for anyone touching her extending even to her husband. It was no wonder they hadn't been successful at having children of their own.

"I might go and look for your amethyst now." Lily stood up.

"But the weather," said Father. "It's so wild out there."

"Don't let him stop you." Mother's head snapped up. "I need my amethyst."

"She's right," said Lily. "Let me look. Finding that amethyst is her greatest wish."

"Mine too," said Father with a sigh.

Lily slipped from the room before they could see the smile on her face. She could grant both of them their greatest wish if she wanted to. Then she thought of her greatest wish that they were quite happy to deny her.

She wanted to go home.

Let the amethyst stay on the bottom of the ocean. They didn't deserve their greatest wish. And they sure as hell didn't deserve her.

RAPHAEL

THE BEFORE

*R*aphael picked up the bottle and threw it against the wall, watching the elixir splatter and drip down the wall as shards of glass showered his workshop.

Throwing the bottle hadn't made him feel any better. Disappointment was still gripping him around the stomach. It was just so frustrating! He was close. So close. He could feel it. Or rather, he could smell it. His homing elixir was almost right, but almost wasn't good enough. The children of Wintergreen didn't need to almost find their way home. They needed to be able to march all the way back to the safety of their families.

He reached for his broom, scolding himself for losing his temper. This workshop was usually his sanctuary. A peaceful place connected to the main apothecary where women sorted the bounty picked from the garden, distilling the oils into bottles, just like the one he'd thrown at the wall. It was in here that he experimented with his healing elixirs. A job he normally enjoyed.

He swept the glass into a neat pile and dabbed at the wall with a cloth.

A noise at the door startled him and he turned to see a thin woman with a dirty face and bright red hair worn in a messy braid that hung over her shoulder. She was dressed in trousers and a long shirt, like a man might wear. Most unusual. He'd never seen a woman dress like that before. There was a determination in her eyes that made him think he'd also never met a woman quite like this before.

"How long have you been standing there?" he asked, wondering how much she'd seen.

"Only a moment." She strode toward him and put out her hand, again, just as a man might do. "I'm Micah. Are you the Alchemist?"

He nodded as he took her hand and shook it. "I am. But you may call me Raphael."

"I've come a long way to see you." She pulled up a chair at his workbench without asking. "I thought my feet might fall off. Walked all the way from Forte Cadence, crossed the river and everything."

"All by yourself?"

"Well, I wanted to, but I'm afraid Tallis came with me. He's my husband. I told him I'd be all right on my own but he's very persistent."

"And where's your husband now?" he asked.

"Sipping tea in your gazebo with three women waiting on him. Your workers are very hospitable."

"Did they tell you where to find me?" It was unusual for anyone to be allowed this far into the apothecary, although the women who worked for him were intuitive. They'd be able to tell if this strange woman posed a threat.

"They did. Not until I explained who I was, of course. They're quite protective of their Alchemist." She tugged at the lapel on her shirt and he noticed how filthy her fingernails were. This was a woman who liked to dive into life headfirst. He couldn't help but like her. Whoever she was, he knew she'd tell him before long. She didn't seem the sort to favor small talk.

"Would you like to tell me who you are over a cup of tea?" he asked.

"Had a tea already, thanks. I'm here to talk to you about something, if you don't mind." She leaned forward and he noticed something very familiar about her. He tried to figure it out, without staring.

"What would you like to talk about?" he asked.

"I probably should've introduced myself properly." She clasped her hands together on the workbench. "Let me start again. My name's Micah and I'm the sister of Prince Jeremiah, who's married to Queen Rose of Wintergreen. I believe you met them both at your sister Jasmine's wedding to King Ari?"

"Oh!" She didn't look much like her brother at all, let alone someone who was related to royalty. But then again, he supposed neither did he. "I've heard about you."

Now it was her turn to look surprised. Or perhaps curious. "What have you heard?"

"Just that Prince Jeremiah has a sister who's as feisty as she is brave." He crossed his arms and grinned at Micah who shrugged off the description, seeming to neither accept it nor dispute it.

"I'm here to talk about my missing niece, Princess Lily," she said, getting back to business.

Raphael found himself reaching for the nearest stool to steady his legs. Of course! That was why she looked familiar. She was like an older version of the girl in his vision. Which made sense now that he knew she was Lily's aunt.

"Lily," he said, his mind swirling with the coincidence of the timing of Micah's visit. No sooner as he'd had the vision of Lily, her aunt had turned up wanting to talk about her. But there was one thing he'd learned for certain in his life, and that was that there was no such thing as a coincidence.

"You've had the vision too, haven't you?" She put her palms on the workbench and looked at him with wide eyes.

"Too?" he asked, feeling his heart pick up a beat. "Have you seen her?"

She nodded slowly, drinking in his reaction. "The first time was in a dream. But then... well, now I'm seeing her when I'm awake. She comes to me at odd moments, always in the same way. I keep seeing her, over and over and I'm sure she's calling to me."

"Tell me what you see." He leaned forward now, seeking more details. "What's she doing in the vision?"

"She's underneath the water. She's reaching out to me, seeming to want me to help. She has a purple stone held in her hands and she looks so sad."

Raphael drew in a deep breath, trying to absorb the shock of Micah's words. This was the same vision. There was no doubt about it. It was hard to decide if he was relieved or disappointed that it'd been shared by someone else. It'd felt like a private moment between them, but apparently, it wasn't. Had he read too much into the way it'd made him feel?

"You've seen her too," said Micah. This time it wasn't a question. It must be obvious by the look on his face.

But what did this mean? He'd had many visions over the years but none of them had ever been shared by anyone before, except his mother, but she'd been dead since he was a young boy.

"The same vision," he said. "All of it, just as you described."

"We need to help her." Micah stood, wringing her hands and pacing. "I'm going to Feldspar and I want you to come with me."

His stomach clenched at the mention of Feldspar, having become more and more certain that this was where Lily was being held captive. It was the only place that made sense with both his head and his gut.

"I can't," he said. "I wish I could, but I can't."

"But you have to!" Micah's pacing stopped and she went to him. "She's asking for our help."

He hated to disappoint her like this, but there was no other way. He'd thought of little else in the past days and had come to this same conclusion every time.

"Many people need my help, not just one."

"Who?" Micah's face was like thunder now and he found himself taking a step back. "Name me one person who needs you more than Lily right now."

"My nephews. My sister worries they'll be taken. I'm working on an elixir to keep them safe. And all the other children of the kingdom."

"Your sister worries they'll be taken?" Her jaw had fallen open now. "What about my brother? His daughter actually was taken. Aren't we better off helping those who need our help right now than those who might need our help one day, or they might not? And besides... Wouldn't your nephews be safer if we were able to work out exactly who was behind this and put a stop to them?"

Micah's words hit him in the chest and stung. He hadn't thought of it like that.

"But I'm so close with this elixir. With just a little more work I think I can get it right."

"You didn't look like you were very close when you threw it against the wall." Micah stared at him intently, tapping a foot on the floor as she waited for him to react.

He felt the blood rush to his face, realizing she'd been watching him longer than she'd led him to believe.

"My brother told me you're a good man." Micah's voice softened as if she realized she'd been pushing too hard. "That's why I came here. I thought you'd agree to come with me, but if you refuse then I'll go alone."

Raphael suspected her husband might have something to say about that, but he held his tongue. It must be nice to love someone so much you'd follow them from kingdom to kingdom just to keep them safe.

A strange feeling pulled at his gut and an image of Lily filled his mind. He pushed it away reminding himself that this vision was nothing special to him. Micah had had it too. It didn't mean he had any special connection to that beautiful girl under the water. He was as alone now as he'd ever been.

"I had a friend called Gabrielle." Micah's voice wavered with emotion. "She was old and wise. She knew things nobody else knew. I told her about my dream and she was the one who suggested I come here to talk to you. Telling me that was the last thing she ever did."

"I'm sorry for your loss," he said. "But I can't abandon my elixir because of the last words of a woman who didn't know me."

"Ever since she died, my visions have been stronger," said Micah. "This will sound crazy, but it's almost like she passed them on to me. That was when the dream I'd had while I was asleep started to come to me during the day. Have you ever heard of anything like that happening?"

"My mother." Raphael's voice dropped to a whisper. "It happened when my mother died. The visions I'd been having grew and multiplied and became more real. I thought it was connected to my grief but since then I've wondered if maybe she passed them on to me somehow."

"Raphael, I don't know why I was sent to talk to you, but I can feel it's the right path. You have to come with me to find Lily. You've seen her, too. There's nobody else in the world who'll know where to look like you can. We've got a better chance of finding her together than we do alone."

Raphael looked at the shattered glass on the floor in the corner of the room. Could he really leave now when he was so close to finding the right balance of ingredients for his elixir?

But wasn't that what Micah was suggesting? That the combination of their skills would be a better balance than one of them going alone? But was the two of them the right balance or were they still missing an ingredient?

"Have you heard of the Evernow?" asked Micah.

He nodded. "The feeling of being happy right now where you are, not wishing for the past or the future."

"That's right," she said. "And do you have your Evernow?"

Raphael let out a slow breath as he shook his head. There was no way he could call the way he'd been living his Evernow. Even before his vision of Lily, he'd be yearning for something more, as if he knew he was missing something but didn't know what. Would finding her be the thing that filled that empty space in his heart?

"Come with me," urged Micah. "We're meant to find her, I know we are. Why else would we be having these visions?"

She made an excellent point. His life had changed the moment he'd had that vision. But could he really abandon his work here in the apothecary to chase after a dream?

"How are you going to feel if you don't at least try?" she asked, clearly not prepared to give up until she had the answer she'd come here for. "Please Raphael, you're meant to come with me. I know it."

"Okay." His brows shot up, almost as if he'd surprised himself with his answer. But how could he say no when she'd put it like that? She was right. He had to at least try to find Lily. She was clearly crying out to him for help.

"Okay, as in you'll come with me?" A twitch of excitement flittered across her face.

"I'll come with you, but not to Feldspar," he said, as a different plan formed in his mind.

Micah tiled her head, clearly confused.

"We'll go to The Sands of Naar," he said. "To the very place Lily disappeared to see if we can follow her trail."

Micah was hopping from foot to foot now. "I like that! Yes, it's a deal. I agree. Although, I'm sure the trail will take us to Feldspar."

Raphael tried to smile but his lips wouldn't cooperate. He had too many worries right now for something as frivolous as a smile. He'd just made one of the biggest decisions of his life with absolutely no idea if it would lead him to his Evernow or his death. This journey was going to be extremely dangerous. Whoever had Lily was unlikely to release her without a fight.

Micah went to Raphael and gripped both of his arms so tightly he was sure he'd be left with bruises. "I knew you'd help me. Gabrielle was right. You're a good man. We're going to get Lily back!"

Raphael nodded, still coming to terms with what he'd just agreed to.

"I'm going to go and find Tallis," said Micah. "I'll be back!"

As he watched her skip from the room, he hoped more than anything that whoever Gabrielle had been, that she was right to send

Micah his way. Was it too late to change his mind? He could chase Micah out the door right now and tell her he'd made a mistake.

Why then, were his feet planted firmly to the floor?

It seemed that he'd made his choice.

LILY

THE BEFORE

*T*he cold wind whipped at Lily's dress as she raised it over her head, leaving her standing on the rocks in her undergarments. The cold worked its way into her bones. Father was right. It wasn't the weather for swimming, but she didn't care. She wanted to touch the amethyst again and feel the smoothness of its surface. Maybe she'd be able to dislodge it this time. Although, that wasn't such a good idea. She couldn't risk Mother getting her hands on it again.

She plunged into the freezing water and swam to the ocean floor with her hands outstretched. Making her way to the rocks, she suppressed a shiver and reached out for the amethyst, surprised to find that it was warm. It hadn't been like that last time. She'd have noticed. Especially given the way it was taking the chill off the water.

Her shivering subsided as her fingertips caressed the warmth of the smooth stone and she saw her Prince once again. Golden hair, fair skin, strong hands, and a kind face. There was someone else with him this time. She closed her eyes so that she could see better.

Aunt Micah! He was talking to Aunt Micah. She wasn't at all sure what they were talking about, but it was clear that her aunt wasn't happy about it. Her arms were crossed and she was tapping her foot on the floor. Was this a lovers' quarrel? Surely not. Aunt Micah loved Tallis. She felt a pang in her gut at the thought of her uncle who used to make her giggle as a child, pretending he was a dragon.

She concentrated on every detail of her vision, knowing she was going to need to come to the surface for air. She'd have to figure out the meaning of this later.

With one last look at her Prince and her aunt, she broke contact with the warmth of the stone and kicked her way back up to the surface.

Sitting on the rocks, she dragged in large gulps of air, noticing her father's boat heading away from the lighthouse. It seemed his visit had come to an end. He never stayed long and sometimes she wondered why he bothered to come at all. Was it worth all that trouble for one glance at his wife? Perhaps it was. After all, she'd gone to a whole lot more trouble just to see the face of her Prince once more.

She was shivering now but decided the warmth of the stone was preferable to returning to the lighthouse.

Plunging back down, she went to the rocks and touched the amethyst again. But instead of the warmth of only moments ago, it was cold, just like when she'd first found it.

She ran her fingers over it and an image of her Prince came to mind. He was reaching out to her, and with her fingers pressed against the stone, it almost felt like they were touching. Aunt Micah was no longer there. It was just the two of them once more.

There were so many questions she wanted to ask him. *Who are you? Where are you? Do you see me? How do you know my aunt? Can you help me?* But with no way to ask him any of these from under the ocean, instead, she locked eyes with him and pressed her fingers harder to the amethyst, talking to him with her eyes.

He was even more handsome than she'd remembered. His blond

hair was messy and his blue eyes clear. He had a fine layer of stubble on his chin and a strong line to his jaw. He was a little older than her but not nearly as old as her aunt. He wasn't her aunt's lover. She was ashamed for even thinking such a thing. There was something in his eyes that said he was a man who belonged to no-one. Or was it possible that he belonged to her?

Breaking contact with the amethyst, she went to the surface for air. Her body shivered harder this time and she wrapped herself in her blanket as she made her way back to the lighthouse. There was no use in her Prince saving her if all he found was a frozen corpse.

She climbed the spiral staircase of the lighthouse, passing the empty kitchen on her way to her bedchamber.

Peeling off her soaking wet underwear, she crawled underneath the blankets of her bed and curled into a ball, waiting for the shivering to stop.

Why did it always have to be so cold on this small island made from rocks? It hadn't been cold in the mines. Quite the opposite, with the warmth of all those small Fossickers digging for treasures, a lantern in one hand and a pick in the other.

Lily had found it a hard life, crawling underneath the ground and hoping the earth didn't fall on her head and crush her. Many of the Fossickers perished and they all lived in fear. Lily often felt guilty at having been plucked from that horrible existence when those beside her had no choice but to continue on until they grew too tall for the narrow passages of the mines. If they were lucky, they were returned to the families they'd been stolen from. Children taken from the other kingdoms were never sent home. They'd have to leave Feldspar to do that and they were needed here to work. It was no surprise that the population was declining with people refusing to have children, knowing they'd be ripped from their arms as soon as they were old enough to dig.

Lily's shivering continued, although now she was uncertain if it was from the cold or the memory of how easily she'd been lured from a life that she'd loved into one that she never wanted.

As she drifted off into a troubled sleep, one image kept creeping in her mind. It was the lighthouse crumbling and crashing into the ocean, just like she'd often wished it would. This tower of misery didn't deserve to stand.

She pushed the image away. Wishes didn't come true. If they did, she'd be home right now.

AZRAEL

THE BEFORE

*A*zrael smoothed out the blankets on the bed, knowing she was going to need it, but not quite certain yet who it was for.

The bed was more like a wide shelf, dug out of a wall of sand. Azrael had once slept in this particular bed when she'd been rescued from the desert and brought to the Colony. She'd been half dead. Actually more than that. There'd been only a tiny strand of life she'd been hanging onto. But the healers of The Sands of Naar had worked their magic on her and brought her back to health.

Now, she was a healer herself. Thankfully, desert rescues were rare these days with Empress Rani and Colonel Aarow in charge. People were no longer released into the desert for the crime of touching another person, which meant the healers could concentrate on helping people with other less preventable ailments. Life expectancy in the kingdom had doubled over the past decade and Azrael was proud to have played a pivotal role in this.

She went to the bed carved into the adjacent wall and smoothed down the blankets on that one too.

"How many are coming?"

Azrael spun around at the sound of her mother's voice.

"Two," she said. "A man and a woman."

"Would you like me to stay and help?" asked her mother.

"Yes please, Freya," she said, unable to break the habit of calling her mother by her first name. "We can heal one each."

"You should heal whoever's in worse shape," said Freya, tying her long gray hair back as she prepared herself for work.

Azrael nodded. There was no point in denying that she was the more powerful healer of the two of them, even though Freya had taught her everything she knew. It was Freya who'd healed her when she'd first been brought here, although she hadn't known she was her mother back then. It was the first time she'd seen her since she'd been torn from her arms moments after her birth and it had taken them some time to figure out their connection. But they'd made up for lost time now and were as close as any mother and daughter could be.

"Tell me again what you felt." Freya rubbed her hands together, preparing them for the healing. She knew Azrael didn't see things. She felt them in a way that was hard to explain.

"I woke this morning unable to shake the feeling that a man and a woman are trying to reach us on foot. They've been walking through the desert for days now. They need our help."

"And you sent Jinn and Toran to fetch them?" asked Freya, nodding.

"Just in time, too, I'd say," said Azrael.

The door swung open at Azrael's words. Toran held a woman in his strong arms. Her eyes were closed and her long red hair swung free, like a lick of fire. She was wearing men's clothes, which made Azrael like her immediately. This was a woman who valued practicality over tradition. Azrael didn't need to lay her hands on her to know that her spirit was strong.

Jinn was supporting a man with golden hair and fair skin that'd turned pink in the sun. His blue eyes were open and he scanned the room, attempting to smile at Azrael, but not seeming to have the energy to pull it off.

"Azrael and Freya will help you now," said Jinn, leading the man to one of the beds.

Toran gently laid the woman down on the other bed.

Azrael moved toward the man with golden hair. He groaned softly as he stretched out his legs.

"We'll get out of your way," said Jinn.

"Thank you," said Azrael, without turning around. She needed to focus on their two patients now. Jinn and Toran understood that.

"I'll take the male." Freya put a hand on her shoulder. "The woman's in worse shape."

Azrael shook her head. "She's not. He's sicker than he looks. Don't be fooled just because his eyes are open and hers are closed."

"Okay." Freya stepped away and went to the woman, taking a sponge soaked in water and running it over her cracked lips.

"What's your name?" Azrael asked the man.

"Raphael," he said. "I'm Queen Jasmine's brother."

"Wintergreen!" Azrael looked at Freya. "They've come from Wintergreen."

Raphael nodded, his eyes seeming to find it difficult to stay open.

"My name's Azrael and I'm going to heal you. Have you heard of our healings before?"

He nodded.

"My mother's going to work on your friend. Can you tell us her name?" Healings were always better when a name could be used as it strengthened the connection.

"Micah. Sister of Prince Jeremiah of Forte Cadence."

"More royalty." Freya raised her eyebrows at Azrael.

"You're both going to be fine," said Azrael. "Don't try to talk now. Please, just close your eyes and let us work. When you wake up, you'll be feeling a lot better. Does that sound good?"

He nodded again, his eyes closing and his head lolling to the side, as if he knew he was safe now and could submit to her care.

She scanned Raphael's body with her hands hovering just over him. A tingling sensation stung her palms. So many of his energy centers were blocked, which was to be expected given how close he was to death. All except the area between his eyes, where his energy boomed like thunder.

Azrael drew in a gasp, realizing that she was dealing with someone quite special here. Raphael wasn't just the brother of the Queen of Wintergreen, there was something about him that was far more impressive. Raphael was intuitive, his powers just as strong as Azrael's, if not far stronger. If only he could open his eyes and tell her what he'd seen to bring him to the Colony. It must certainly be something important.

But it wasn't his areas of strength that she needed to focus on right now. If she wanted him to open his eyes, then she needed to work on his weaknesses.

She placed her hands lightly on his stomach where his energy force was weak, a sure sign of his depleted health. She moved her hands through his energy pattern, pulling the field up and out, resetting it as she went.

When she was satisfied, she moved to the next most urgent center, moving swiftly and confidently up and down his body, kneading her hands through his energy until she felt some of his strength returning as the knots unraveled.

Raphael may be tall and lean, but his mind was strong. He was unlike anyone she'd healed before. She watched him sleeping now and reached for a sponge to dab at his lips. He was dehydrated and exhausted, but he was going to live.

"How's Micah?" she asked Freya, turning her attention away from Raphael for the first time since she'd begun her healing.

"She's coming back to us."

Freya stepped back so that Azrael could scan Micah with her hands.

"Amazing work, as always," she said, feeling the clean flow of energy.

She paused over the space between Micah's eyes, wondering if it was possible that she shared Raphael's gift.

There was certainly a strong pull of energy, far stronger than any ordinary person, but nowhere near as strong as she'd felt in Raphael.

"She has the sight, like you," said Freya. "Does he have it, too?"

"He does. Far stronger than I've ever felt on anyone else before."

She watched as Freya went to Raphael, carefully scanned his head, then looked across at Azrael with shaking hands. "He... I've never felt this before."

"I know."

"What do you think it means?"

"That, I don't know."

Why had a man with such a gift come seeking their help? Especially a man who already had strong connections within his own kingdom. And why had the sister of the Prince of Forte Cadence come with him?

It was then that Azrael was hit with her very first vision. So clear that she stumbled back and sat down on a chair carved into the sand.

"What's wrong?" Freya rushed to her side.

Azrael held up her hand to show that she was okay as she closed her eyes and concentrated on what she was seeing in her mind's eye.

"I see a girl," she whispered. "She's under the ocean holding a purple stone. She looks like Micah, only younger. She's... reaching out to me. I think she wants my help."

The vision faded and Azrael's eyes sprang open as all the pieces of the puzzle fell into place.

If Micah was the sister of the Prince of Forte Cadence, she was also the aunt of the Princess who went missing from Rani and Aarow's wedding, here in the desert.

"What is it?" asked Freya.

"They've come to look for Princess Lily," she said. "Micah's her aunt and she's brought the most powerful man she could think of to help find her."

"But why did they come to us?" Freya crouched in front of her, eyes wide as she sought her answer.

"Perhaps they want to see for themselves where she went missing," said Azrael.

"Or perhaps they want a healer to come with them," said Freya.

Azrael shrugged. "I'm not sure about that."

"I can't lose you again, my daughter." Tears poured down Freya's cheeks.

"They haven't yet asked me to go anywhere." Azrael slipped from her seat and wrapped her mother in her arms.

"But they will ask you," Freya said into her dark hair. "Now that they've seen the power of your healings."

"We don't know that," said Azrael, fighting the feeling that Freya might be right. These two strangers had come here for a reason. But only time would tell if that reason involved her. Would she go with them if they asked?

Princess Lily's disappearance wasn't her problem. But then again, nor were the people who came to her for a healing, and she helped them. Everyone's problems were connected in one way or another.

It seemed she had a lot to think about.

LILY

THE BEFORE

"*A*ngel! Get up, you lazy girl. Angel!"

Lily was in a forest filled with fog. This is how she knew she was dreaming. She hadn't seen a tree since she'd left Forte Cadence with her parents. She couldn't even see a tree when she strained her eyes from the highest balcony of the lighthouse.

But why could she hear Mother's voice in the forest? Ignoring her, she looked around at the trees and saw there were three people standing before her. Her Prince with the golden hair, Aunt Micah, and a woman with dark hair who wore a beautiful robe like the women who'd been at the wedding in the desert. Three angels coming to save her.

"Angel! You need to look for my treasure. Wake up!"

Lily turned her head to the side, forcing her eyes open. She was hot. So hot. No, she wasn't. She was cold. So cold. She was shaking. Was that why she was so tired?

"Angel! Stop this right now!"

She was in her bed with Mother's angular face hovering over her.

"I don't feel too g—" Lily clamped her hand over her mouth as a cough exploded from her chest.

Mother leaped back, her mouth pursed and her hands waving wildly.

Lily wanted to go back to the forest. It was quiet there with her angels. They didn't screech at her to tell her to get out of bed. They wanted to help her.

"Get up right now!" Mother had one hand on her hip and the other was waggling at Lily.

"I think I'm sick." Lily groaned and clutched at her chest as she tried to breathe.

"Sick! That's impossible! Who have you seen to catch a germ from? The King doesn't carry germs." Mother leaned in again, peering at Lily's face as if she could assess her health with her eyes.

The shivering worsened and Lily clutched at her blankets, trying to pull them higher.

"You lazy girl! You don't want to help me find my treasure today. You're faking it. You don't love me. After all I've done for you." Mother made loud, messy sobbing noises that grated on Lily's ears.

Lily coughed again and curled herself into a ball, trying to warm herself up by protecting her core.

"How did you make yourself so hot?" she asked. "I can feel the heat coming off you from here."

"I'm not hot. I'm cold. Please, leave me alone." Lily wanted to cry but that would take too much energy so she concentrated on trying to stop her shivering to distract herself. "I'm sick, Mother."

"But my treasure! You have to look for it."

Lily thought for one crazy moment about flinging herself into the water to keep Mother quiet. At least she'd be able to see her Prince. Maybe that would heal her? But she was too sick. Going into the water like this wouldn't heal her. It would kill her. If she wanted to see her Prince, all she had to do was slip back into the forest.

"Tomorrow," said Lily, her breath short now and a stabbing pain taking up residence deep in her chest. "If I'm well."

"You can't be sick. What will I do if you're sick? What will your father do?"

Lily had no energy to answer.

"You need to get better." Mother swept from the room, leaving Lily to wonder if it mattered if swimming would kill her. She was certain she was dying anyway.

But then Mother flew back into the room and pointed to the cup of water beside her.

"Drink it," she said. "Your father went to the trouble of leaving it there for you when he visited earlier."

Lily took a few sips of water, then her coughing resumed as she remembered how her real mother had cared for her as a child by placing a cool cloth on her forehead and rubbing her back until she fell asleep. Maybe if she closed her eyes, she could pretend her mother was caring for her now.

"I'm going to tell you a story." The uniquely high pitch of Mother's voice made it impossible to pretend she was anyone else. Her beautiful mother hadn't talked like that. "Stories make me feel better. It will work on you, too."

Lily closed her eyes and waited to see what would happen. Mother had never told her a story before. No doubt it was going to be the story of Ella and the wicked stepmother, although with a dark-haired Prince in place of the one with golden hair that Lily had substituted him for last time.

"Once upon a time…" Mother paced the room, not seeming to know how to continue.

Curiosity got the better of Lily and she fought the urge to slip back to her forest.

"Once upon a time there was a girl," said Mother. "She had one brother and a father and her mother was dead."

Lily's ears pricked up. This wasn't a story she knew.

"The girl's house was ugly, her clothes were ugly and everything in her life was ugly, too. But she longed to be beautiful. She wanted hair that grew so long it hung to her waist and to have jewels everywhere, just like the ones she'd fossicked for as a child."

Lily peered out from underneath her blankets.

Mother clapped her hands. "She wanted jewels on her hands, on her dresses, in her hair, on every wall of her house. She wanted to see beauty everywhere she looked. It was my greatest wish."

Lily wondered if she realized the story had just slipped into first person. Now, at least, she knew where this story had come from. She was hearing the story of Mother's life. Lily hadn't really thought much about what her life had been like before she'd become the Queen. Had she really been a Fossicker?

"The girl grew into a young woman and learned that the new King was looking for a bride. And more than anything in the world, the girl wanted to be the Queen. It was her greatest wish."

It seemed to Lily that the girl had a few greatest wishes, but she knew better than to point this out. The forest was beckoning her to slip back under its canopy and she fought back, having never heard the story of Mother's life before. This may be her only chance to find out what events had turned her into the selfish Queen she was today.

"The girl knew the King would never love a girl as plain as her, but she went to the castle anyway, just like Ella in your story."

Lily opened her eyes now, hanging on Mother's words. So, this was why Mother loved the story of Ella and the Prince so much. And why she'd always seen herself as the Princess rather than the wicked stepmother. Given the King had dark hair, it was also why she'd insisted the Prince in the story had the same.

"The girl did her best to look nice. She'd brushed her hair and borrowed a dress from a friend that wasn't quite as plain as the ones she owned. And her brother spent all his savings on a necklace for her with a jade stone tied to a leather cord. The girl went to the castle and was upset to see all the other fancy girls in the line. It wasn't fair! Her friend's dress may be better than the ones she owned but it was still ugly. And the necklace her brother had given her was hideous in comparison to the sparkly treasures the other girls wore."

Lily was unable to suppress the cough that rattled through her chest. How horribly ungrateful of Mother. It sounded like her brother had given up everything for that necklace.

Mother paused her story while Lily coughed, tapping her foot on the floor. Lily only hoped she continued with the story, keen to learn how the King came to choose her for his bride.

"As the girl got close to the front of the line, she saw something most unusual," said Mother. "The King was holding a purple amethyst in his hand and one of his guards was passing a second identical amethyst to each girl as she reached the front of the line."

Lily coughed again, but this time out of surprise. There were two amethysts! Never had she imagined there was more than one. But how much of this story was truth and how much was embellishment? Perhaps when she was better and had a clearer head, she'd be able to figure that out. It was taking all her energy right now just to listen.

"As each girl was handed the amethyst to hold, the King would look at her and call out for the crystal to be passed to the next girl in line. So, the girl in our story got to the front of the line and the guard handed her the amethyst. She turned it over in her hands and felt its warmth. And then the strangest thing ever happened..."

Mother paused. It was the longest pause in the history of pauses and eventually Lily found the energy to speak.

"What strange thing happened?"

"And that's the end of the story," said Mother, clapping her hands, her face pale and her eyes darting around the room.

"But it didn't end," said Lily.

"It's a story! I don't know how it ends, just like you've told me before." Her tone was harsh, back to the way she normally spoke, instead of the sing-song voice she'd used while she'd been telling the story.

"You said a strange thing happened," said Lily.

"This wasn't a good idea. You're better at stories than I am." Mother left the room once more, leaving Lily in emotional anguish as well as physical.

What strange thing had happened when the King had given Mother the amethyst? And were there really two identical stones? If so, where was the other one? Did the King still have it?

It was all too much to try to figure out right now. What she needed to do, was make sure she remembered these details for when her fever broke. Because she wasn't sure what Mother had just told her or why, but she was certain that it was important.

She closed her eyes and slipped back into a sleep so deep the forest couldn't be found amongst the black fog that surrounded her.

RAPHAEL

THE BEFORE

*R*aphael's eyes sprang open and he drew in a sharp breath as he sat up. Where was he?

"It's about time you woke up," said Micah looking surprisingly well as she approached his bed. Was it a bed? He was lying on some kind of shelf dug out of a wall made from sand.

"Are we underground?" he asked.

Micah nodded. "Cool, hey? Apparently, you walked all the way down here, climbing into that very bed yourself. Don't you remember it?"

"Just the vaguest of memories. Give me time." He lay back down and smiled. His sister, Jasmine, had been to the Colony and told him all about it. An underground oasis in the middle of the desert. The people were protected by the harsh elements down here and had access to fresh water in some kind of underground river.

"We only just made it." Micah brushed the fabric of the trousers she wore. They were different from the ones she'd arrived in, as was her shirt. He looked down to see that he was wearing the same loose-fitting trousers and was bare from the waist up.

"Where are our clothes?" he asked.

"Torn to shreds in the wind." Micah shrugged. "Thankfully, they didn't replace mine with a dress."

"And my elixirs?" He'd carried a bag of oils to aid them on their journey. Not that they'd been much use in the end. The elements had been far harsher than he'd expected.

"They're over there." Micah went to a table where a familiar hessian bag sat on top. She picked it up and set it down next to him on the bed.

"How did we get it all so wrong?" he asked. "I thought you said Jeremiah whispered for our safe arrival?"

"He did." Micah laughed. "And here we are, safely arrived."

"We should have listened to Jazz," he said. His sister had warned them of the treacherous journey, suggesting they travel as a larger party with more supplies, like she and Ari had done when they'd made the journey to that fateful wedding all those years ago.

"We should've," Micah agreed. "But we thought we knew everything. We thought a whisper and a bag of oils were enough. This is why I've been thinking…"

"About what?" he asked, cautious of Micah and her ideas.

"What if a healer comes with us?" Her eyes burned with enthusiasm.

"Comes with you where?"

Raphael sat up quickly again at the sound of a stranger's voice. There was a woman with dark hair and eyes like night standing in the doorway. Although, somehow, she wasn't a stranger. Had he heard her voice while he'd been asleep? Had she been the one to heal him?

"To the washroom," said Micah, glancing at Raphael, seeming to be trying to tell him something with her eyes. "We need you to come with Raphael to the washroom. I'm afraid I'll get lost if I take him."

The woman smiled, despite not seeming to believe Micah. "I'd be happy to take you, Raphael. I'm pleased to see you awake. I'm Azrael, I'm one of the healers."

"Did you heal me?" he asked.

She nodded and smiled. "Mostly you healed yourself, but I did help you along the way."

"Thank you." He reached into his bag for an elixir to clear his mind. It was all so confusing right now. Coming here had either been the biggest mistake of his life or the best thing he'd ever done. He'd thought he might have dreamed of Lily while he'd been asleep but he'd not had a single vision of her since he'd left Wintergreen. Had something happened to her?

He found the bottle he was looking for and waved it under his nose.

"May I?" asked Azrael, reaching out her hand.

He handed her the bottle and she held it to her face, breathing in cautiously.

"It helps you think clearly," he said. "It has rose and lemongrass and cedarwood. A few other things too, but I won't bore you with that."

"Raph," laughed Micah. "I don't think there are too many rose bushes out here. Or lemongrass sprouting out of the sand. I doubt you're boring her."

"Oh." Raphael felt heat rise to his cheeks. "Of course not."

"It smells beautiful," said Azrael. "I'd love to go to Wintergreen one day."

"You'd be very welcome at our apothecary any time," said Raphael. "If Grimm doesn't burn it down while I'm gone. Not sure it was such a good idea leaving him in charge."

Azrael's brow wrinkled ever so slightly. "What's an apothecary?"

"That's the place where we make the oils," he added, realizing if she didn't know what a rose bush was, she was hardly likely to have heard of an apothecary.

"Why did you come here?" Azrael looked from Raphael to Micah, seeking an answer. "Nobody comes here without a reason."

"It was my idea," said Micah, letting out a long sigh and sitting down on the edge of his bed. He shuffled over to make more room for her, happy to let her speak for now. "I wanted to see where my niece went missing."

Azrael nodded. "I can take you to the place as soon as you're well enough. But why now, Micah? Lily went missing years ago."

"Well, you see, Raph and I have both been having visions of Lily. She's sitting on the bottom of the ocean clutching—"

"A purple stone," finished Azrael.

"You've seen her, too?" asked Raphael, unable to stop his jaw from gaping.

"Yes," said Azrael. "That's what you were talking about just now, wasn't it? You're going to look for her and you want me to come with you."

"We need a healer," said Micah, glancing at Raphael. He nodded, letting her know he agreed it made sense to convince Azrael to come with them. Especially if she'd had the same vision they'd had.

"We don't know what state Lily's in," continued Micah. "I don't feel confident we have the powers to bring her back on our own. Our journey here proved that. Will you come with us?"

"To be honest, I wondered if you were going to ask me to come with you," said Azrael. "Our kingdom let Lily down in the worst possible way. We failed to look after her when she was here as our guest. Instead of the kingdoms uniting in the way they were meant to, her disappearance sits between us like a wedge. Your brother and his wife can never forgive us, and nor should they."

"Does that mean you'll come with us?" asked Raphael, a lightness sweeping through him. They had a much better chance of succeeding with Azrael on board, not just for her healing but it seemed her intuition was finely tuned as well.

"I've been thinking about it and admit that I'm tempted," she said.

"You must come," said Micah. "We need you. It's so important you say yes."

Raphael smiled. He'd been on the receiving end of Micah's begging before. It was far more amusing to watch from the sidelines.

Azrael sighed, seeming to be wavering to the side Micah was trying so hard to push her to.

"You said yourself that your kingdom was responsible for Lily's disappearance," said Micah. "This is the perfect way to earn the forgiveness of the other kingdoms."

Raphael coughed, trying to warn her that she was now pushing too hard.

"It wasn't The Sands of Naar's fault," he said, when she failed to take his hint. "They weren't the ones who took her."

"But they can be the ones to help get her back," said Micah. "You're a healer, Azrael. You help people. Isn't this what you do? Please say you'll come with us. We'll be so much stronger with the three of us."

"Do you think that maybe there's someone missing?" asked Azrael.

"Yes… Lily's missing," said Micah. "I don't understand."

"No, someone missing from our search party," said Azrael.

"She means The Bay of Laurel," said Raphael, certain he knew what she was getting at. "If Azrael comes with us, we have a Whisperer, an Alchemist and a Healer. We need a Guardian as well."

"Not a Guardian." Azrael held up her hand. "The herbalist. I can heal people when they get sick, but what if they were so healthy, they didn't need healing in the first place?"

Raphael let out a long breath as he processed this, shaking his head as he realized she was right. One of their herbalists would be far more useful than a Guardian.

"We can travel to Feldspar via The Bay of Laurel," said Micah.

"But how do we know we're going to Feldspar?" asked Raphael. "We don't really know where Lily is. That's why we came here, so we could pick up on her trail."

"I've stood in the exact place she was last seen many times," said Azrael. "I'm certain that's where she was taken."

"That's what I think, too," said Micah. "She has to be there."

"I still want you to show us where she disappeared," said Raphael, not willing to agree just yet. It'd been dangerous enough journeying to the desert, a place of peace. Crossing the sea to go to one of their enemies was far more perilous.

"Of course," said Azrael. "And if we all agree, we'll go to talk to the herbalist. If she refuses to go with us to Feldspar, I'm certain she'll give us some tonics to strengthen us for our journey."

"So you're definitely coming with us?" he asked. It sounded like she'd made up her mind.

She nodded. "Micah's right. I took an oath to help people and Lily needs my help."

"The herbalist will feel the same way," said Micah, leaping to her feet and pacing. "She'll come with us. She has to."

"Nobody has to do anything," said Raphael. "That's the whole point of this. Lily was taken against her will. We're here because we chose to be."

"I didn't mean we were going to force her." Micah rolled her eyes a little more dramatically than Raphael thought was necessary. "I just meant we'll convince her how important this is."

"Who's their herbalist?" asked Raphael. "I thought she was an older woman."

"That's right," said Azrael. "But she no longer works alone. I believe she's training Princess Philippa in the hope she'll take over one day. Either one of them would be a suitable choice."

"Philippa?" asked Raphael, having trouble placing that name.

"Also known as Pip," said Azrael. "Sister to King Tate."

"Right," said Raphael, certain that name sounded more familiar.

"It's meant to be!" Micah clapped her hands. "We're all siblings of a monarch."

"I'm not," said Azrael.

"I thought the Empress was your sister?" Micah seemed puzzled. "I heard someone say something like that."

"We're sisters in our hearts," said Azrael. "We've been through a lot together."

"Were you there when Lily went missing?" asked Micah.

"I was." A darkness crossed over Azrael's eyes. "I can show you the exact spot."

"How about we start with you showing me where I can clean myself up?" asked Raphael. "I smell like some kind of elixir gone wrong."

Azrael and Micah both laughed and a realization struck Raphael.

He was no longer lonely. He was about to travel to The Bay of Laurel with these two intriguing and strong women beside him so they could rescue the girl who'd captured his heart in much the same way she'd been captured, in that it'd happened without his consent.

"Come on," said Azrael, motioning from the door.

He swung his legs out of the bed and went to her, wondering why people tried so hard to shape their own destiny. It seemed to him that destiny was powerful enough to unfold all by itself.

MICAH

THE BEFORE

*M*icah paced the passageways of the Colony feeling more than a little claustrophobic. She could never live underneath the ground. There wasn't enough room for her to move and breathe. The only thing that had ever come close to making her feel like this was when she'd been a Whisperer and forced to shave her head, dress in an orange robe and live in total silence.

Although, at least down here in the Colony, she wasn't in fear of her life. Nobody was going to cut off her head for talking when she wasn't supposed to. Which was lucky as talking was her most favorite thing to do. After fidgeting, which she knew she did all the time, including when she was asleep. Or eating. Or spending time with Tallis.

Oh, Tallis! The thought of him sent her legs pacing faster and she decided to see if she could find the passageway that led to the entrance of this strange underground world. She knew it would be hot outside but she desperately wanted to see the sun again. And maybe it would distract her from thinking about her husband, who she was missing a whole lot more than she'd thought she would.

Perhaps she should've let Tallis come with her. He'd certainly wanted to and she'd had a tough time explaining to him that this was something she needed to do without him. Thankfully, Tallis wasn't a jealous man. She didn't know many husbands who'd allow their wife to walk into the desert with another man. But Tallis knew their relationship was stronger than ever. They'd been through so much together, from the days they were starving children running wild, to the sensible grown-ups they were today.

She turned a corner and felt the slightest of inclines. That had to be a good sign. As long as her footsteps kept going up, she had to reach ground level eventually. Or sand level might be a better way to put it.

It was good to have her energy back. She'd heard the healers were good at what they did, but she hadn't realized just how effective their treatments were. To think that they were able to do all that work just with the palms of their hands.

"Want some company?" asked Azrael, appearing beside her.

"You have a habit of doing that!" Micah put her hand to her heart and laughed.

"Doing what?" Azrael tilted her head.

"Sneaking up on people."

"I didn't sneak." Azrael laughed and Micah noticed how pretty she was with a smile on her face. "You were just deep in thought."

"I'm trying to find the way out of this maze you live in."

"Ah, then you're on the right track. It's just up there." Azrael pointed. "Need some fresh air?"

Micah nodded, falling into step beside her.

"Took me a while to get used to it down here, too," said Azrael.

"You mean you weren't born down here?" she asked, yet again surprised to learn this about Azrael.

"No, I was sixteen when I arrived. I grew up in the Capital."

Micah had heard all about the circular city in the middle of the desert known as the Round, connected to the Colony by an underground tunnel.

"I'm told it's beautiful there," said Micah.

"It is now." Azrael's voice was hard. "But I don't like going there. Too many bad memories."

"Freya's your mother, isn't she?" asked Micah.

"She is," said Azrael. "But I didn't meet her until I came here. It's kind of a long story."

"My mother's dead," said Micah, flatly. "And my father. And the baby that was in my mother's belly."

"I'm so sorry." Azrael nodded at her with solemn eyes.

"Me, too." Micah swallowed down her pain. "But at least I got my brother back. And now I have Tallis. He's my husband. Do you have a husband?"

"I don't want a husband," said Azrael, the hard edge creeping back into her voice.

"I didn't really, either." Micah bit down on her lip as she said this. "It took Tallis a long time to convince me to marry him. I like to be free and he promised to always respect that. I guess he wore me down with that kind heart of his."

"Kind is good," said Azrael.

"It is," she agreed.

"Here." Azrael pointed to a steep slope with a doorway at the top. "Brace yourself for the heat. You might want to adjust your veil first."

Micah tried to copy what Azrael was doing with her veil as she lifted it from her neck and draped it over her head and looped it over her shoulders. But Micah got herself tangled in such a knot, all she could do was stand there and laugh.

"Here, let me." Azrael lifted the veil from Micah's shoulders and fixed it. Her movements were swift and gentle and she did it all without making any contact with Micah.

"I've noticed you don't usually touch people unless you're healing them," said Micah.

"It's just a habit." Azrael smiled but offered no explanation. "Come on."

She opened the door and held it for Micah who stepped through, wincing as a blast of heat hit her in the face.

"Intense!" she said through her veil.

"Follow me." Azrael walked away from the Colony and up a steep dune.

Micah dug her feet into the hot sand and followed. It was no wonder she and Raphael had nearly perished out here. How had Lily survived?

They walked to the top of the dune and Micah's mouth fell open at the spectacular view before them. The red sand dunes rolled across the landscape in every direction. It looked like the world had been turned upside down and the sky had turned red.

"It's so…" She found herself unable to find a word that would do this kind of view justice.

"I know." Azrael laughed with her eyes and led Micah across the top of the dune to a place where the sand was being shaded by a giant sail. She sat down and patted the sand next to her.

Micah cautiously sat down, afraid the sand might burn her, only to find that although it was hot, it lacked the ferocity of the sand they'd just trudged across.

"This is where the wedding was," said Azrael. "Under this sail. We were all looking down over this dune when Lily vanished."

Micah scanned the vast desert, understanding for the first time why it'd been so hard to search for a missing child out here. The way the steep dunes dropped away without warning and the brightness of the sun meant it was impossible to get a full picture of the landscape. And that was without sand blowing in her eyes.

"It seems so empty, but there are a thousand places to hide," said Micah, trying to imagine what it must have been like for Lily out here all by herself.

"Especially given we didn't know what direction to start looking for her." Azrael swept her hand out across the dunes. "She was here one moment and gone the next."

"It will be good for Raphael to see this." Micah hoped he'd be able to sense more than she could, which at this stage was nothing. She had no idea where Lily could have gone. Coming here had been of no help at all. Except for meeting Azrael and convincing her to join them. She still wasn't sure how they'd even managed that.

"The desert's a beautiful place as long as you respect it," said Azrael.

"I don't think I could live here," said Micah. "But I can see why you love it."

Azrael pulled a face. "I love it here as much as I can love it anywhere."

"Life was cruel to you before you came here, wasn't it?" asked Micah, a few things clicking into place.

Azrael nodded. "No crueler than it was to you, I'm sure."

"Is that why you agreed so easily to come with us?" she asked, certain she'd almost figured things out. "We thought we'd have a tough time convincing you."

"Partly. But it was true what I told you. Our kingdom let your niece down. And when I saw her in that vision, she looked so sad. I know what it's like to be taken from your mother and spend your life feeling trapped. If I can save one person from experiencing that, then I will."

"You're so calm. So wise." Micah kicked at the sand in front of them and instantly regretted it when it flicked back at her.

Azrael laughed. "I wasn't always like this. I used to be quite feisty as a girl. A bit like you, actually. But healing people has taught me to temper that energy and use it only when it's needed most."

"I wish I could learn to do that," said Micah, struggling to imagine Azrael as a feisty young girl. "Everyone's always telling me to keep still. I need to be more like you."

Azrael shook her head furiously at this. "No, don't. Be like you. Exactly like you. That's who you're meant to be. Never compare yourself to anyone. Lily doesn't want two of me rescuing her. She wants her Aunt Micah."

"I liked being an Aunt," said Micah, edging toward something she'd wanted to ask Azrael about when Raphael hadn't been around.

"You'd be a great aunt," said Azrael. "Fun and brave. You would've taught Lily how to be the best kind of Princess."

"I wanted children of my own." Micah pushed back the tears that stung at her eyes. "But it seems no child wanted me. I've lost two babies now. Neither of them lived long enough to be born alive."

"Oh, Micah!" Azrael moved closer to her, although she stopped short of taking her hand.

"D-do you think you can heal me?" Micah stifled a sob, determined not to let it out. "I mean, that p-part of me?"

"I can try. I promise you I'll try," she said. "You know that Raphael might have some oils to help you as well. And I'm sure The Bay of Laurel would have a tonic."

"Please don't tell anyone." Micah felt heat in her face and not from the hot desert sand. "I don't want anyone to know. I haven't even told Jeremiah or I'm sure he would've whispered for a baby for me. I don't want the Whisperers making wishes for me when there are so many other people in worse situations. Like Lily."

"We're going to get her back," said Azrael. "And of course I won't tell anyone."

Micah nodded. "Thank you."

"There you are!"

They spun around to see Raphael approaching. "I was told I might be able to find you out here."

"This is the spot, Raph," said Micah, jumping to her feet. "The wedding happened under this sail. See if you can feel anything."

Raphael paced around, scanning from left to right. Every now and then he'd stop and close his eyes.

"Do you think he senses anything?" whispered Azrael.

Micah shrugged. "I have no idea how his visions work. Maybe?"

After some time, Raphael returned to them, shaking his head.

"I was sure I'd feel something," he said. "But…"

"It's okay, Raph!" said Micah, hating the crushed look on his face. "I couldn't feel anything either. Nor could Azrael."

"I was sure I would," he said.

"Then it looks like we're off to The Bay of Laurel as planned," said Azrael.

Micah clapped her hands. The kingdoms were uniting at last, not just by words and promises but by combining their powers to turn the bad into good.

With any luck, the herbalist would have had a vision of Lily, too, and would be as easy to convince as Azrael had been. Or Princess Philippa.

But for some reason, she found it impossible to imagine Princess Philippa without seeing an image of her shaking her head.

PIP

THE BEFORE

*P*ip shook her head and firmly crossed her arms. "Absolutely not."

"Why not?" asked Ariel, pushing the tonic toward her.

Pip sighed. She trusted Ariel more than anybody. She wasn't just her teacher and mentor, but her friend. Although, just because she trusted her didn't mean she had to drink everything she put in front of her.

"It will make you strong," said Ariel.

"I'm strong enough!" Pip shook her head. It was Ariel's mission in life to fatten her up after she'd become dangerously thin when she was younger.

"Just drink it, Pip." Ariel blinked at her with an expression of pure innocence.

"Ariel, I love you and I know you care about me, but I make my own tonics now." Pip pushed the tonic back to her. Being fat was just as unhealthy as being too thin.

"You need your strength," said Ariel.

"Why?" Pip narrowed her eyes and stared at Ariel, certain she was up to something.

"I'm not sure." Ariel blinked and looked away. "I just have the feeling you're going to need to be strong for whatever life throws at you next."

Ariel often said things like this and usually, Pip knew better than to ignore her. But this was different. She knew how to take care of herself.

"I'll make myself a strengthening tonic later, okay?" she said. "I promise."

Ariel huffed as she lifted her tonic to her lips and drank it herself.

"I didn't want to waste it!" she said, wiping her mouth with her apron. "I don't mind getting fat."

"So you admit it! You did add something in there for weight."

"I admit it," said Ariel. "What are you going to do to me? Throw me in the dungeon?"

Pip didn't laugh. The idea of being thrown into the dungeon wasn't funny ever since it happened to her brother, Tate. Not that he'd stayed there for long. When their father died, Tate had not only been released, but he'd been crowned King of The Bay of Laurel.

"No dungeons," said Pip. "I'm going to send you to the garden to pick me some more thyme instead. Please?"

"Very happy to do that for you." Ariel lifted her long skirt to her ankles and swept out of the kitchen to her beloved herb garden, while Pip got busy sorting through a basket of celery she'd picked that morning.

Silence. That was better. Pip had spent years as a recluse closed away in her bedchamber. But things were different now. She'd been lured from her room by Edison—a man who'd told her that he loved her but turned out to love nobody but himself. However, he was dead now and the only part of that Pip was sorry for was that Ariel had lost her son. She'd deserved so much better than a selfish son like that. So had Pip.

Despite the way things had gone, Pip was glad for the role Edison had played in her life. Without him, she was sure the only way she would've ever left her bedchamber would've been as a corpse.

Pip smiled as she reached for a bunch of celery and sliced into it, her knife moving swiftly through the stalks like they were made from butter. She tasted one of them to check how bitter this crop was, pleased to find the flavor was mild.

This kitchen was where she belonged, not in the palace wearing fancy dresses and fending off proposals from potential suitors more interested in her title than who she was as a person. She had her tonics, she had Ariel, and she had her nephew and nieces in the palace. Living amongst the Guardians in the village on the outskirts of the palace grounds was where she felt most comfortable.

"Hey there."

She looked up from her chopping board to see a Guardian leaning on the doorframe. Not just any Guardian, but Griffen, a man who sent a whole rush of confusing feelings racing through her brain. He was tall and blond, like all the Guardians, but there was something about him that'd always stood out to Pip. Perhaps one day she'd work out what it was.

"Hey," she said, focusing fiercely on the celery, hoping he hadn't seen the blush she knew had spread to her cheeks. He must think she was permanently the shade of the beetroot tonic she served the Guardians once a week.

"Need any help with that?" he asked.

"I'm fine thanks." She winced at the way her voice had squeaked when she talked.

"Wise," he said. "I'd probably chop off one of my fingers if you gave me that knife."

He held up his enormous hands and she laughed. As a Guardian, he was built for strength and power, not dexterity.

"Do you need me to bring anything in or out for you?" He seemed to be looking for a job. With peace spreading across the kingdoms, the Guardians weren't needed as much to protect the kingdom. Instead, they got involved in distributing the tonics to the wider population to ensure everyone had the opportunity to grow to be strong.

"Not today, thank you." She breathed in, pleased her voice had returned to a more regular tone.

"You know I'm always happy to help."

"I know that." She smiled and went back to her chopping. Griffen was such a kind man. Always helping Pip and Ariel by carrying heavy supplies or going to the Bay to collect some of the rarer ingredients they needed. They had Ariel's husband, Jacob, to help them too, but often he was busy weaving belts or making dolls for the children in the village or spending time with Tate. It was a strange connection that Jacob had with Tate, but Pip never questioned it, knowing Tate saw Jacob as the father he'd never had. And perhaps for Jacob, Tate was like the son he'd lost.

"The tonic was delicious this morning," said Griffen, not seeming to want to move from her doorway. "It had a bit of a kick to it."

"Wonderful." She picked up the celery pieces and added them to the large pot on her stove. "I tried adding a pinch of chili powder this time. I was worried it might be too much."

"It was perfect." He grinned at her in a way she couldn't interpret.

"Did I say something funny?" She tilted her head and willed her cheeks to return to their normal pale complexion.

"No," he said, the grin still plastered to his face.

"Then why are you laughing?"

"I'm not laughing." He left the doorframe to approach her.

As he got close, her stomach pulled into the kind of knot she hadn't felt for such a long time. Not since she'd thought she'd been in love with Edison. She'd promised herself she'd never fall for a man's charms again, but Griffen was the kind of man who sent promises flying out the window.

He reached for her and it was like time slowed down, then stopped. She waited to see what he was going to do.

"You have celery on your lip." He put a gentle hand on her face and swiped her lower lip with his thumb.

Her cheeks burned like fire now. "You said you weren't laughing at me."

"I wasn't. You looked... cute. Green's your color." He pulled his hand away from her face and her heartbeat picked up as if to keep pace with the blood supply needed to keep her cheeks so flushed.

"Celery isn't cute," she said, licking her lip where his thumb had just been.

"Pip, I'm supposed to marry a Guardian," he said in a rush. "My parents are tired of waiting. They want a decision soon."

"Oh." She swallowed, scolding herself for how uncomfortable she was with this idea. She had no claim on this man. There were plenty of beautiful female Guardians who must be lining up to marry Griffen. She'd known this was going to happen one day. She just hadn't known that the idea of it would hurt so much.

"I told them I don't want to marry a Guardian." He blinked twice, searching her face for a reaction.

"Why not?" she asked, barely able to disguise her relief.

"Why do you think?" His hand returned to her face and he brushed a lock of hair away from her face. "Pip, surely you must know how I feel? I'm certain you feel the same."

"Griffen." She looked up at him. As a Guardian, he'd been bred to be stronger and larger than an ordinary person. The top of her head reached his chest, making her feel tiny.

"Yes, Pip." His voice was gravelly, taking on a husky tone she hadn't heard before.

"Griffen, please," she begged. "I don't understand what's happening here? What are you doing?"

"I'm about to kiss you, that's what's happening." The blue of his eyes flashed with irresistible mischief.

She sucked in a breath and blinked. This couldn't be real.

"Is that okay?" he asked.

She nodded, a slight movement of her head but enough to send Griffen's mouth crashing to her own.

His lips were warm and strong and she responded by kissing him back with more passion than she'd ever kissed a man before. Although, given that Edison was the only other man she'd kissed, this wasn't all that surprising.

So, this was what a kiss was supposed to be like. It wasn't the meshing of lips, it was the meshing of every ounce of your being.

A series of tiny pulses raced through her body. She wasn't just kissing Griffen's mouth, she was kissing who he was as a person. His tongue sought her own and tears stung her eyes at how vulnerable and beautiful the intensity of his desire made her feel. He wasn't kissing a Princess. He was kissing her.

He broke away, slowly peppering her with delicate kisses as he drew back. Now, there was another kind of grin altogether on his face. One that could never be mistaken for amusement.

Her hand fluttered to her mouth and she took a step away to catch her breath.

Ariel came back into the room at that moment with a large bunch of thyme in her hands.

"Am I interrupting anything?" she asked.

"I was just helping Pip out with something." Griffen winked at Pip then dipped his head at Ariel and left.

Ariel set the thyme down on the workbench and stifled a laugh.

"Well," she said. "I was wondering how long it would take him to make his move. Good for Griffen!"

"What do you mean?" Pip abandoned her side of the workbench and went to Ariel, grabbing her on the arm. "You knew how he felt?"

"Oh, my word!" Ariel laughed. "The whole village knows how that man feels about you. And how you feel in return, I might add."

"But... I didn't..."

"Your cheeks don't turn that color for anyone else, my dear Pip. He's a good man. I'm happy for you."

Pip looked down at the workbench. She wasn't ready to talk to Ariel about her feelings for Griffen until she'd made sense of them inside her own head. How was it possible for a whole village to know more about how she felt then she did?

"There are some people in the garden who want to talk to you," said Ariel.

"Who?" Ariel had Pip's attention now. Nobody ever came here to talk to her. "Are you sure it's me they asked for?"

"I'm sure it's you," said Ariel, smiling. "Go on. These aren't the kind of people you want to keep waiting."

Pip removed her apron and smoothed down her dress.

"Do I look okay?" she asked Ariel.

"Pip, you're beautiful. I'm not sure how many times I need to tell you that before you hear me. Now, go on." Ariel put a gentle hand on her back and steered her from the room.

She went out into the herb garden to see three strangers standing beside the parsley patch with two Guardians hovering close by.

"Princess Philippa," said one of the Guardians, walking over to her.

She winced, really not liking that title, but she understood the Guardians called her this out of respect. Except for one Guardian who always called her Pip. The same one whose lips had been connected to hers only moments ago.

Her hand fluttered to her mouth again, as if it was obvious to everyone else what she'd just been doing.

"You have some visitors," said the Guardian. "May I present Raphael, brother to Queen Jasmine of Wintergreen; Micah, sister of Prince Jeremiah of Forte Cadence and Azrael, a healer from The Sands of Naar."

Once again Pip found herself speechless. This was no ordinary group of visitors.

"My brother's in the palace," she said, not understanding why the Guardians had brought them directly to her.

"We asked to speak to you first," said Raphael. "But it would be an honor to speak to Prince Tate and Queen River when we're done."

The Guardians remained close enough to let her know they were there if she needed them. Any one of them would lay down their life to protect her if required.

"Please leave us," said Pip, with a wave of her hand. Whatever this strange collection of visitors was doing here, they meant her no harm, that much was obvious.

The Guardians nodded and left.

"What brings you here to see me?" she asked, unsure who to direct her question at. Raphael with the golden hair and kind eyes? Micah with the dirt-stained face and feet that couldn't keep still? Or Azrael with the wave of calm that surrounded her?

It was Micah who stepped forward. "We've travelled a long way. Please, before we discuss what we came here to talk to you about, could we trouble you for something to eat or drink. One of your famous tonics perhaps?"

"Of course." Pip clapped her hands together. "Please, excuse my manners. Come in. We can sit in the kitchen."

"Are you sure your herbalist won't join us?" asked Azrael.

Pip wasn't sure how to answer this. "Did you come to speak to her?"

"We wanted to speak to both of you," said Azrael. "But she said we were best to speak with you."

"Meant to, not best to," corrected Micah.

"Perhaps we can talk first then," said Pip. "And then I can decide if Ariel needs to be persuaded to join us."

She led them through the garden, her mind swirling at the possibilities for their visit. Was it a tonic they were after? Whoever needed it must be very sick. Because clearly, neither whispering, magic elixirs made from oils, nor healings had helped.

Or did this have something to do with Ariel's earlier comment about her needing strength for what lay ahead? Whatever the case, she was going to need to tread very carefully here.

Tate had always told her he believed in her. It seemed the time had come for her to start believing in herself.

RAPHAEL

THE BEFORE

*R*aphael took a seat at Princess Philippa's table, his feet throbbing from the long journey. It'd been days of walking, riding on wagons and sleeping under trees, but they'd made it here at last. If it weren't for the healings that Azrael performed on them each night, he doubted they would've made it at all. The elixirs Raphael dabbed onto their collars had helped by giving them hope and focus, but it was the healings that'd kept them strong. They'd arrived in The Bay of Laurel in far better shape than they had at the Colony.

Except now that he was seated in front of the person they'd come here to talk to, he was filled with doubt. No matter how hard he tried, he couldn't imagine this Princess agreeing to come with them to Feldspar. The way she'd reached out to stroke the leaves of the herbs as she'd moved through the garden had shown him how connected she was to her home. It was like she had invisible threads tying her down, in much the same way he felt about his apothecary. And it was clear that the herbalist didn't want anything to do with them.

Raphael shot Micah a look, trying to communicate all of this in a glance, but of course, that wasn't possible and she seemed to take the desperation in his eyes as a sign that he wanted her to get on with the asking, rather than delay it.

"Thank you for seeing us, Princess Philippa," she said.

"Please call me Pip." The Princess set down a tall glass of tonic in front of them. "I insist on it."

"Thank you, Pip," said Azrael, the first to pick up her glass and down the muddy liquid.

Raphael followed suit, having no reason to distrust the Princess. The Bay of Laurel had joined the alliance with the other kingdoms. They were on the same side.

The tonic was bitter and Raphael winced as he swallowed it down. It was thick too, like drinking a heavy soup, working to satisfy both his hunger and his thirst.

He smiled at Princess Philippa—Pip now— to show his appreciation. She was an unusual looking woman, not quite what he'd expected. She was extremely petite, which meant her features stood out from her face with a bird-like sharpness. With dark blonde hair and pale blue eyes, she had a delicateness about her, like she could do with drinking a few more of her tonics herself.

"Oh my goodness," said Micah, wiping her mouth on the back of her hand. "You must've used a hundred lemons to make this!"

Raphael grimaced. "It's delicious," he said, to cover the bluntness of Micah's words.

"It's not meant to be delicious," laughed Pip. "It's meant to return you to strength. Micah's right. There are plenty of lemons in there, although perhaps not a hundred."

"I feel better already," said Azrael, although Pip was distracted by a man who was standing in the doorway watching them.

He wasn't tall enough or blonde enough to be a Guardian and Raphael studied his face carefully for a sign of who he might be. His hair was dark and tied back in a failed attempt to make him look tidy.

His eyes had a serious glint in them despite the smile on his face and his clothes looked expensive, yet well worn. Raphael had never quite seen a man of such contradictions before.

"Tate!" said Pip, going to the man and taking him by the hand to lead him to the table.

Raphael stood from his chair so quickly it fell backward, as he realized who this man was.

"Your Highness," he said, dropping to a bow.

Azrael and Micah let out simultaneous gasps and stood. Micah curtseyed like an expert, while Azrael copied her with some awkwardness.

"This is my brother, King Tate," said Pip, although Raphael couldn't help but notice they looked nothing alike. He looked more like he could be Pip's brother than her actual brother did.

"Please sit back down," said Tate pulling out a chair and joining them. "My Guardians told me of your arrival. You've traveled a long way to reach us here."

Raphael picked up his chair and sat down, not sure if the King's presence was going to help or hinder them with this conversation. He seemed a man who could be trusted, but would he allow his sister to do something as dangerous as to go with them?

"I didn't realize you'd be joining us," said Pip, running a hand through her blonde waves of hair.

"I confess I was curious," said the King. "Do you mind?"

"Of course not," smiled Pip.

"Actually, we were hoping that your herbalist might join us, too," said Azrael. "She insisted we speak with Pip but this involves her."

"Just a moment." King Tate nodded and left the room. Ariel may have been able to refuse to speak to them, but Raphael imagined she'd be unlikely to refuse her King.

He took another sip of his tonic while he waited. This time he was expecting the bitterness and the shock of it was far less.

King Tate returned and took his seat once more. "She'll be here shortly."

"Let me introduce you to everyone," said Pip.

Micah tapped her foot on the floor as Pip made the introductions, leaving Raphael smiling at her impatience to get on with things. If her determination were an indicator of their potential success, then he was very confident of the outcome.

"I believe you've met my brother," said Micah.

"How is Jeremiah?" asked the King, a shadow of grief flickering across his face. "And Queen Rose, of course."

Micah shook her head as sadness spilled into her eyes. "Doing as best they can in the circumstances, as I'm sure you understand."

"Terrible." The King shook his head and Raphael noted the genuine sadness that took hold in his dark eyes. "I can't imagine anything worse than losing a child."

"Tate and River have a son and three daughters," said Pip, her face filling with pride. "And another on the way."

"Actually, I think our Alchemist here may have had something to do with that," said the King, turning his attention to Raphael.

Raphael's eyebrows shot up as he snapped to attention. "I beg your pardon, Your Highness, but I'm not sure what you mean."

"Do you remember many years ago when you were only a young Alchemist, a man from our kingdom came to ask you for a fertility elixir for his King? My father, of course."

Raphael felt his face flush at the memory. He hadn't given the man a fertility elixir as requested, instead handing over an oil blend that would provide calm. The man had seemed a little overwrought. And he hadn't asked nicely…

"I do," said Raphael, cautiously.

"Well, it certainly did the trick." The King laughed.

Raphael decided to keep quiet about the elixir for now. The King didn't need to know that it had nothing to do with Queen River's apparent fertility. Perhaps her just believing she was fertile had been what did the trick in itself.

"It's okay," said King Tate. "We know you didn't give us the right elixir. Our herbalist, Ariel, worked that out. I just always found it funny that it worked anyway."

Raphael let out a breath, relieved that this wasn't a secret he was going to have to keep. "I apologize for attempting to deceive you."

The King waved his apology away. "No harm done. Now, tell me, how is your sister, Queen Jasmine? And King Ari, of course."

"They're very well, thank you. They have three sons. Very spirited children, but healthy and happy."

Raphael yelped as Micah kicked him under the table. They'd agreed to use the despondent nature of their siblings to play on Pip's sympathies so she'd be convinced to help them. He'd totally forgotten. King Tate had the sort of face it was hard to lie to.

"Are you okay?" asked Pip.

"Sorry, yes, just a sore back from the journey." He rubbed his lower back for effect. "I was just about to say that my sister is well, apart from her constant worry that one of her sons will be taken, just like Princess Lily. It's been very difficult for her. And King Ari, of course."

"I'll never forget the day she went missing," said King Tate. "Nor will my wife. We think about Princess Lily every day, wondering where she might be."

"The people of my kingdom feel very responsible," said Azrael.

"You're from The Sands of Naar?" asked the King. "Are you also a sibling of the royal family?"

"I'm a healer," said Azrael, shaking her head. "Although Empress Rani is like a sister to me."

"You were at the wedding, weren't you?" asked the King. "I remember you in the search for Lily."

Azrael nodded. "I'll never forget it, either. It fills me with great sadness."

"Which is why we're here," said Micah, tapping her fingers on the table. "We're on our way to Feldspar to bring Lily home."

"Feldspar?" It was Pip who spoke now, leaning forward in her seat and looking at them one by one.

"We've looked everywhere else," said Azrael. "She must be there. We're certain of it."

"But how do you know she's still alive?" asked Pip. "Sorry, I don't mean to be rude, but it's been an awfully long time since she went missing."

Raphael's heart sank at these words, for they were confirmation that Pip hadn't shared the vision they'd had of Lily, calling for help on the bottom of the ocean. It would make things so much easier if she had.

"Princess Lily's alive," said Raphael, firmly.

"I think so, too," said a female voice behind them.

They spun around to see Ariel walking into the kitchen with a man Raphael assumed was her husband.

"I'm Jacob," said the man, setting down a heavy crate of potatoes. "The herbalist's husband. Hope you don't mind me being here, Tate?"

Raphael tried to stop his eyebrows from raising at the informal way Jacob had just addressed the King. But when he looked closer, blocking out the distractions of the room, he saw something quite different pass between them. Something that only someone with his intuition would be able to pick up on. These men were father and son. But how was that possible?

"Thanks, Jacob," said King Tate.

"He's not staying," said Ariel. "And nor am I. Please, forgive me, but I told our guests earlier that it's Pip they need to speak to. Not me."

"Ariel, why do you think she's still alive?" asked Micah, remaining as on task as always. "When Princess Phillipa seems to think otherwise."

"Hard to explain," said Ariel, smiling kindly as she took a step toward the door. "When I think of her, I see a light, when I'm sure I'd see darkness if she were no longer with us."

Micah glanced openly at Pip, and Raphael was certain if she could stick out her tongue at the Princess, she would.

"We also think she's alive," said Azrael. "We're certain of it."

"Please, Ariel. Will you stay and talk with us?" asked Raphael, intrigued by what she'd just said.

"I'm not meant to." She cast a glance around the table, her eyes lingering just a beat longer on the King, before leaving the room.

"Leave her be," said King Tate. "If she believes she's not meant to be here, then I trust that's for the best."

Raphael took this in, sorting out the threads between these people in his mind's eye. The same connection that existed between the King and Jacob extended to Ariel, too. But how could that make any sense? And why didn't the thread connect to the King's own sister, Pip?

"So, I'm guessing you'd like our support with your search?" asked Pip, getting the conversation back on track. "Is it tonics that you're after? Because I can help you with that."

"Not exactly," said Micah. "It's—"

"It's Guardians then, isn't it?" said the King. "We can spare as many as you need."

"That's very kind," said Micah. "But I'm afraid it isn't your Guardians we'd like to take with us."

King Tate and Pip tilted their heads simultaneously.

"What then?" asked the King.

"We'd like Pip to come with us," said Raphael. "Or Ariel."

Pip's mouth fell open.

"Me?" she asked. "To Feldspar?"

"That's right," said Micah. "It's time we brought Princess Lily home."

Pip was shaking her head now and shrinking back in her chair.

"I'm afraid that's not going to be possible," said the King. "Pip isn't fond of travel."

Raphael looked toward the window, trying to sort out the jumble of thoughts racing through his head. If Pip refused to go with them and Ariel refused to even speak to them, then why had they come here? This had been a total waste of time. And one thing he knew for certain, was that time was running out.

LILY

THE BEFORE

*L*ily groaned as she struggled to open her eyes, determined to chase away the dream she kept having of the lighthouse falling into the ocean. How long had she been asleep? Was she still asleep? No, she was in too much pain for that. Her head was thumping.

Seeing a glass of water beside her bed, she reached for it and gulped it down. A damp cloth slipped from her forehead to the floor and she noticed her blankets were clammy. She must have had a terrible fever.

She sat up and waited for the room to stop spinning. Vague memories rushed back to her of Mother telling her a story to put her to sleep. She couldn't remember Mother ever telling her a story before. Normally, it was the other way around.

Feeling cold, she slipped her feet back into the bed. It was so warm in there. Her bed never felt like this. Did she still have her fever?

Her bare feet touched something warm and solid and she slid her hands down to feel what it was, surprised to find a large gemstone tucked in beside her.

She pulled it out above the sheets and gasped. It was Mother's treasure! There was no doubt about it. This was the purple amethyst she'd found hidden under the ocean and it was warm, heat pulsing out of it in waves.

Before she had time to wonder how it'd gotten there, an image of her Prince hit her so strongly she had to lean back against her pillow and close her eyes.

Her Prince calling to her, clearer and closer than he'd ever been before. Lily searched for a sign of Micah or the woman with dark hair who'd also come to her in her dreams, but this vision was of the golden-haired man alone.

She drank in his angelic features. His mane of blond hair, his crystal blue eyes, his fair skin. When she looked at him, she saw love. Her love. This man was meant for her and she couldn't explain why.

The intensity of her feelings bubbled and grew. Was this because she'd seen him a few times now, or because he was getting closer? Was it possible he was on his way to her? She wasn't sure how much longer she could wait. If Mother kept sending her into the freezing ocean, she was certain to fall ill again and she wasn't sure she could survive it next time. But now that she had the amethyst, was there even any need to go under the water again?

There was a flash of color in her doorway and she hid the amethyst under her blankets, the vision of her Prince fading. Was there even any need to hide it? Surely Mother was the one who'd given it to her. But how had a woman who didn't know how to swim managed to retrieve it?

Mother swept into the room.

"Angel!" she gasped, rushing over to Lily's bed. "You're awake. Oh, thank goodness."

Lily blinked up at her. "Mother."

"I thought you were going to die." Mother went to pull up Lily's blankets, then stopped herself.

"Not dead yet," said Lily.

"I don't know what I would have done without you." Mother's face filled with pain. "I couldn't possibly stay here all by myself again."

"You could live in the palace with Father." Lily bit down on her tongue. She didn't have the strength for an argument, so why was she starting one?

"I can't live there!" Mother's voice raised into the familiar screech. Lily's illness had almost been worth it just to have had a rest from that tone for a while. "You know I can't live there!"

"Why not?" Lily cursed herself. There she was going again, not being able to help herself.

"This is my palace! My treasures are all here!" Mother tore at her hair with her bejeweled fingernails. "You're here, you selfish child! Can't you see that all of this is for you?"

This time Lily bit down her words, but that didn't stop them racing through her mind. *What if I don't want to be here? What if I were no longer here? What if I... got away?*

"Thank you, Mother," she said, instead, grateful to be rewarded with a few moments of silence for her compliance.

"Do you think you're well enough to look for my treasure today?" Mother's face lit up.

Lily's hand went to the amethyst to check she hadn't imagined it. It was still there, under the blankets, pulsing with warmth. This didn't make sense. Was this the one from under the water, or was it something different? They looked identical.

A memory scratched at the surface of Lily's brain, as if trying to break through. Something about the treasure...

"Are you well enough?" asked Mother again.

"I'm not sure." As subtly as she could, Lily tucked the amethyst into the waistband of her undergarments, covering it with her nightdress. If Mother didn't know she had it, then she needed to keep it that way.

"It's been five days!" Mother's face contorted. "Five days of lost opportunity! I knew you did this on purpose. You don't care if I ever find my treasure again."

"I do care." Lily rubbed at her throbbing temples. "I'll look for it. I'll look for it right now."

Mother stood up and clapped her hands. "I'm so pleased you're better, Angel."

Lily peeled back the blankets and swung her feet out of the bed. Looking for the treasure would keep Mother quiet for a while. And it might satisfy her curiosity. Would there be a dark, cold space where the stone had once been? Or were there two stones when she'd thought there had only been one.

A memory of a story Mother had told her when her fever had been high, slammed into her chest with such force she gasped.

"What's wrong?" asked Mother from the doorway. "You'd better not be sick again."

"Nothing." Lily smiled to mask the rush of details that were sliding into place in her mind. The King had two identical amethysts and had given one to the girl in the story. A girl who was undoubtedly Mother. The stone had glowed with warmth when she'd held it.

"You're smiling," said Mother. "Why are you smiling?"

"Just happy to be feeling better." Lily swept past Mother, went to the kitchen to take an apple from a bowl and bit into it as she clomped down the staircase.

The treasure was a twin stone. Which meant that either someone had placed the amethyst from the ocean in her bed while she'd been sick, or she'd somehow come into possession of the King's stone. Perhaps the Fairy Godmother had visited her while she'd slept.

This thought only put an even wider smile on her face. Something big had happened and now it was her job to put the pieces together and figure out what it was.

Her head might be thumping and her body might be weak and aching, but there was nothing that was going to stop her diving into the water to find out which amethyst had been warming her bed.

She went outside, pleased to see the sun was shining today. Was that a sign? But with the warmth of the amethyst pressed to her body, she wasn't likely to get cold today. It felt even warmer now that she was outside. Was that just the contrast to the cool air or was the stone itself getting warmer?

Raising her face to the sun, she let the rays caress her as she took in some fresh air, pleased to be feeling so much better.

Finishing the apple, she tossed the core onto the rocks for the gulls to pick over and clambered over the rocks to the water's edge.

"Hurry, Angel!" called Mother, watching her from her balcony.

Lily lifted her nightdress over her head, angling her body so that Mother couldn't see the amethyst held tight by her waistband.

She dived into the water, enjoying the rush of the cold water as it washed the sweat and fever from her body. Kicking down, she went to the rocks that held Mother's treasure, untucking the amethyst from her waistband and holding it in her hand. She hadn't been imagining it. The amethyst wasn't just warm now. It was hot.

And there it was. Still there. The twin stone to the one she held in her hand. Reaching out, she grazed her fingertips over the surface. It, too, was burning hot, the water around her more like a warm bath than the freezing ocean.

She pressed the stones together to see what would happen, half expecting an explosion of light or the heat to intensify to the point she could no longer touch them.

A vision of her golden Prince burst into her mind. Her ribs ached with the force of it as it demanded her attention. She held onto the amethyst with one hand and reached out to her Prince with the other, hoping he could see her, too.

Aunt Micah was standing behind him, next to the woman with dark hair. But there was someone else this time, standing back a little, blurred by a shadow as if she hadn't quite made up her mind if she was with them or not. Four angels now.

Quickly running out of air, Lily forced the amethyst into the gap in the rocks beside its twin, making sure there was no chance of it coming loose. She couldn't risk Mother finding it and taking it from her. Keeping it safe from her was the single most important thing she could do.

The vision had vanished the moment the amethyst left her hand, but the feeling of the Prince remained as she pushed back up to the surface.

She wasn't sure just yet what power the amethysts held or what having them both in her possession meant, but she was closer than ever to working it out.

"Did you find it?" called Mother, her voice being carried by the wind.

Lily shook her head as she looked up at her standing on the balcony, remembering the dream she'd had about the lighthouse falling.

A shudder ran through her. What if the dream hadn't been a dream at all? What if she was being warned? If that lighthouse were to fall, she'd never survive it. Was she a fool to sit here waiting for her Prince to save her? Perhaps she'd be better off to find a way off this island and save herself before it was too late.

But how?

PIP

THE BEFORE

"*A*bsolutely not," said Tate.

"Wait." Pip held up her hand and looked at Micah. "You want me to go with you to Feldspar?"

"That's right," said Micah. "We need to use the lessons each of our kingdoms has learned to get Lily back. Whenever one of us has tried to find her alone, we've failed."

"And how do you think my sister can help you?" asked Tate. "Surely you're better off taking some Guardians with you."

"She can make tonics," said Azrael.

"You can bring tonics with you," said Pip, trying to figure out if the idea of going on such an adventure excited her or terrified her. Then she thought of Griffen and what had just passed between them, and she knew there was no way she'd ever leave him.

Azrael's shoulders visibly slumped. "It's important you come with us. It's hard to explain why, but we all feel very strongly about this."

"That's not a very convincing argument." Pip smiled, not wanting to burst their bubble, but it was true. They wanted her to uproot her life and put herself in danger all because they said they had a feeling about it.

"Would you excuse me a moment, please?" Raphael stood and bowed to Tate.

Tate nodded at him and Pip noticed Micah shoot Azrael a panicked glance as Raphael left the room. Clearly, he was up to something and whatever it was, it wasn't part of their plan.

Pip looked toward the window to see what direction he'd gone. Nobody traveled the sort of distance he had to talk to her, only to excuse themselves from the room the moment the topic had been raised.

"Where's he gone?" Pip directed her gaze at Micah. She was the one who seemed to be running this farce.

"I don't know." Micah may be impatient but she wasn't dishonest, that much was clear.

"Perhaps we should wait for him to return to discuss this," said Pip.

"I'm not sure there's much to discuss," said Tate. "We want to help you find the Princess. That's sincere. But I can't let my sister go with you. It's far too dangerous."

"Tate, please," said Pip. "Let me make up my own mind. I thought you believed in me?"

"I do. But…" Tate looked at her, confusion spilling into his eyes. "But you never leave the Guardians' Village. I didn't think…"

"You didn't think I'd like to decide for myself." Pip crossed her arms. Perhaps she should talk about this in private with Tate once she figured out why she was getting annoyed. It wasn't so much that she disagreed with the decision Tate was making for her, more that it was important to her that she be in control of her own future.

"I don't understand," said Tate. "You've always made your own decisions."

Micah and Azrael were shifting in their chairs now and studying their glasses of tonic intently, clearly feeling uncomfortable at the personal direction this conversation was taking.

"So, you're saying you want to go to Feldspar?" asked Tate.

"No! I'm not saying that at all." Pip shook her head, realizing she'd made a mess of this conversation. "I'm just saying that I'd like to be the one to decide."

"We need you," said Micah, leaning across the table. "Please, come with us. If Feldspar is behind this, as we suspect, then they can't get away with it. They can't just come into our kingdoms and take our children. It's not right."

As Pip let out a sigh, she looked across at the window to see Ariel talking to someone. Leaning over in her chair she could just see a wisp of white-blond hair. Ariel looked distressed, grabbing at Raphael's sleeve as if begging him to do something for her.

"Would you excuse me for just one moment," said Pip.

"Not you, too!" said Micah, under her breath.

"I'll just be a moment." Pip left the kitchen from the door that would take her out just behind where Raphael and Ariel were talking.

She walked quietly through the herb garden, although she needn't have bothered. Ariel and Raphael were so deep into their conversation, they were unlikely to notice if a tornado appeared.

"She can't know!" Ariel was saying. "Please."

"She has a right to know," said Raphael.

Pip stilled her steps and listened. Who was this *she* they were talking about?

"It makes no difference," said Ariel. "She never wanted the throne anyway."

A sick feeling twisted in Pip's gut. Were they talking about her? As Tate's younger sister, she'd been second in line to the throne at one stage. But now that Tate had a brood of heirs it was something she didn't need to worry about. She could think of nothing worse than becoming the Queen.

"If you come with us to Feldspar, you have my word that your secret is safe," said Raphael.

"That's blackmail." Ariel stepped back and Raphael's face filled with anguish.

"I'm sorry," he said. "You're right. It's just that I'm desperate. We all are. We have to get Lily back and I think you're the best person to help us."

Pip's eyebrows shot up. So, Raphael didn't want her to come with them. He'd rather have Ariel. Had he noticed that Ariel had talents that Pip didn't possess? Talents that Ariel would be unable to pass down to her no matter how much time she spent in her kitchen. Even though she didn't want to go, she felt a little offended.

"And if I don't come with you, then you're going to tell Pip?" asked Ariel.

Pip stepped quietly behind a rosemary bush, keeping her breathing to a minimum.

"I won't tell her," said Raphael, raking his hands through his hair. "It's not my place. And if she never wanted the throne as you say then it's of no consequence if she finds out that Tate's claim to it is false."

Pip's hands flew to her mouth to hide her gasp. Tate's claim to the throne was false? How could that be possible?

"Tate's a wonderful King," said Ariel. "The most wonderful. I couldn't be prouder that he's my son."

This time it was impossible for Pip to hide her reaction and she stepped forward shaking her head as she tried to process what she'd just heard.

"Tate is your son?" she asked, her eyes fixed on Ariel. "But how?"

Ariel staggered back and rested on a raised garden bed, hanging her head in her hands.

Tate chose that moment to come marching into the garden.

"What's going on?" he asked. "I saw you from the window. Are you ill, Ariel?"

"Don't you mean Mother?" asked Pip.

Tate's eyes opened wide and he looked from Ariel to Pip.

"Raphael worked it out," said Ariel, shaking her head. "Then Pip heard us talking just now."

"I don't understand," said Pip, her world crashing down on her.

"I swapped them as babies," said Ariel. "I knew the Prince was evil, so I swapped him for my own child. I did it for the kingdom."

"You're talking about Edison?" asked Pip. "You're telling me that your son—the man I was forced to marry—was actually my true brother, and Tate is the son of a herbalist? That's ridiculous."

But the looks on the faces around her told her that no matter how ridiculous it sounded, it was true.

"Why didn't you tell me?" she asked Tate, aware that her voice had risen to a shriek. "How could you keep this from me?"

"Some secrets are better off not having to be kept," said Ariel. "Don't blame Tate. It's not his fault. Blame me."

"Would you have wanted the throne?" asked Tate. "Because if I thought you did, then I'd have told you. I promise I would've."

"I don't want your throne!" This was the truth. Tate may not be her brother but he knew who she was and what she did and didn't want. "But it would be nice to have been told the truth, instead of being treated like a child. You always treat me like a child. Making decisions for me and keeping secrets from me. I've had enough of it!"

"I'm sorry, Pip." Tate took a step toward her with his arms outstretched, and Pip turned and ran.

She didn't want to feel his arms around her. She didn't need his comfort. He'd lied to her in the worst possible way!

She ran from the garden into the Village, then for the first time in many years she took the path that led to the hedge that separated the Village from the palace grounds.

Ignoring the aching in her chest from the sudden burst of activity, she pushed on, running right through the palace gardens and out into the cornfields beyond. This was where she'd seen Tate escape to in the early mornings when she'd been closed up in her bedchamber. She never did find out what had drawn him to the cornfields, no matter how many times she asked him, but perhaps there was something here that would bring her solace.

She ran down a row of corn, brushing at the leaves as she passed them and throwing herself on the ground when she was sure she was hidden from the world. She needed to be alone. Away from Tate and away from Ariel. Away from everyone who'd looked her in the face and lied to her over the years.

Tate wasn't her brother. Edison, the awful man she'd married who'd died at their wedding feast had been her flesh and blood. How could this possibly be true?

A strange grinding noise caught her attention and she crawled along the ground to see a rabbit caught in a steel trap. It was thrashing about, desperate to find its way out.

"Oh, you poor little thing." Pip went to the trap and got to work on the release mechanism.

As soon as she'd pried open the jaws of the trap, the rabbit rushed out and ran like a flash of black lightning as far away from her as possible.

It was then that Pip started laughing. All these years when she'd asked Tate what he'd been doing in the cornfield in the morning, he'd winked at her and told her he was saving the rabbits. She'd thought he'd been joking. Suddenly, she knew without a doubt that he'd been telling her the truth, He *had* been saving the rabbits.

Her laughter dried up with the thought that although he hadn't lied to her about the rabbits, he'd been lying to her about something so much more serious. He'd lied to her about who he was.

Maybe it was time she learned a lesson from that rabbit in the trap. Perhaps she was just like that poor creature, only the trap was her own doing. She'd holed herself up in her bedchamber for years, only to finally break free and hole herself up in the kitchen instead. She'd never seen the world. She'd never even seen anything outside the palace gates.

Maybe the arrival of these three strangers was meant to happen? Maybe instead of sending them away and staying in the safety of her kitchen, she was actually supposed to go with them. Ariel certainly seemed to think so, with her insistence that Pip was the one they were meant to talk to.

At any rate, going with them would get her away from Tate and Ariel and everyone else who'd lied to her and allow her to sort out her head.

But how could she leave Griffen? Unless…

"Pip! There you are!"

Tate was standing before her, his hair flying in all directions and his chest heaving for breath.

"What are you doing?" he asked.

"Saving some rabbits," she said, holding up her bloodied hands.

"I did tell you that's what I was doing." He sat next to her on the ground, keeping a safe distance, no doubt worried he'd scare her away again.

"Why didn't you get rid of the traps?" she asked. "You could've outlawed them."

"I did," he said, shaking his head. "Guess I might have to check on the farmers a little more often. I didn't know some had started using them again."

"How long have you known?" asked Pip. "About Ariel."

"Not until after I'd already been crowned," he said. "I really thought I was doing the right thing not telling you, Pip. I couldn't see how it would benefit you."

"You can't protect me forever, you know," said Pip.

"I know. I'm sorry." He shuffled a little closer to her and her heart broke to think he wasn't really her brother. "You were right with what you said back there. I need to stop treating you like a child."

"I've decided to go." Pip reached for Tate's hand.

"To Feldspar?" He looked stricken.

She nodded. "It's time I saw the world. It's time I did something. Something more than this."

"Is there anything I can do to stop you?" he asked, wrapping an arm around her shoulders. "Because I really don't want you to do this."

She shook her head. "I need to do this."

"Then I want you to take a Guardian with you," he said. "To keep you safe."

She smiled. "I was hoping you'd say that. Because I know just the one."

AZRAEL

THE NOW

*A*zrael slipped off her shoes and dug her toes into the sand. They'd made it to the shoreline. Somewhere across that large expanse of ocean and over to the east was Feldspar. The kingdom nobody knew much about except that when you got close, you'd see a line of dead trees. But what was behind those trees? Or perhaps more importantly, *who* was behind them?

Pip collapsed onto the sand next to her and Griffen knelt down, asking if she was okay. That man took his job as a Guardian very seriously. King Tate had asked him to look after Pip and he'd hovered over her the whole journey. Although, it was becoming obvious there was something more between them.

They'd all played their part in getting them safely to this point. Pip had been able to identify foods along the way that they could safely pick and eat. And the tonics she'd filled their waterskins with had gone a long way to keeping them fueled with energy. Azrael knew that Raphael was disappointed Pip had come in place of Ariel, but

Ariel had been very insistent and they were lucky to have any kind of herbalist come with them. They weren't in a position to be fussy about which one it was.

Micah had taught them how to whisper, explaining that although the whispers were most powerful when the Whisperers in the palace conducted them, they were all able to send their wishes into the sky. Before they'd set off, they'd sat in a circle and held hands, whispering for their safe arrival and the successful return of Lily. Saying the words out loud had filled them with confidence and Azrael had heard each of them continuing the chant at various times as they'd walked.

Raphael had sprinkled various elixirs on the inside of their wrists and the collars of their clothes and Azrael could feel the focus that they gave her.

And she herself had been tasked with performing healings each evening to restore them to health. They made an excellent team and the journey didn't seem like it would've been possible without each of them doing their part.

"Can you heal her?" asked Griffen, looking up from Pip's side.

Pip looked tiny next to Griffen. All wispy blonde hair and delicate frame lying back on the sand. Her eyes were closed and she was groaning softly. But to give her credit where it was due, she'd managed to walk all the way here, when before that she'd never left the grounds of the palace.

Azrael knelt down beside Pip and placed her hands on her, working on the energy centers that needed her attention most. She wasn't in peril. She was just exhausted. They all were.

"How are we going to get over there?" asked Raphael from the shallows. He'd thrown off his shoes so he could enjoy the coolness of the waves lapping at his ankles.

"We'll find a way," said Micah, running straight past Raphael and plunging into the water.

"You're crazy!" laughed Raphael.

"It's beautiful in here." Micah scooped up some water and splashed it onto her face.

Finishing up with Pip, Azrael decided to join her. The sun was high in the sky and there was plenty of time to dry their clothes before the cold night air settled in. It would feel nice to have clean skin.

She waded out past Raphael and sat down in the water beside Micah, grinning at her. "Not sure I'd call this beautiful."

"I would." Micah skimmed her hand over the water, splashing Raphael, laughing when it hit him in the face.

Raphael shook his head and smiled, before diving into the water and making his way over to them.

"Come and join us!" Micah called to Pip and Griffen.

"Pip's just resting for a bit," called back Griffen.

"Anyone else think something's going on between those two?" Micah asked in a hushed voice.

Raphael nodded so vigorously it made Azrael laugh. She didn't have many friends back home, apart from Empress Rani. She had her little sister, Bindi, who was a lot of fun. And her mother, of course. But Micah and Raphael had come to feel like friends of her very own. Micah with her irrepressible courage and determination and Raphael with his wisdom and gentle soul. He was so unlike any of the men back home and she wasn't sure what to make of that.

When she'd been younger, she'd thought that she was in love with Rani, but those feelings had faded over the years as she'd seen Rani marry and give birth to her twin daughters. If Raphael lived in the Colony maybe she'd fall in love with him? But then again, maybe not. She looked over at Griffen hovering over Pip. Did she want that for herself? Not especially. Perhaps she wasn't destined to be in love with anyone. Was it wrong that for her that was what felt right?

"What are you thinking about?" asked Micah.

"I'm wondering if we should've taken King Tate up on his offer to give us a boat," said Azrael, not willing to share her true thoughts.

"Too conspicuous," said Raphael. "We don't know what weapons they have. There has to be another way."

"We need to get on one of their boats," said Micah. "Have I told you about the time I stowed away in a crate to get to my brother, Jeremiah?"

"Only several dozen times," teased Raphael.

"This is a little more serious than that," Azrael gently reminded her.

Micah's face fell and she looked away. "If I'd been caught, I'd have had my head chopped off. Is that serious enough for you?"

"I'm sorry," said Azrael, realizing there was so much they didn't know about each other's lives. "I didn't mean..."

"I know," said Micah quickly. "It's okay."

"Think we could whisper for a boat?" asked Raphael.

Azrael breathed a sigh at the diversion.

"Great idea!" said Micah. "But there'd be more power with five of us."

They stood and squeezed the excess water from their clothes. Azrael held her arms out to the sun and looked at her goosebumps. She was cold but clean. With any luck, soon she'd also be dry. Thankfully her dress wasn't heavy and would dry quickly.

Wading their way through the water, they went back to Pip and Griffen. Pip looked far healthier now than when they'd arrived. Azrael was pleased she responded to healings so effectively.

"What's wrong?" asked Griffen.

"We're going to whisper for a boat," said Micah. "Like the whisper we did before we left to ask for our safe journey here."

"Is that the best idea we have?" Pip let out a long sigh.

"We need a boat," said Raphael. "And yes, whispering is the best idea we have. Unless you fancy yourself a good swimmer?"

"Let's whisper," said Pip, allowing herself to be helped to her feet by Griffen.

They stood in a circle and grasped hands, focusing on their goal just like Micah had taught them.

Azrael brought the image of a boat to mind, imagining what it would feel like to see a boat on the horizon and how she'd fold herself up into a ball as she hid herself somewhere below the deck as it traveled to Feldspar.

"The Whisperers are whispering," said Micah.

"The Whisperers are whispering," they all repeated. "The Whisperers are whispering. The Whisperers are whispering."

"A boat has come ashore," said Micah.

Azrael smiled. She liked how the whispers were said in present tense as if they'd already taken place, rather than them being something they were willing in their future.

"A boat has come ashore," they all repeated. "A boat has come ashore. A boat has come ashore ..."

On and on they chanted until their voices were hoarse and Micah indicated that their work was done.

They let go of each other's hands, although Azrael noticed that Pip and Griffen continued to hold onto each other.

"If you're going to have a swim, you'd better do it now while the sun's still out," said Azrael, pleased that her dress was already almost half dry.

They nodded and wandered off to the water.

"Will it work?" asked Raphael.

"The whispers always work," said Micah.

"But haven't you been whispering for Lily's safe return for years now?" asked Azrael. "And that was with proper Whisperers doing it."

"Yes," said Micah.

"But..." Azrael didn't have the heart to finish her sentence. If that whisper hadn't worked, then why should they expect to see a boat come ashore?

"But nothing," said Micah. "We whispered for her safe return and that's exactly what's going to happen. There are no timelines on whispers. Sometimes they happen straight away and sometimes you have to wait."

There was a scream from the water and they spun around to see Pip pointing toward the horizon.

"A boat!" Pip jumped up and down, her face lit with joy.

Azrael squinted in the direction she was pointing, blinking when she saw what had caused the excitement.

There really was a boat, far out on the horizon. And if Azrael's eyes didn't deceive her, it was headed straight for them.

MICAH

THE NOW

Seeing that boat on the horizon was the happiest moment of Micah's life. Actually, no, that was a lie. Seeing Jeremiah for the first time after cheating her way into the palace as a Whisperer had been the happiest. Or was it when she'd seen the evil King fall from the balcony of the Arena? Perhaps it was when she'd realized she was in love with Tallis?

These jumbled thoughts made her smile. Because the truth was that no matter how miserable the start to her life had been, it had also been packed with happy moments. Moments that had made surviving all the misery worthwhile.

Knowing that nothing happy could come from a boat from Feldspar, they'd hidden behind some bushes back from the shoreline and watched and waited, their fear increasing with every moment that passed. All they needed was an opportunity to climb aboard and hide themselves. Griffen would be the hardest to hide, due to the sheer size of him.

Pip and Griffen had gone off in search of some food, saying they needed strength for what lay ahead. They'd returned with a large parcel of walnuts, tied up in a cloth Pip had brought for the purpose. Micah's mouth had watered when Griffen laid them out in front of them, cracking them one by one with his huge hands.

"The boat's taking forever," said Pip, straining her eyes as she looked out to sea.

"My brother found some walnuts once," said Micah, ignoring Pip as she crunched down on a walnut. The floury taste stuck to her tongue and she swallowed it down, despite her stomach feeling sick with nerves. "He wears one of the shells around his neck. Says it's his lucky walnut."

"And is it?" asked Pip, taking half a walnut from Griffen's outstretched hand.

"He hasn't starved to death yet." Micah slipped a walnut shell into her pocket, deciding they needed all the luck they could get right now.

"Your brother's married to the Queen," said Pip. "He's hardly likely to starve to death."

"Keep your voices down now," said Raphael. "Sound travels across water."

As the boat got closer, they saw it was only small, not the sort they were expecting at all. It had two large sails and what looked like a cabin underneath.

"That thing can't hold more than half a dozen people at most," said Griffen, peeking out from between the branches.

"We should have whispered for a bigger boat," said Pip, keeping her voice low.

Micah tugged at her hair, her fingers getting caught in the knots. Her swim earlier may have made her clean but it'd done little to tame the wildness of her hair. Hopefully, it made her look fierce.

"We'll figure something out," said Azrael. "At the very least, this will give us an idea of the kind of people we're dealing with."

"We need to overpower them," said Griffen, turning back to them. "And take their boat. It's the only way. There's nowhere to stow away on there. It's too small."

Micah realized he was right. The closer the boat got, the smaller it seemed. Large enough to hold them, but definitely not to hide them.

"I don't like violence," said Azrael, visibly shaking.

Micah shot her a sympathetic look. Overpowering someone would be difficult for her. Hopefully, it didn't come to that.

"Let's wait and see how many of them we're dealing with," said Micah, prepared to do what she had to do, but the thought filling her stomach with dread. "Maybe we'll get lucky and there'll only be one or two."

"I have an idea," said Raphael, shuffling about in the bag of elixirs he had slung over his shoulder. "I didn't want to use this, but I brought it with me, just in case."

He retrieved a small brown bottle and held it out for them to see.

"What is it?" asked Micah, her nose twitching as if she could smell it through the glass.

"It's a sleeping elixir," said Raphael. "Similar to one that was used on me as a child to kidnap me."

"You were kidnapped?" Pip's jaw fell open.

"It's a long story," said Raphael. "But I can tell you firsthand that it works. What if we wait to see how many men we're dealing with and we put some on a cloth to hold over their noses and knock them out. By the time they wake up, we'll have their boat and be halfway to Feldspar."

"You're a genius, Raph!" Micah clapped a hand over her mouth, realizing she'd forgotten to keep her voice down.

"Shhhh." Griffen's eyes widened and he pointed down the beach.

There were two people walking toward them. One tall and one short. A child?

Micah squinted to try to get a better look, then decided she'd have no choice but to wait until they got closer.

"Are they meeting the boat?" asked Raphael, his voice little more than a whisper.

Micah nodded, not trusting herself to speak.

They hunkered down behind the bushes, their eyes moving

between the figures walking toward them and the boat, which was getting close to shore now.

The two figures got near enough for Micah to see that the taller one was a man. The shorter one was indeed a child. A boy with a rope tied around his waist, the other end held by the man.

It took all Micah's will to stay quiet. Her blood was boiling. This boy was a prisoner! Memories of being held prisoner as a Whisperer flooded back to her. There was nothing worse than taking a person's freedom. It was almost as bad as taking their life. Sometimes it could be even worse.

The boy was small, maybe only four years old. His face was dirty and streaked with tears and his brown hair was standing up in clumps. The man wore black trousers and a long black jacket with a strange black wide-brimmed hat sitting crookedly on his head.

He was sneering at the boy, pulling at the rope whenever his little legs slowed, jerking him forward.

"Ow!" the boy complained, only to receive a blow across the back of his head.

Every muscle in Micah's body tensed as her rage built up in her stomach and threatened to explode.

Azrael put a hand on her arm and Micah looked across at her in surprise. Azrael was saying something under her breath as she held onto Micah and a wave a calm spread through her body, not enough to quell her anger, but enough to stop her from revealing her position and running down the beach to give that vile man a blow across the back of his head.

"Wait," said Griffen, so quietly Micah barely heard him. He was squatting, perched on his feet ready to leap out if needed.

Pip had tears of her own running down her cheeks. No child deserved to be treated this way.

Another wave of rage raced down Micah's spine as she realized this was likely how Lily had been treated when she'd been taken. And suddenly Raphael's idea of a sleeping elixir didn't seem like such a good idea after all. It was too kind. That man deserved to feel the pain he was inflicting on that small boy.

The man came to a stop several feet away from their hiding spot and waved to the approaching boat, confirming their suspicion that he was the cargo this boat had come to collect.

The boy sat down on the sand beside him and brought up his knees so he could rest his head on them.

He looked so tiny, curled up like that and Micah glanced at her companions who were all visibly distressed.

Raphael shook his head at Micah, no doubt sensing her strong desire to attack. As much as she didn't want him to be right, he was. They didn't know how many men were on that boat or what weapons they had. The best way to defeat these men and rescue the boy was to wait. They had to be smart about this, just like when Micah worked with Jeremiah and Rose to rescue the Whisperers. If they'd rushed in, their plan would never have worked.

The boat beached itself in the shallows and an anchor was thrown overboard to secure it to the sand.

Two men clambered off the boat and strode through the shallows toward the shoreline.

It was at this moment that the boy turned his head scanning the bushes as he searched for a way to escape while the men were distracted. His eyes landed on their hiding spot, his eyes widening to see five sets of eyes peering out at him.

Micah leaned out from behind the bushes and pressed her finger to her lips, locking eyes with the boy.

They stared at each other for a few moments as something passed between them. A silent conversation with an offer of trust.

The boy nodded ever so slightly and turned his face back to the ocean. Micah pulled back behind the bushes, feeling safe that their position wouldn't be revealed.

"Only one child!" called one of the men as he stepped onto dry sand. "Hardly worth the trip."

"That's all I could get this time," said the man holding the rope. "Damn parents holding onto them too tightly these days. Not this one, though. No parents left to hold onto him. Easy one to grab."

Micah's heart broke all over again. Once, she'd been a child with no parents left to hold onto her. No child should have to be responsible for their own survival like that.

Raphael tapped her on the leg to get her attention and held up three fingers, then pointed at the men.

She nodded.

Then Raphael pointed at himself, Griffen and then Micah, indicating the three of them were to be the ones to launch the attack.

Micah nodded again. There was no arguing with that. They needed their three strongest if they were going to succeed.

As Raphael readied the elixir by tipping it onto three pieces of cloth he'd removed from his bag, Pip got their attention by pointing to herself and Azrael and waving her hands above her head.

Realizing she was suggesting that they cause a distraction, Micah and Raphael nodded wildly. This would give them the opportunity to sneak up behind them and place the cloths over their noses. Griffen was shaking his head, protecting his Princess as best he could, but the look on Pip's face stilled his protests. She seemed determined to do her bit to help.

They waited until the three men were standing on the shore passing a flask around and Micah, Raphael, and Griffen walked slowly away from bushes, looping around to get themselves into a better position. Raphael stepped on a branch and the three men spun around when it cracked in half.

It was then that Azrael and Pip burst out from the bushes waving their arms.

"Help us!" said Pip.

"Wild boars!" added Azrael.

"Where?" The man with the rope hauled the boy roughly to his feet and Micah held steady, deciding this was the man she was going to target. Nothing would give her greater pleasure than sending him sinking to the sand. Perhaps she'd cover his face a little longer than was strictly necessary.

Pip and Azrael pointed in the opposite direction to where the others were hidden and the men braced themselves for a wild boar to run out onto the sand.

Micah looked at Raphael and Griffen, and Raphael nodded, sending them running as quickly and quietly as they could down the sand, while Pip and Azrael shrieked and hollered to hold the men's attention.

Micah went straight for the man with the rope, reaching around him to hold the cloth to his face. His hand clamped down on hers and tried to pull it away, but what Micah lacked in strength, she made up for in determination and she managed to hold on.

The boy kicked at the man's shins, and the man shrieked and kicked back at the boy, sending him flying to the sand.

In her peripheral vision, Micah could see Raphael had managed to subdue one of the other men and Griffen was laying the other down on the sand for his big sleep. But for some reason, the man at the other end of Micah's hand wasn't giving up. Something was wrong. Either she wasn't doing it right, or the elixir wasn't working on him.

The man broke free of her hold and turned around, grabbing Micah by the shoulders before pulling back one of his fists and aiming it directly at her face.

Micah ducked and spun around, landing her foot directly in the man's groin with force.

Excitement surged through her as he howled and doubled over, and she went back for him, hoping to land another kick.

But just as her foot rose from the sand, she spotted something shiny in the man's hand. He'd pulled a long knife from his belt as he'd righted himself and was ready for her.

She ducked again, knowing she didn't have the time that she needed to escape his blade.

Just before it made contact with her, Griffen appeared behind him, twisted the knife from his hand and held it at his throat.

Micah fell back on the sand next to the boy, her heart beating faster than it ever had before and her breath coming in short gasps.

"What are you doing with the boy?" Griffen asked, still holding the blade to his throat.

The man squirmed and a trickle of blood ran down his neck into the rough fabric of his jacket.

"He's for the King," the man said.

"What does a King want with a boy?" asked Micah, leaping up from the sand.

"For the mines. He can fit in the tunnels."

"Why not use your own children?" asked Griffen. "Why take from other kingdoms."

"We don't have enough." The man wriggled and more blood spilled to his jacket.

"What happened to the Princess you took in The Sands of Naar?" asked Micah. "Is she in the mines?"

"I don't know." The man glared at Micah.

"You do know," said Griffen.

The man reached for Griffen's wrist, his movements sudden as he tried to wrench the knife from his hand.

Micah stumbled back as blood gushed from the man's throat.

Griffen let go and the man fell to the sand, lying still as a red stream ran from his throat.

"You killed him," said Pip, her eyes wide.

"I had to," he said. "He'd have killed us all if we gave him the chance."

"Some people are better off dead," said Micah, not feeling in the least bit sorry for this awful man.

It was then that she looked down to see the boy had risen to his feet and looped one of his arms around her leg and was holding on tight.

She squatted down and undid the rope around his waist, cursing at how tightly it had been knotted. He had sores all around his middle from the friction.

"You're safe now," she said.

The boy nodded at her, his dark eyes full of trust and sorrow as tears streaked their way down his cheeks, making new trails in the dirt.

"Where are you from?" she asked.

"The Valley of the Blessed."

Micah's eyebrows shot up. "That's where I live. I've never seen you before."

The boy shrugged. There were a lot of people in the Valley. It wasn't so unusual not to have seen someone before.

"What's your name?" she asked.

"Gabe."

She gasped. This couldn't be a coincidence. It was Gabrielle who'd sent her on this quest to bring Lily home. And now this boy carried a variant of her name.

"Where are your parents?" she asked, reaching out to brush away his tears.

"They went cold and the man took them away. Then the other man came and took me."

"Which man?"

"That one there." He pointed at the corpse on the sand. "He was mean to me."

"He was." Micah swallowed. "But now that I've found you, I'm not going to let anyone ever be mean to you again."

"Are you going to look after me?"

Now it was Micah's turn to let her tears fall. "Yes, Gabe. I am."

RAPHAEL

THE NOW

"Why didn't your elixir work on him?" Griffen asked Raphael, pointing to the man bleeding out on the sand.

Raphael looked at the man's two companions who were lying unconscious either side of him.

"I'm not sure," said Raphael. "But if I had to guess, I'd say he has no sense of smell."

"Is that a thing?" asked Pip. "I've never met anybody before who couldn't smell."

"I've only ever met one other," said Raphael. "Elixirs didn't work on him either."

"Well, the knife seemed to do the job well enough," said Azrael, her face pulled into a permanent grimace.

"Thanks for what you did, Griffen," said Raphael. "It wasn't pleasant but you saved us."

Griffen gave a tight smile along with a nod. "Come on, let's check out this boat."

Raphael followed Griffen and Pip over to the boat, while Azrael went to Micah and Gabe to see the extent of their injuries.

"We need to pull down the sails," said Griffen, wading into the water. "I've seen boats like this in the Bay. These grooves on the side are for oars."

"Why couldn't we just sail across?" Pip crossed her arms against the cool breeze that had picked up.

"Unless one of us knows how to sail, that's going to be difficult," said Griffen.

"He's right," said Raphael. "We could end up anywhere. Plus we'll be easier to spot with those sails flapping about."

"Wouldn't they just assume we're them?" Pip pointed to the three men on the sand.

"And what if they prepare to greet us?" Griffen shook his head, his eyes full of worry. "We need to arrive in secret. Preferably at night."

"Surprise is the best weapon we have," said Raphael, noticing that Griffen had tucked the knife into his belt. That wouldn't hurt as a weapon, either.

"If we leave now, we can make a good start before nightfall." Griffen went to Pip and gently lifted her from her feet, cradling her in his arms as he walked toward the boat. "If we row through the night, we can hopefully make it before sun-up."

"Thank you, Griffen," said Pip as he set her down. Her face was flushed and she turned away quickly to hide it.

Raphael was certain he'd never made anyone's face flush like that before. It'd never bothered him, mainly because he'd never wanted to elicit that reaction from any of the women in his life. But Lily... would Lily feel that way when she met him? Because when he saw her in his visions, she managed to turn all his feelings on their head, swirl them into a ball and send them tumbling through his senses.

"Raphael," called Griffen, motioning for him to climb aboard.

Raphael shook his head awake and climbed over the edge of the boat. It tipped with his weight, then steadied itself. They'd better hope the seas were calm. This thing would be torn apart if the waves picked up much strength.

"Will the boy come with us?" asked Pip.

"Well, we can't leave him here," said Raphael, doing his best to be polite.

"Poor thing," said Pip, her eyes glued to Gabe, who was lying with his head in Micah's lap while Azrael worked to heal him. "I was just worried we might be bringing him into even more danger."

"I hope not," said Raphael. "But I don't like our chances of separating him from Micah and you try keeping her away from Feldspar. This whole quest was her idea."

Pip nodded. "We can all watch over him. He looks the same age as one of my nieces. I can help with him."

Griffen was busy working out how to pull down the sails, so Raphael detached an oar from the side panel of the boat and set it in one of the grooves. Balancing the weight of the smooth timber, he dipped it into the water. They'd have their work cut out for them to push this vessel through the water. They were all going to need to contribute, including Pip. Gabe could be let off, of course. One oar alone weighed more than that skinny boy.

But with a belly full of walnuts, washed down by the last of the tonic in their waterskins, they should have the strength to do this. Pip had been right to make sure they ate while they'd been waiting for the boat to approach.

Micah and Azrael were making their way over to the boat now. Micah was carrying Gabe in her arms, his skinny legs wrapped around her waist as he hugged her tightly around her neck. It didn't look like he was ever going to let go. Although, it really didn't seem like Micah cared. Anybody who didn't know them would assume they were mother and son.

He got another four oars ready.

"We need to get moving," said Azrael. "The men are starting to stir. Well, except for the one with the... neck."

Raphael put out his hands and helped Azrael aboard. Once she was safely settled, he reached for Micah.

"Pass Gabe to me," he said, seeing the boy's arms tighten around Micah's neck in response to his offer.

"It's okay." Micah lifted Gabe into the boat then clambered aboard herself. The moment she took one of the seats, Gabe scrambled onto her lap.

Raphael was going to need to go easy on that boy. It seemed his trust in men had been destroyed. Perhaps over time, he could show Gabe that not all men were like the one who'd tied that rope around his waist.

Having finished stowing away the sails, Griffen looked around the boat, scratching his chin.

"We need to balance our weight and our strength," he said.

Griffen was twice the size and three times the strength of any of them, which made things a little more difficult, but with a bit of shuffling about, they figured out that if he and Pip sat on the left and Raphael, Azrael, Micah, and Gabe on the right, they were roughly even.

Raphael jumped out of the boat to push them off the sand and deeper into the water, climbing back aboard when he felt them float free. He was dripping wet, but there wasn't a lot he could do about that.

He slid back into his seat at the stern of the boat and took hold of his oar, just as Gabe let out an almighty scream that almost stopped Raphael's heart.

Spinning around, he saw that Gabe was pointing to the shoreline. One of the men had gotten to his feet and was stumbling around on the sand.

Gabe screamed again and the man's head snapped up and his eyes found focus.

"Row!" called Griffen, hauling his oar through the water.

Raphael did the same, pleased to see the rest of his companions were also doing their best to get the boat moving. Micah was struggling with a terrified child on her lap, but she seemed to be making more headway than Azrael who was still trying to gain some traction with her oar in the water. Pip was fumbling in a panic, but with a powerhouse like Griffen behind her, her slack was more than being made up for.

"Row!" Griffen called again.

This time they all pulled together and the boat shot across the water.

Daring a quick look behind him, Raphael saw the man trudging through the water toward them with his fists in the air. They needed to get into deeper water as quickly as possible.

"Row!" Griffen's voice boomed across the water and Raphael pulled on his oar with as much strength as he had.

A wave crashed into them, pushing them back toward the shore, but undeterred, they pulled on their oars again.

"You need to be our lookout!" Micah said to Gabe, gently ejecting him from her lap so she could put her full effort into the task. "Stand beside me and tell us if the man gets close."

They pulled on the oars again, and the extra power Micah was exerting became obvious and they mounted a building wave and slid forward in the water. But the man was closing the gap now, finding it easier to push one body through the waves than this heavy boat.

"He's catching up!" shouted Gabe, taking a step closer to Micah.

"Row! Row! Row!" Griffen kept up the chant to keep them in time and they moved forward some more, almost over the worst of the waves now. If they could get lucky and catch a break in the waves, they might just get away.

Listening to Griffen shouting at them to row gave Raphael an idea. Griffen's shouts were no different really to their earlier whispering for a boat. They were all wishing to row faster and Griffen was calling out the words and sending them into the sky, but somehow it wasn't quite right.

"The boat is moving fast!" called Raphael as loudly as he could, only to be met with a few puzzled glances. "Let's whisper for it! Come on. The boat is moving fast!"

Griffen dropped his chant and joined in with Raphael, and soon they were all shouting. "The boat is moving fast."

Raphael wasn't sure if it was his imagination or if it was really happening, but the strength in the next stroke of their oars seemed to gain momentum.

"The boat is moving fast!" they called again on the next stroke and found they moved faster still.

Soon, their momentum built and they were gliding over the breaking waves and out to flatter water.

"We're doing it!" shouted Gabe, taking his job seriously. "He's given up!"

"The boat is moving fast!" they continued to call, not wanting to be too confident. They were working as a team and they were gliding faster over the water than it seemed possible for five people to do alone.

Renewed hope filled Raphael's soul. They were going to Feldspar and they were going to get Lily back. He didn't know if she'd love him in the same way he'd come to love her, but that didn't matter. All that mattered was that she was safe. Because nobody—absolutely nobody —deserved to be taken from their home against their will.

I'm coming, Lily. I'm coming.

LILY

THE NOW

*L*ily slipped out of the lighthouse and pressed her back against the door. She was certain neither Mother nor Father had heard her leave. They were too busy sipping on the tea she'd made them in the kitchen, before asking to be excused so she could have a nap. Given she was still recovering from her illness, they'd agreed, despite their usual insistence that she join them for the entirety of Father's visit. Sometimes Lily wondered if they were afraid to be left alone.

Her heart thumped wildly as she scanned the rocks along the shoreline, her eyes resting on Father's six oarsmen, who were sharing a flask of what she was certain must contain a spirit of some sort. Hopefully, the alcohol would put them in a good mood, for they were about to have to make a decision and she hoped their answer was a resounding yes.

She drew in a deep breath to try to calm her nerves. The plan she'd come up with was crazy, but she could do it. She just had to be brave like Aunt Micah.

Deciding there was no point in waiting for her heart rate to slow down, she waved at the oarsmen, motioning for them to come over to her. She couldn't risk going to them. If Mother or Father decided to look out the window or went to the balcony, she'd be ruined. Speaking to her Father's oarsmen was strictly forbidden.

The oarsmen looked at each other, raising their eyebrows. One of them punched another on the shoulder, no doubt misinterpreting what Lily wanted from them.

She motioned again, this time with more urgency. She didn't know how long she had. Sometimes Father's visits stretched for hours and other times he was gone only moments after he'd arrived. Given that Lily had left him alone with Mother, she doubted he'd stay for long.

One of the older men said something to the others and ambled over with his hands jammed in his pockets. She willed him to hurry but he seemed to only be able to travel at one speed. Slow.

"Quickly," she called, as loudly as she dared. "I need to talk to you."

"We ain't supposed to talk to the likes of ya," he said when he was close enough. "King's orders."

"Then why are you talking to me?" She stared at him and crossed her arms.

He shrugged.

"What's your name?" she asked.

"Norris." He crossed his arms and eyed her closely.

"You were on the boat that brought me over here, weren't you?" she asked. "I remember you."

He nodded. "What ya want, Princess?"

"I have something for you." She reached into the bag she had slung over her shoulder and produced an enormous ruby. "I have six of them. One for each of you. Worth enough for you to never have to row the King over here ever again."

Norris's eyes widened. "Keep talkin'. You ain't giving it to me for nothin' I presume."

She tucked the ruby back in her bag. "Take me back with you. Hide me under a blanket in the back of the boat. Get me there without the King seeing and the rubies are yours."

"The King will have me head if he finds out." Norris scratched at his beard in a most unbecoming way.

"Then he'd better not find out." She swallowed, but the lump in her throat was stuck fast.

"Need to discuss this with me associates." He shook his head with a look of wry amusement.

"Be quick about it." She suppressed a huff. "If Father sees me out here, the deal's off."

She watched as Norris made his way back to the other oarsmen, walking somewhat faster now that there was a ruby at stake.

The men stood in a circle, the wind carrying their words away from Lily out to the ocean. Even Mother Nature was working against her. Did this plan have a hope of succeeding? But she had to try something! She couldn't just sit here waiting for the lighthouse to crash into the ocean. She didn't even know that her Prince was coming for her. Maybe she was seeing him in her visions because she was supposed to go to him.

Escape had always seemed impossible. The seas were too rough and land too far away, no matter how good a swimmer she was. Otherwise, she'd have tried it years ago. So, she'd decided the only way was to stow away on Father's boat. If she could get to Feldspar, maybe she could find her way across yet more water back to the shores of Forte Cadence.

Home.

After what felt like approximately one hundred years but couldn't have been more than a couple of minutes, Norris marched back to her.

"Tomorrow," he said.

"I'm ready to go now." She locked eyes with him.

"Not going to work I'm 'fraid. Not everyone agrees. We need a sensus."

Her brow furrowed as she tried to work out what a sensus was, then it hit her.

"A consensus, you mean?"

"Don't go getting all fancy and correcting me grammar now, Princess. I said tomorrow. I'll make it good by then."

Lily's shoulders slumped. She couldn't wait until tomorrow. The lighthouse could fall at any moment. It had to be now.

"Tomorrow won't do," she said. "The deal's off. It was a today-only offer."

"Flamin' heck! Okay, wait 'ere." Norris stomped off, back to his *associates* where a heated conversation took place. The sort that was held with fists and boots as well as words.

Lily grimaced. She hadn't expected to be the cause of such angst when she'd come up with this plan. But she swallowed down her regret. She'd suffered far worse than this over the years.

One of the younger men stumbled backward as Norris landed a blow on the side of his head. He picked himself up and held out his palms, nodding slowly as his eye immediately bloomed a shade of purple.

It seemed a sensus had been reached.

Norris came back to Lily carrying an empty sack that'd been used to deliver food supplies to the lighthouse when they'd arrived.

"Get in." He held it open for her and waited.

Lily threaded one of her trembling legs into the sack, then the other, curling herself into a ball at the bottom, with her small bag of belongings clutched at her stomach.

Norris closed off the top of the sack and darkness surrounded her.

"Lucky there's nothin' of ya," he muttered, as he hauled her into the air.

Her plan had worked. Well, so far it had. There was still a possibility that one of the men who hadn't wanted to be a part of it would tell the King. She mustn't get overly confident. Not yet.

Although, a tiny part of her was celebrating. She may not have struggled as much as she should have when she'd been captured in the desert, but she was sure as hell fighting now.

Aunt Micah would be proud.

MICAH

THE NOW

*M*icah's arms ached from pulling the oars through the water, but there was no way she was going to admit to it. Each stroke took her closer to Lily. She could feel it in her soul. Gabe was stretched out at her feet, fast asleep. She liked the comfort of having him close. It gave her strength whenever she felt it wane.

She wasn't the only one starting to struggle, having heard several groans from her companions. All except Griffen who she was sure would be able to row for days if required. The Guardians were quite a strange creation. Was creation even the right word? Probably not, as that made them seem like they weren't human, when Griffen clearly was. She'd seen glimpses of fear, love, courage, and vulnerability cross his eyes. He was just stronger and bigger than the average human, a result of generations of tonics and training. As long as that strength was used for good instead of evil, then it was a good thing, she supposed.

Much like the Whisperers. When they'd been used for evil, the consequences had been devastating. But now they were being used for good, Forte Cadence was flourishing. All despite having a Queen who ruled with a broken heart.

Whispering for the boat had certainly worked well. Although, in fairness that could've been a coincidence. Certainly, she doubted the increased speed of their rowing had had nothing to do with them shouting to the universe. That'd been fear driving them. They'd all known it wouldn't end well if that man had made it to the boat. Griffen would have had to kill him and they didn't need another death on their hands. This quest was about restoring life, not ending it.

"Are we nearly there?" asked Pip.

Micah was certain that Pip had been skimming her oar over the top of the water for some time now. Although, the way Griffen was rowing behind her, it didn't seem to be making all that much difference.

Azrael was rowing at a steady pace, her hands strong from all the healings she'd performed. Raphael was seated behind Micah and putting in an impressive effort. Although he was a slender guy, he was stronger than he looked, with larger hands and a wider arm span than Micah, giving him an advantage. For a group of people who'd never rowed before, they were doing remarkably well.

"It's hard to tell," said Azrael in response to Pip. "Too dark now to see the land."

"Then how do we know we're not going in circles?" asked Pip.

"I've been watching the stars," said Raphael. "We're been heading east this whole time."

That answer seemed to satisfy Pip who fell silent once more.

"I'm sure it won't be much longer," said Micah, trying to convince Pip as much as herself.

As soon as the words were out of her mouth, the boat hit sand and they came to an abrupt halt.

"Sandbar?" asked Micah, not daring to believe they could have arrived.

"Land," said Raphael. "Quiet, everyone."

He was right. So much for them arriving in stealth. Here they were talking loudly as they'd drawn right up to the shore. They could only hope they'd arrived in a deserted part of the kingdom where nobody kept watch.

Gabe stirred at Micah's feet. Not being able to see him in the dark, Micah sat forward and put her hand on his chest.

"It's okay," she whispered. "We're here."

Gabe scrambled onto her lap and wrapped his arms around her neck.

"Shhh," she hushed, rubbing a circle on his back.

Why had he chosen her to be his person? Was it because she'd been the one to attack the man at the other end of his rope? Or was there more to it than that? Had he sensed her desperation for a child and decided he could fill that hole in her life? Whatever it was, she didn't plan on letting this boy down. Not now and not ever. Hopefully, Tallis would understand. He knew how hard her childhood had been. He'd witnessed it with his own eyes and experienced hardships of his own. He'd accept Gabe into their lives and be his father. She didn't need to have birthed this child from her body to be his mother.

A gentle breeze swept Micah's hair into her eyes and she pushed it away. If only it were a full moon to light their path.

"What do we do?" whispered Pip.

"I think we wait for sun-up," said Griffen. "Get some rest. I'll keep watch."

Micah wasn't sure how he was going to watch in the dark but held her tongue. He was right. Climbing out of the boat in the pitch dark would be too dangerous. They didn't know what was out there. If they got moving at first light, they'd be in a much better position.

Maneuvering herself out of her seat, Micah sat on the bottom of the boat and leaned against the side with Gabe snuggled into the crook of her arm. It was hard and uncomfortable, but her arms were grateful for the rest.

"I'm hungry," he whispered in her ear.

Remembering that she'd filled her pocket with shelled walnuts, she reached in and took out a handful, guiding Gabe's hand to her own.

"Eat these," she said, her own mouth watering, but not willing to eat any herself. Gabe needed them more than she did.

She nestled back against the side of the boat, listening to Gabe crunch on the walnuts as the boat gently rocked in the water.

Putting her hand back in her pocket, she took out her lucky walnut shell, wishing she had a string to tie it around her neck.

Closing her eyes, she filled her mind with Lily, begging the universe to give her a clue as to where to find her.

She gasped when a vision came to her, stronger than ever before. Lily was begging for help with her eyes once again, only this time she wasn't under the water. She was standing on some rocks holding what looked like several large rubies in her hands. Then just as quickly as the vision appeared, it vanished.

Her eyes sprang open and darkness engulfed her once more.

"Did anyone else see that?" she asked, keeping her voice low. The others had had visions before. It was possible they'd seen this too.

"I did," said Raphael.

"See what?" asked Pip.

"Lily," said Raphael. "She's in trouble. Worse than before. She's in the dark."

"So are we," Pip pointed out.

"This was different," said Micah. "Azrael, did you see it?"

But the gentle snoring she heard in reply told her that the only thing Azrael was seeing were her dreams. Perhaps she was dreaming of Lily.

"We have to get off this boat and go to her." Micah started to struggle to her feet.

"Quiet!" said Griffen, the urgency in his voice stilling her. "I can hear something out there."

Silence descended on the boat and Micah leaned forward as if that helped her to hear better.

A branch cracked in the distance and there was the distinct sound of somebody cursing.

They weren't alone.

LILY

THE NOW

*L*ily squeezed her eyes closed, despite being inside a dark sack. It was hard to breathe and she had to try to slow down the intervals she took between gasps. She concentrated on an image of her golden Prince and Aunt Micah, hoping to let them know that she was coming. She tried to bring the dark-haired woman to her mind as well but it was hard to remember her face. Perhaps when she was less stressed, she'd be able to. Maybe the woman who'd been standing in the shadows would reveal herself, too.

"Majesty's comin'." Lily was unsure if Norris was talking to her or his men. Not that it really mattered. His words meant it was too late for her to back out.

"None of youse is gonna say nothin', do ya hear me?" he hissed. "I know where all of youse live. Never forget that."

Lily cringed all over again. She'd wrongfully thought if Norris was an oarsman to the King, he'd be of a respectable nature. It appeared not. Although, she doubted this oaf of a man showed Father his true nature.

The boat tipped and rocked as the men climbed on board and Lily held her breath, certain Father would be able to hear the hammering of her heart. She was really doing this! It was happening. She was getting off that island and soon she'd be far away from Mother, never to have to clean her treasures or tell her another bedtime story ever again.

The boat set off with a jolt and Lily knew that one of the oarsmen would have pushed them off the sand and jumped aboard, just as she'd seen from her balcony countless times, never once imagining that one day she'd hide herself aboard. What had given her the courage to flee like this?

Aunt Micah may have inspired her with the stories she'd heard of her bravery but it was more than that. It was her Prince.

There was no doubt about it. The look in his eyes that had filled her with courage. They were destined for each other. She'd known it the moment she first saw him and she knew it now. She had to get away from the lighthouse before it was too late. He needed her as much as she needed him.

She was just like Ella in the story. She'd run away from her evil stepmother and by some kind of luck or magic, she was on her way to find her Prince. Except, there'd been no Fairy Godmother. She'd had to do it all herself. And instead of slippers made from leumarian seeded crystal, she had a bag full of rubies. She had to hope now for the same happy ending as Ella.

The boat headed further out to sea. It would almost settle into a calming rhythm if it weren't for the unpredictable tumbling of the waves. She was rolled back and forth and had to stop herself from gasping out loud as her spine bashed against the bottom of the boat. She reminded herself of the importance to keep quiet and clenched her teeth, squeezing her eyes closed even harder and wincing with each bump.

The boat reared up over a particularly large wave and Lily rolled back, twisting her shoulder in an awkward angle, unable to stop herself from yelping. Then came a blow to her ribs with what felt like the end of an oar, no doubt a warning to keep quiet. Bringing her hand to her mouth, she bit down on her sleeve to muffle her cries.

There was no need for such violence! An awful man like Norris didn't deserve a giant ruby to sell on the black market. How could she have trusted him with her life?

The boat crashed back down, only to rear up again over another wave. This time, Lily kept her cries to herself as her shoulder connected with the hard timber. She couldn't remember her trip over to the lighthouse being quite as rough as this. Although, that day had been calm, and she hadn't been hiding inside a sack that smelled like potatoes.

A scuffle broke out just in front of her and she resisted the urge to peek out of the opening of the sack, instead listening intently to the fast moving of feet, a loud crack and then a scream.

"Man overboard!" cried a deep voice.

There was more frantic scuffling, then the boat pulled back and turned.

Lily hugged her knees to her chest. She'd never heard of anyone falling overboard, although she supposed this wasn't the sort of conversation Father would make with her. Did it happen often? With seas this rough, it was going to be impossible to pluck anyone out of the water. Whoever it was would be dragged away by the current in no time.

A sick feeling that had nothing to do with the rocking of the boat gripped Lily around the middle. What if the man overboard was Norris? These men were sure to tell the King and she'd be sent back to the lighthouse with no way to ever escape again. This was her one chance.

As the boat was being tossed around on the waves, she knew there was nothing she could do except listen and hope that horrible Norris had somehow survived.

"What happened?" Father shouted over the angry ocean.

"I don't know!" shouted Norris. "He just fell in!"

Relief slid through Lily's core to hear his voice. He hadn't fallen overboard. The deal was still on. Then, guilt replaced the relief as she realized she'd just been happy to hear of another man's deadly misfortune.

"There he is!" someone else called. "Over there!"

The boat jolted from side-to-side as the men shouted at each other, between grunts as they tried to direct the boat to the man. Their words were whipped about by the wind and tumbled around the boat.

"I can't see him!"

"He went under!"

"Hurry!"

"It's no use!"

"Keep trying!"

"He's gone!"

Lily took the opportunity to move the opening of the sack so she could peer out at the chaos surrounding her. Men were leaning overboard and others were pulling on their oars with desperate looks plastered to their faces.

She saw Father sitting in the bow of the boat, running his hands through his dark hair as his eyes scanned the angry ocean

Until his eyes landed on her.

Lily held still. He couldn't possibly know she was inside this sack if she didn't move. Surely, he couldn't tell.

But Father continued to stare, until Norris stepped between them and broke his gaze.

Lily remained frozen, her heart hammering so fast now she was certain it must be making the hessian of the sack move up and down. She tried to slow it down but it only seemed to beat faster. Never had she felt this much fear, not even when she'd been lured away from her parents in the desert.

"We need to get back to shore," Norris said to his King. "It's too rough out here. We must keep you safe."

"We can't leave him," Father replied, his focus now on Norris

"We have no choice," said Norris. "We'll all die trying to find him."

Lily saw Father give Norris one quick nod as he smoothed down his jacket and looked forward once more.

He hadn't seen her. She was okay. Her plan was still working.

After a short heated discussion about the rights and wrongs of leaving a man behind, the men took their seats and hauled on the oars, pulling and pushing until the boat was over the worst of the sea and they entered the dock where Lily had left from all those years ago. A dock that she never thought she'd see again.

Worried now that someone would see her peering from the sack, she lay back against the side of the boat, keeping her movements slow and measured, and buried her head in her hands. Her heart rate had slowed now and her breathing steadied.

Without the anger of the sea, she could hear the panting of the men as they tired from all that hard work, no doubt deflated to have lost one of their crew. Perhaps grateful that it wasn't them.

"I saw you," hissed one of the men. It was hard to tell if it was Norris, but she thought not.

"Ya saw nothin', ya hear me," came the reply, which was unmistakably Norris.

"You pushed him," the other voice insisted. "I saw you."

"He was gonna tell," said Norris. "Ya want that ruby, or not?"

Lily fought the urge to vomit. Norris had been so desperate for the ruby that he'd pushed a man overboard. This was her fault. If she'd stayed where she was in the lighthouse, that man would still be alive.

The boat came to a sudden stop and Lily lurched forward, allowing herself to roll, in fear of being seen moving within the sack. She lay as still as she could, wondering how many bruises she'd get out of this. But none of that mattered. She was alive when some poor man was not. She was going to need to find a way to help set that right. Maybe deliver the ruby to his family? But how could a gemstone ever replace a loved one? The simple answer was that it couldn't.

There was the sound of men climbing onto the dock and helping the King out of the boat.

Lily lay still, waiting for Father to walk away so Norris could let her out of the sack. Her stomach had pulled into such a knot she wasn't sure how it was ever going to unwind itself. She'd actually done it! She was on the mainland where Mother couldn't reach her. And once she'd paid her debt of rubies, she'd be free.

"Is everything okay, Your Majesty?" asked Norris, his voice wavering.

What was Father doing to make this man so nervous?

"Follow me to the palace, Norris." Father's voice was laced with something completely different from nerves. Was that menace?

"Yes, Your Majesty."

Great. How was Lily going to get out of this sack now? Would one of the other men be kind enough to let her out?

"Oh, and Norris," said Father. "Please bring my daughter with you."

KING STERLING

THE NOW

King Sterling smiled, enjoying the impact his words had just had on Norris. If he'd reached out and slapped him it probably would've had less effect. Norris's shoulders had visibly stooped as his face fell apart, unable to be held together by the smugness of what he'd believed to be a victory.

This man had taken him for a fool, which made Norris the real fool here. It also made him a murderer. Did Norris really think he hadn't seen him toss his fellow oarsman into the water? The whole boat had seen it. And as for that sack that'd moved and groaned at Norris's feet... If that hadn't been obvious enough, hitting the sack with his oar had sealed Sterling's suspicions. It was definitely a person and there was only one possibility as to who it could be. Did Angel really hate living in the lighthouse that much? And what exactly had she offered Norris in exchange for her transport?

He watched as Norris clambered back into the boat and scooped up the hessian sack, throwing Angel over his shoulder. She wasn't bothering to disguise her movements now and thrashed about in protest. Norris climbed back up to the dock and followed Sterling along the worn timber planks, heading toward the shoreline.

"Father!" Angel shouted from within the bag. "Let me out of here! Please!"

"Not yet, my Angel," he said, smiling. "Let's get you safely to the palace first."

Norris went red in the face from the effort of carrying the squirming sack and shifted it from his shoulders to cradle Angel in his arms.

"Stop ya movin'," he growled.

"That's no way to talk to a Princess," said Sterling, keeping his voice level.

Angel yelped, no doubt being squeezed beyond her limits. As much as Sterling didn't like the idea of his precious daughter in pain, it seemed necessary. A good way for her to learn what happened when you tried to outsmart a King.

Sterling nodded at the guards waiting for him at the end of the dock.

"Make sure this one follows me," he instructed, nodding toward Norris.

"Yes, Your Majesty," said one of the guards, breaking away to walk beside Norris.

Sterling walked on ahead, knowing he had some decisions to make. Not just what to do with this murdering idiot traitor of an oarsman, but what to do with Angel.

Eileena would be angry when she realized Angel was missing. That girl was her greatest treasure and the glue that held their family together. When she'd first told him about her vision of a daughter, he'd thought it was sweet. But, of course, he'd also thought this daughter would be the fruit of his loins, not a girl he'd had to pluck from the mines when his wife's womb had remained stubbornly void.

He hadn't realized at the time who Angel was. He'd selected her for her tender age and red hair. It wasn't until much later that one of his informants had told him about the search for Princess Lily of Forte

Cadence and he'd made the connection. But it had been too late by then. Eileena had already bonded with her. Besides, Angel had been so young when she'd arrived in Feldspar, she'd barely be able to remember her former life. There was no use in returning her.

Sterling swallowed, aware of a lump in his throat. This was a lie and he knew it.

He heard a squeal come from behind him and turned to see Norris struggling to keep hold of the wriggling sack.

He quickened his footsteps. Angel remembered her life, all right. And that's why she was fighting so hard right now. It was time he had a serious talk with that girl. Time for him to remind her just how lucky she was.

He made his way through the gates and across the dirt expanse that surrounded the palace. He knew other kingdoms had lush gardens in their palace grounds, but this was foolish. People could hide behind trees. It was better to be able to see exactly who or what you were surrounded by.

He walked toward the palace entrance, remembering how it used to feel to return home knowing his Queen was here. It was so empty now without her.

He'd been surprised all those years ago when he'd placed the other half of his twin love stone in the hands of what he'd thought was an ordinary girl and it'd glowed brightly. He'd looked down at the other stone in his hand and known that this plain-looking girl was destined for him. She wasn't just his future Queen, she was his true love. The amethysts could not be argued with.

When he'd looked at Eileena for the second time with this knowledge safely tucked away, he'd realized that she wasn't plain at all. She was... beautiful. He'd made it his life's mission to keep her happy. Although, admittedly, back then he hadn't known just how difficult this was going to be. But that didn't matter, for he'd have tried anyway. Because when Eileena smiled with her eyes, he smiled with his heart, the warmth of their connection penetrating even the darkest corners of his soul. He could never be truly at peace unless he knew she was, too.

He kicked at a rock, sending it flying across the dirt. His whole kingdom looked like this; barren and cold. There was even a line of dead trees across the southern shoreline, which was pleasing. Let his enemies think there was nothing of value here.

He walked up the wide marble steps and nodded to the guards who held open the palace doors, bracing himself for the emptiness inside. He'd move to the lighthouse to be with her, but it would be too difficult to rule a kingdom from across the sea. And too heartbreaking to live with a woman who was the ghost of the loving wife she used to be.

She'd become an angry soul, blaming him for not having been able to provide her with the child she'd yearned for, going so far as to have moved to the lighthouse saying she couldn't stand to be around people. He'd thought when he'd brought her Angel that maybe she'd soften and come back to the palace, but it seemed he'd been too late.

She'd thrown away her love stone, having given up waiting. He tried so hard not to be offended by this, but it was difficult. Throwing that amethyst away was the equivalent to her throwing away her love for him.

He strode into the grand entrance hall, pleased to hear that Norris was following.

"Let me out, Father! Please!"

He smiled at Angel's stubbornness, wondering if she'd brought the amethyst with her. The one he'd slipped into her bed when she'd been sick. Maybe she'd also brought Eileena's stone, which he half suspected she'd found a long time ago. He knew it hadn't gone far from the lighthouse by the way his own amethyst had glowed with warmth whenever he'd ventured near.

He'd given Angel his amethyst so it would make her well and she could use it to find the twin stone. As his only child, she was supposed to inherit the amethysts anyway. Surely, she must have known he was the one to put it in her bed? But instead of asking him about it, she'd tried to run away, leaving him with no love stones, and no daughter.

He looked around at the entrance hall, the sparkling of the emer-ald-lined walls a direct contrast to the brown stone walls of the outside. Eileena had thought it was beautiful here when she'd first arrived. He'd been so pleased, thinking she'd make it her home forever. Now, when he looked at the emeralds, all he saw was his broken heart.

Making his way to his throne room, he braced himself for the shine of the diamonds that covered every surface of the room. The guards opened the door for him and he had to squint at the sparkling light that burst out, every facet of every stone reflecting off the giant diamond-encrusted windows that lined this long rectangular room. His father's father's father had first had the idea to decorate the throne room like this. Or had it been his father's father's father's father? He couldn't remember now. All he knew was that it'd taken many generations to mine enough diamonds to complete the dazzling effect. This had been Eileena's favorite room in the palace. When she'd moved to the lighthouse, she'd asked him to remove the diamonds and bring them to her.

This was the one request of hers that he'd denied and she'd been furious with him. She still was.

But they belonged to the palace. They weren't his to give.

A scream behind him reminded him of why he'd come to the throne room today.

Angel.

Had she been his to give?

Going to his throne, he took a seat and ran his fingertips over the diamond-encrusted armrests as he waited for Norris to set down the squirming sack at his feet.

"Undo it," Sterling commanded.

Norris did as he was told and unknotted the string that held the sack closed. As soon as it was partially open, Angel's hands burst through as she tore the sack down over her head then shoulders. She was gasping for air, clutching at her stomach, her eyes full of tears and rage. Her orange hair was tangled into wild knots that stood on end and she had scratches and bruises on her forearms where the torn sleeves of her dress had been pushed up.

"My daughter," he said.

"I'm not your daughter," she spat back.

His eyebrows shot up so quickly that his head jolted back and hit the back of his throne. Damn diamonds! They might look pretty, but they were sharp.

"What did you say?" he asked, rubbing the back of his head. Angel had never defied him like this.

"I'm not your daughter." She crossed her arms and glared at him.

Sterling clicked his fingers to get his guards' attention and motioned for them to take Norris and leave the room.

"Put him in a cell," he said. "I'll deal with him later."

"But…" Norris's mouth flapped open to protest, until he realized that he had no grounds to complain. What had he expected for kidnapping the King's daughter? A bag of jewels and a pat on the back?

The guards dragged Norris from the room.

"Close the door behind you," Sterling instructed. "And take that sack with you. It smells like potatoes in here."

"I smell like potatoes." Angel sniffed at her clothes and shook her head in disgust.

"Well, you chose to get in there," he said, keeping his voice level. He rarely raised his voice, priding himself on his ability to rule the kingdom with measured calm. "Unless you're trying to tell me you were taken against your will?"

Angel's stony eyes were her response. Yes, he had this story right. This had been her idea.

"Your mother will be very worried to find you missing," he said.

"She's not my mother." A look of hatred crossed her eyes and he wondered how he'd gotten everything so wrong. He'd thought she'd been happy in the lighthouse.

"She raised you," he said. "That makes her your mother."

"My mother is Queen Rose of Forte Cadence." Angel crossed her arms and stared him down. "And my father is Prince Jeremiah."

He bit down on his tongue, trying to regain his calm, then noticed she had a small bag around her shoulders.

"What's in the bag?" he asked. If the amethysts were in there surely he'd be able to feel their warmth from here.

She lifted the bag from her shoulders and tipped it out, sending half a dozen large rubies scattering across the floor.

"Is that all you have with you?"

She nodded. "I want to go home. Please, Father."

He smiled. At last, she was being compliant.

"I'll take you back in the boat in the morning," he said. "The seas are too rough right now."

Her face lit up. "You mean it? You're going to let me go home?"

"Of course. I told you that Mother will be worried."

Angel's legs crumpled beneath her and she collapsed to the floor, burying her head in her hands.

"I want to go home," she said, looking up at him. "To Forte Cadence. That lighthouse isn't my home."

His heart sank. Perhaps he was the fool that Norris had taken him for. Of course, she was talking about the home she'd been born to.

"Please, Father." She grabbed at the bottom of his long cloak and pulled at it, pleading with him. "Please, let me go home."

"Angel," he said, as gently as he could. "Your home is the lighthouse."

"It is *not* my home," she said. "And my name's Lily."

He sighed deeply, realizing what he had to do. He'd been far too soft on this girl.

She needed to learn to appreciate how good she had it in the lighthouse. Life was all about contrasts. Sometimes you had to experience the bad before you knew how good you really had it.

"Guards!" he called.

Two guards burst through the door, ready to do his bidding.

"Take my daughter to the Terrace," he said.

The guards looked at him, unable to hide their shock. Only the worst criminals were sent to the Terrace. He hadn't even sent Norris there.

"You heard me!" He bit down on his lip, realizing he'd almost raised his voice. "Leave her there until I tell you otherwise."

"What's the Terrace?" asked Angel as the guards seized her by the arms.

"It's where you're going to think," he said. "When you're ready to tell me your real name and where your home is, you can call for me."

"My name is Princess Lily of Forte Cadence!" she shouted as her feet lifted from the floor as the guards hoisted her into the air.

"You are Angel of the Lighthouse!"

Damn it! He'd definitely raised his voice that time. But somehow, she hadn't seemed to have heard. A few nights on the Terrace should sort her hearing out...

PIP

THE NOW

*P*ip shuffled a little closer to Griffen on the boat. If he was right and there was someone out there, they were in grave danger.

"Wait here," he said, landing a light kiss on her forehead and rushing silently off the boat, sliding into the water. Her heart ached at the loss of having him by her side. He wasn't just her protector, he was her best friend. She knew her other traveling companions found her irritating, even though they were happy to eat the food she brought them. Micah would've died on day one if Pip hadn't stopped her putting that poisonous berry in her mouth. But Griffen didn't find her irritating. She could feel the protection he offered her came from a place of love as well as duty.

If they somehow managed to make it back to The Bay of Laurel alive, she intended to ask Tate for permission to marry him. It was strange to have to ask for his stamp of approval but the King needed to approve all royal unions. She expected he'd say yes. After all, he himself had married a Guardian and look at how successful that union had been. River had turned out to be the perfect match for him. Besides, he probably wasn't in much of a position to say no to anything she wanted, given she was the true ruler of the kingdom. But she didn't want to think about that any more than she wanted it to be true.

She wrapped her arms around her middle and waited, using every ounce of her being to send Griffen silent wishes of protection. If only she could ask the others to whisper for his safety. But they couldn't make a sound right now. Perhaps sending good thoughts to Griffen was the same as whispering? Maybe it was the intent that the universe picked up on instead of the words themselves.

Gabe made a small whimpering sound and Micah hushed him. That poor child had been plucked from danger only to be directly deposited into even more. But at least he had loving arms around him now. Pip was fond of children too and would've been happy to care for Gabe, but something about the look in Micah's eyes had made her back off. It was a look of longing and hope as if Gabe was the child she'd been waiting for all her life. Pip wasn't going to interfere with that.

A gentle breeze pushed a dark cloud across the sky and the moon broke through, casting soft light across the boat and Pip saw Gabe on Micah's lap with his arms wrapped around her neck. Azrael sat quietly in front of them and Raphael was sliding into the water, his eyes scanning the shoreline for Griffen.

She watched as Raphael waded through the cold water and scrambled up onto the sand, disappearing behind a line of what looked like dead trees. Then, almost as if the clouds had decided they'd seen enough, they raced across the sky and covered the moon, once more shrouding them in darkness.

They waited. Waited some more. And then waited for what felt like eternity.

It was Micah who eventually broke the silence.

"Should we go after them?" she whispered, her voice so soft it sounded more like the flutter of wings than an actual voice.

"No," said Azrael.

"We have a better chance if we stick together," said Micah, daring to raise the volume of her voice a little this time.

"Not always," said Azrael. "Sometimes it's better to divide in order to conquer."

There was certainly in Azrael's voice, making Pip wonder what conquering she'd done in her past.

"Gabe," said Micah. "I need you to stay with Pip for a moment. I'm just going to check on the others."

"No!" His voice was high pitched and panicked.

Pip winced. If their enemies hadn't known their location before, then they were certain to now.

"I'll take care of you," said Pip, not bothering to lower her voice after that. "Come to me, Gabe."

She held out her hands and Micah placed the squirming boy on her lap. She held onto him tightly, resisting his attempts to get away from her.

The boat rocked as Micah slid into the water, the sound of her retreat fading with each moment that passed.

"Hush," she said to Gabe, doing her best to soothe him. "It's okay. She'll be back soon."

"That's what Mother said about Father." Gabe buried his face in Pip's shoulder. "And he never came back."

Pip rubbed his back. This poor boy had been through too much. She'd lost her own mother at a similar age and although the years had dulled the pain, it had never gone away. At least she no longer felt responsible for her mother's death, having worked hard to let that go.

Coming to terms with what she'd learned before setting out on this quest was proving a little more difficult. The brother she'd loved and respected all her life was of no relation to her at all. And the man she'd despised for his evil heart, was linked to her by blood. What kind of person did that make her? A little bit of both? She was trying to be a good person. Maybe if she could help rescue Lily and bring her home, she'd be able to believe that she was worthwhile.

"What do you think's happening?" asked Azrael. "It's been ages."

"I think we should go and check," said Pip, feeling her heart rate pick up. "We don't want to be sitting out here when the sun comes up. We'd be better off to hide in the bushes while we wait."

"Come on then," said Azrael, not needing any further convincing.

"Micah," Gabe whispered in her ear. "Let's go find Micah."

Pip squeezed Gabe a little tighter.

"Hold on," she told him as she climbed over the edge of the boat.

The water was cold and she held Gabe up high to keep him dry. Griffen had told her to wait on the boat, but surely, he hadn't meant for her to wait all night, not knowing what had happened to him.

She could hear Azrael ahead of her in the water and she followed behind, not wanting to lose her.

"Are there bad men out there?" asked Gabe.

"I don't know," said Pip, being as honest as she could. If the men they'd met on the beach earlier were anything to judge the inhabitants of Feldspar by, then they were in for trouble.

Stepping onto the sand was a welcome relief and Pip set Gabe down, her aching shoulders thanking her. She wasn't as strong as Micah to be able to carry him across the sand. Gabe gripped her hand tightly and she squeezed him in return.

If only the clouds would move a little and allow them some light, but they stubbornly curtained the moon, with no sign of shifting.

Pip jumped as someone grabbed her on the arm.

"It's only me," hissed Azrael, sliding her hand into Pip's. At least they wouldn't lose each other now.

The ground sloped upwards and they trudged through it until they felt bracken breaking underneath their wet shoes. Stepping as quietly as they could, they made their way forward.

Pip let go of Azrael's hand, needing to wave it in front of her as she walked, certain she was about to crash into one of those dead trees she'd seen earlier. Azrael clung onto the back of her dress instead.

Pip squinted ahead, not sure if she was imagining a white light in the distance.

"Do you see that?" she asked as quietly as she could.

"Yes," Azrael whispered back.

The light grew brighter and Pip felt herself being pulled toward it. There was something about it that made her want to touch it.

So fascinated was she with it, that she didn't notice at first when Gabe let go of her hand.

They were only separated for maybe three or four beats of her heart before Pip's hand reached out for him. Then she was reaching with her other hand, taking frenzied steps in a circle as she tried to find him.

"What's wrong?" asked Azrael, still clinging to the back of her dress.

"Gabe," she said. "I can't find him. He let go of my hand."

Now Azrael was turning in circles.

"We have to find him," said Azrael, no longer caring about keeping her voice down as they scrambled about in the dark, their empty hands finding nothing but frigid air.

"Gabe," Pip dared to call out. "Gabe!"

But no sooner had she shouted the words as she was grabbed around the waist. A large hand clamped itself over her mouth and as she struggled to break free, Azrael let out a bloodcurdling screen.

Struggling now to breathe, Pip kicked at her captor, only to feel her feet lift off the ground as she was thrown over someone's shoulder and carried through the trees, deeper into the night.

RAPHAEL

THE NOW

*R*aphael sat forward, straining his ears. There'd been a scream. Was that Pip? Or maybe it'd been Azrael? It couldn't have been Micah, given that she was next to him. So was Griffen, although he'd never suspect him of letting out such a high pitched sound. Men like him didn't scream. They bellowed. And it was hard to either scream or bellow when your mouth was gagged.

The sun was starting to come up now and in the faint light, he could make out where they were being held captive.

The three of them had been imprisoned inside some kind of large cage made out of gnarled tree branches. Their hands were tied behind their backs and their ankles strapped together.

He pushed at the gag with his tongue trying to dislodge it, but it was too tight. If only he could talk to Micah or Griffen, maybe they'd be able to figure out some kind of plan to get out of here.

There was the sound of a struggle in the trees just beyond and

Raphael squinted, willing the sun to rise faster so he could see what was going on.

The shadows of two men were coming toward them with Azrael and Pip in their arms. Neither of the women were being compliant. Pip, in particular, was thrashing her tiny frame about trying to shout something, her words muffled by the hand across her mouth.

Griffen grunted and threw himself at the cage. It buckled and threatened to snap under his force.

"Break that and I'll break her," warned the man carrying Pip.

Griffen's face filled with anguish as he tried to work out his next best move. Raphael knew he'd come on this journey to protect Pip, but that was a little difficult when he was tied up in a cage. There was a bloody gash down the side of Griffen's face. Raphael hadn't seen how he'd been overpowered, but it must have been one almighty struggle.

He watched now as the men threw Pip and Azrael on the ground with no care for their welfare. Two more men appeared with several lengths of rope. One of them had a torn shirt and a black eye, most likely the result of being on the other end of Griffen's struggle.

Micah squirmed beside Raphael, making muffled screams through her gag. Raphael gave her a look to try to warn her to be quiet, before realizing that her distress was no doubt due to Gabe's absence. Didn't she realize this was a good thing? If he wasn't here, then he at least had a chance, whereas it seemed the rest of them were doomed.

The men gagged Azrael and Pip, then trussed up their wrists and ankles. Opening the door of the cage, they threw them inside. Raphael rolled forward trying to break Azrael's fall, remembering how much it'd hurt when he'd been hurled inside, seeing that Griffen had done the same for Pip.

The door was re-tied with heavy rope and the men took several steps away.

It was cramped in here with five of them now, but at least they were together. Except for Gabe, although hopefully, he was somewhere safe. Micah's tear-filled eyes darted around the dead forest in the morning light, looking for him.

Pip shook her head at Micah, but it was impossible to tell if that meant Gabe was safe, or... otherwise.

Griffen shuffled over to get closer to Pip and pressed his forehead against hers. Pip blinked up at him, taking in his injuries, even more visible now that the sun had risen a little higher.

Raphael considered trying to provide Micah with some reassurance, but knew she was too distressed to pay him any attention.

Maybe this wasn't such a bad thing. Because when she was upset, a fire lit inside her. And right now, they all needed to draw on their inner rage if they were going to get out of here alive.

Griffen made a grunting noise and Raphael looked across to see him motioning with his head for them to sit between him and the huddle of guards. The women repositioned themselves and Raphael remained next to Griffen, with no space left to get in front of him.

He watched as subtly as he could to see Griffen straining his arms, his wrists acting as opposing forces to the rope that bound them. Surely, he didn't think he was going to be able to break open the ropes? Guardians were strong but this would take something else. Strength that no man possessed.

Then Raphael saw the glint of metal in the rear of the waistband of Griffen's trousers. The knife! Raphael had forgotten all about that. Had their captors been foolish enough not to check them for weapons before throwing them inside the cage?

Griffen was rubbing the rope against the edge of the blade, his actions fast but subtle enough not to draw attention. The rope frayed a little and he increased the pressure, forcing his wrists apart until the rope broke free, falling on the ground behind him. Now Griffen worked quickly to undo the ropes at his ankles, then got to work on Raphael's wrists. It would be too obvious if he were to undo their gags.

Just as Raphael felt the pressure around his wrists release, the guards broke up their huddle to walk over to them. Griffen returned his wrists to behind his back and blinked at the men with hatred in his eyes. Raphael did the same, desperate to undo his ankle ties and release the others but knowing he must wait.

"This one's going to be our talker," said one of the men, pointing at Micah.

Raphael breathed a sigh, not because he was glad that Micah had been selected, but because neither he nor Griffen had been. If the men noticed they'd managed to undo the ropes on their wrists, they'd be in even more danger.

He studied the man as he opened the door of the cage. Like the other men, he was wearing black trousers with a matching long jacket and a wide-brimmed hat. His skin was fair, although not as fair as Raphael's own, and his eyes were a pale brown. He had a beard, as did the other men and Raphael wondered if this was a fashion statement or a choice to protect their faces from the relentlessly cold breeze they'd so far experienced in Feldspar.

The man made a grab for Micah and pulled her out of the cage. Another of the men quickly closed and secured the door before either Griffen or Raphael had the chance to make a move.

Micah's gag was removed and she stumbled to the ground, sitting there glaring at the men with her red hair like a halo of fire around her angry face.

Raphael took this moment of distraction to untie his ankles, noticing out of the corner of his eye that Griffen was working on Pip's ropes. Once his ankles were free, he shifted behind Azrael as subtly as he could, to work on untying her wrists.

"This one's a pretty one," said one of the men, leering at Micah as he loomed over her. "Even if she's dressed like a man. Can't fool me, though. I see what she's got under those clothes."

Micah kicked out at him with her bound feet, knocking him to the ground. Raphael's fingers paused on Azrael's ropes as he winced, knowing Micah wouldn't get away with such a bold move. Sure enough, one of the other men raised his boot into the air and landed a blow in Micah's ribs.

She let out a loud groan and curled herself into a ball.

Raphael finished releasing Azrael's wrists and moved in front of her with his hands held behind his back so as not to attract suspicion and to cover the men's view of Azrael as she got to work on the rope around her ankles.

"Right. Question time," said one of the men, squatting down just outside kicking distance from Micah. "Who are you? Where did you come from? What are you doing here? And what happened to the men whose boat you arrived in? Got it? You can start talking now."

Micah glued her lips together and shook her head.

"Talk to us, you useless bitch!" The man stood up and raised his boot above her head. "Want another one of these, do you?"

Micah leaped to her feet in one swift action and drove her shoulder into the man's groin, toppling him over.

He howled and cursed as he bent over, clutching his precious manhood. Micah had fallen to the ground again, and as she sat up, she glanced across to the cage, her eyes widening to see something Raphael hadn't yet noticed. He looked across to see Griffen working on the rope that held the door closed, slicing through it with his knife.

Micah pulled herself across the dirt, positioning herself on the other side of the men to the cage, so to look at her they'd need to turn their backs to Griffen.

Raphael shook his head in awe of the most courageous woman he'd ever met. No, scratch that. She was the most courageous *person* he'd ever met. She didn't need a husband or a Guardian to protect her. She was afraid of nothing and nobody. He wondered if Lily had grown up with the same courage burning inside her.

With one man nursing a severely bruised shin and another still hunched over, Micah certainly had the full attention of the four men now.

"Don't like talking much, do you?" said the man she'd kicked first. "Maybe you can show us your appreciation for not killing you in other ways."

The leer on his face spelled out exactly what kind of payment he had in mind and his three friends laughed.

Azrael squirmed beside Raphael, biting on her gag and darting panicked looks at Raphael. They needed to make a move and they had to be fast about it. They outnumbered these men by one, although neither she nor Pip were likely to be much use in a fight, and Micah still had her wrists and ankles bound. But they did have Griffen and he had to be the equivalent of at least three men.

Micah got to her knees, then her feet and smiled at the men, looking at them one by one as she licked her lips, the corners of her mouth an angry pink from where the gag had been. "Which one of you would like to go first?"

She had their full attention now and Raphael watched as Griffen removed the rope from the door and climbed out, holding his knife in front of him. He motioned for Pip to stay where she was, but she wasn't having a bar of that and climbed out behind him.

Raphael was next, then Azrael.

Micah was doing a good job at distracting the men and one of them had stepped forward to make a grab for her. She allowed him to undo the top button of her shirt, then as he got to work on the second, she dipped her knees and bent forward, pushing herself up to her full height with speed and slamming her forehead into the man's face.

The man's nose cracked and blood fountained outwards, splattering the dirt around him.

Griffen moved quickly while shock was still in the air and sliced his knife across another of the men's throats, taking his life before he even knew what was coming.

Raphael had taken a length of rope from the cage with him and slipped it over the man with the broken nose's neck and crossed the ends, pulling as tight as he was able. The man kicked back at him and struggled, but already weakened with pain and blinded by the gushing of blood, he was no match for Raphael and his anger. How dare he put his hands on Micah like that! To think what he would've done if Griffen hadn't managed to get them out of the cage.

He pulled tighter on the rope, having no idea how long it took to kill a man, or what right he had to end a life. But it was kill or be killed. He had no choice here. If they were to get out of this alive and bring Lily home safely, then this scumbag of a man needed to draw his final breath.

The man's kicking lost some of its force, but Raphael held on pulling even harder on the rope until his life flowed out and he crumbled to the ground, blood still running from his nose and pooling around his head.

Raphael spun around to see what needed to be done with the two remaining men, to find Griffen had one pinned to the ground, and Pip and Azrael were holding closed the door to the cage with the other man trapped inside. Micah was sitting on the ground, with her knees pulled up and her head resting on them, still bound by the ropes that had hindered her but not stopped her from protecting herself.

Quickly removing his gag, Raphael went to Micah and undid the rope that bound her wrists.

"Are you okay?" he asked.

Micah looked up at him and he could see a gash across her forehead. "I'm good. Just a bit dizzy. Go and help Griffen."

Deciding to take her at her word, he went to Griffen, helping him drag the man by the feet toward the cage. Together, they threw him inside with his friend.

The two men glared at them through the bars, but with both Pip and Azrael watching their every move, they weren't going to take them by surprise with any sudden moves.

"Look over there," said one of the men, pointing.

"We're not falling for that old trick," said Pip, not taking her eyes off him.

"Your friend's falling for it though," he said. "Or falling over for it."

The two men sniggered and Raphael looked to where they were pointing.

Micah was lying on the ground with her eyes closed, far too still for someone taking a rest.

"Micah!" he cried, rushing to her side.

They'd done the impossible and broken out of the clutches of these evil men. But what exactly had been the price of that?

"Micah!" he cried again, crouching beside her and pressing his fingers to her wrist.

But no matter how hard he searched, he couldn't find a pulse.

AZRAEL

THE NOW

"*D*on't take your eyes off them," Azrael said to Pip, pointing to the two men in the cage.

"I'm watching them, too," said Griffen, taking her place.

"Go! Help Micah," said Pip. "Hurry."

Azrael dashed over to Micah, almost tripping on a tree root, but saving herself and remaining upright. Her wrists and ankles were still sore from that coarse rope, and her mouth dry from the gag, although these were the least of her concerns right now.

"She's not breathing," said Raphael.

Crouching down next to Micah, Azrael put her ear against her face.

"She is breathing," she said, letting out a sigh as the faintest breath of air brushed against her cheek. "Can you untie her ankles while I check her heart?"

As Raphael busied himself with the rope, Azrael pressed her fingers against Micah's bruised wrist. She had to have a pulse if she was breathing? She changed her position to Micah's neck, finally detecting the faintest sign of a pulse. A regular if not concerningly slow heartbeat. Raphael had been too panicked and hasty to detect these signs of life, but Azrael's trained hands knew what to do.

"Help me turn her to her back," she said, and together she and Raphael tipped Micah over.

She held her hands over Micah's body, scanning her as she felt for her energy centers, just like her mother had done when Toran had carried her into their healing room in the Colony.

Her hands tingled as she moved up and down Micah's body. Her energy centers were flowing surprisingly well. She threaded her hands through them anyway, resetting her energy pattern as she pulled the strength of Micah's field up and out.

Once she was satisfied her body was as strong as she could make it, she moved her hands to Micah's head, touching her forehead gently. That was some headbutt she'd given that man. Thankfully she'd used the hard bone at the front of her forehead and not the soft spot on the top of her head. That could have resulted in an injury that not even Azrael was able to repair.

As it was, the trauma she'd experienced to this vital part of her body was impacting her enough, confusing Micah's vital energy that swarmed around her brain. Azrael worked quickly and expertly to knead her hands through this compromised center. Very slowly, the knots blocking the flow began to unravel. She worked hard, pulling and separating the strands, coaxing Micah back to health.

Raphael remained beside her and although she was aware of his presence, he may as well have been a thousand miles away. Her focus was on Micah alone.

Scanning her hands back down the length of Micah's body, she checked for any blockages that might've built up with the shift of energy as she'd rebalanced the center in her brain.

She paused at Micah's core, remembering their conversation in the desert about the babies she'd lost. There was a definite weakness in this area, but now wasn't the time to fix that. Besides, she wondered if she even needed too. Micah had Gabe now. Well, she'd had him before he'd wandered off in the dark.

She moved her hands, making some minor adjustments until she was satisfied she'd done all she could do for her friend. The rest was up to Micah, a woman who'd more than proven how strong she was.

"She's going to be okay," said Azrael, sitting on the ground beside her and running her hands through her dark hair. Every muscle of her body ached. Normally, after a healing like this she'd ask her mother to work on her to bring her own energy centers back in alignment.

"What about you?" asked Raphael. "Are you okay?"

She looked up into the eyes of this sweet man and smiled. "I'm fine. I just need to rest for a few moments."

"May I?" asked Raphael, withdrawing his bottles of elixirs from a bag tucked inside his jacket. "I have an elixir that will energize you."

"Sure," she said, wondering why she didn't have more faith in his elixirs. So far, from what she'd seen they were surprisingly effective.

Raphael withdrew a small green bottle and pulled out the cork, taking a deep sniff before passing it to Azrael.

"What do I do with it?" she asked.

"Put a few drops on your wrist and inhale them. Maybe put a few drops on the collar of your dress, too."

She did as she was told and when she drew in the fresh fragrance, she concentrated on guiding it to the most depleted energy centers in her body, noticing the effect almost immediately. She sniffed again, enjoying the feeling of being revitalized.

"We should give some to Micah," she said, passing the bottle back to him.

"What's happening over there?" called out Pip.

"She's okay!" said Raphael. "We just need a bit of time."

Pip nodded. Griffen did, too, although his eyes didn't leave his two prisoners for a moment.

Azrael watched as Raphael put several drops of his elixir onto the collar of Micah's shirt, then shifted the fabric so it was under her nose.

She breathed it in, each breath seeming to pick up energy, until soon her eyes were blinking and open wide as if she was surprised to find herself exactly where she'd been when she'd closed them.

"It's all right," said Raphael. "You're okay. Take your time waking up. You had a bump on the head, but you're going to be fine. Azrael healed you."

"Raphael helped, too," she said, not wanting to take all the credit.

"Gabe?" Micah closed her eyes briefly, then opened them once more. "Where did he go? Is he safe?"

Raphael looked at Azrael. This was only a question either she or Pip could answer.

"We're not sure," said Azrael. "We saw a white light between the trees. Pip was holding onto him tightly but he broke away. The light vanished and it was so dark. We couldn't see our hands in front of our faces, let alone find Gabe. Then the men grabbed us."

"We need to find him." Micah tried to sit up, but Raphael put a firm hand on her shoulder.

"In a moment," he said. "Don't sit up just yet."

"What happened to the men?" Micah lay back down and put her hands to her temples. "I can't remember it all."

"Two dead. Two in the cage," said Azrael, not sure how many facts to give her all at once.

"Did I kill one?" she asked.

"No," said Raphael. "But the man who touched you is dead."

"Pity." Micah blinked away a disappointed look.

"You wanted him alive?" Azrael tilted her head, confused.

"No, I just wanted to be the one to kill him." Micah grinned at her and Azrael sighed, relieved to see a sign of the old Micah.

"Well, if it makes you feel better, I killed him," said Raphael. "And the only reason I succeeded was because of what you did to him first."

"That does make me feel better." Micah propped herself up on her elbows. "Actually, no. I feel terrible. Did someone hit me on the head with a hammer?"

"It's better if we let you remember for yourself." Azrael stood up and drew her jacket collar to her nose to breath in Raphael's elixir. "You were awesome."

"We have to find Gabe," said Micah. "Every minute counts. Look what happened when we didn't find Lily straight away."

"Then let's get some answers." Azrael stepped toward the caged men. "Besides, we need to get out of here in case some of their friends show up."

Raphael's eyebrows shot up. "Good point."

"You okay to stand?" asked Azrael, returning to Micah and holding out her hands.

Micah raised her eyebrows, aware of Azrael's aversion to touch, then grasped her hands and pulled herself up.

Azrael kept hold of Micah's hands and looked her in the eye, finding that she didn't mind this kind of contact so much. Perhaps this journey was healing for all of them in more ways than one.

"We're going to get Gabe back," said Azrael.

"And Lily," added Raphael.

"And Lily," they repeated together.

"Oh, no you don't!" They spun around to see Griffen wrestling with one of the men through the bars of the cage.

The man was holding a knife and Griffen was grabbing his wrist, trying to shake it free.

Azrael ran for the cage with Micah and Raphael right behind her, just in time to see the second man pull out his knife and swing it into the air.

"No!" cried Pip, reaching into the deep pocket of her dress and pulling out her bag of walnuts. She swung the bag through the bars and hit the man on the top of the head. He didn't crumble like when Micah had broken his friend's nose, but it was enough to distract his attention long enough for Griffen to spin around and take hold of his wrist with his free hand.

As Azrael got to the cage, her jaw dropped at the sheer strength of Griffen as he held these two men by their wrists. King Tate had been right to send him with them.

Pip untied the door to the cage and Micah burst through and wrested the knife from one of the men's hands, just as the other man dropped his, leaving Pip to dart inside and grab it.

"Okay," said Griffen throwing the men into a corner of the cage. "Which one of you wants to be our talker."

MICAH

THE NOW

Micah stepped out of the cage and waited for Pip and Griffen to follow and secure the door once more.

"You didn't check them for knives?" Micah shook her head, unable to believe what had happened.

"I did check them," said Griffen. "But it was hectic and they must've had them well hidden."

"How do you know they don't have more?" Micah crossed her arms and scowled at the men.

"Because if they pull out another knife, I'm going to slit their throats with it." Griffen looked directly at the men as he spoke.

The men held up their hands, blinking innocently.

"What did you do with the boy?" asked Micah, not wanting to waste another second.

"What boy?" They shrugged their shoulders.

"The boy." Surely, she didn't need to spell it out.

The two men looked at each other. Either they were exceptional liars or they really didn't know what boy she spoke of.

"I'm so sorry, Micah," said Azrael, but Micah didn't have time for apologies now.

"The boy who was with us when we were taken," said Pip, stepping forward. "He disappeared when we saw a white light."

"Oh," said both men at once.

"Oh?" Micah jabbed her finger through the bars of the cage. "What does 'oh' mean?"

"Nothing," said the larger of the two men.

Griffen waved one of the knives at them. "The lady asked you a question. Might be a good idea to answer it."

"Lady?" The man laughed, elbowing his friend in the ribs. "Didn't seem much a lady before."

Griffen tore open the door and grabbed the man by the front of his shirt, dragging him out into the open and holding his knife to his throat.

"Too much of a coward to make it a fair fight," the man spluttered. "Give me a knife and I'll fight you properly."

"We don't have time for this!" cried Micah. "Please Griffen. I don't care what he called me."

"I do." Griffen tossed the knife to Micah and she plucked it out of the air by the handle. "I'll give you a fair fight, but not with knives."

The man brought up his fists and shuffled his feet in the dirt. He stretched out his arm to try to land the first blow, and Griffen caught his fist in the palm of his hand and twisted his arm, sending the man thumping to the earth.

The man scrambled to his feet. "Protecting your whore of a girl-friend, are you? Or does she belong to your skinny friend over there?"

He took another swipe at Griffen but this time Griffen landed a blow of his own, his fist slamming into the man's face, sending him to the ground once more.

"I think you killed him," said Azrael rushing to the man's side.

"Careful," said Micah, trying to pull Azrael back. But she was too late. The man's eyes sprang open and he grabbed Azrael around the neck.

"Should'a killed ya when I had the chance," he snarled as he tightened his grip.

Azrael gasped, her hands flying to her throat as she tried to pull the man's hands away.

Micah didn't hesitate. Using the knife Griffen had thrown her, she lunged forward and plunged it into the man's chest.

He groaned as he loosened the grip on Azrael's throat. Then his wide eyes went blank. It seemed she'd gotten him in the right spot. This wasn't the first time she'd killed a man, but it'd been a long time since she'd had to.

Azrael peeled the man's limp hands from her throat and stumbled back.

"You killed him," she said, her eyes wide with either shock or awe.

"Thanks for saving one for me." Micah pulled the knife out of the man's chest and wiped it on her trousers.

She knew she shouldn't joke about a man's death but this piece of work had tried to kill a woman as she'd been checking on his welfare. She'd done the world a favor by removing him from it.

"Three down, one to go," said Pip, glaring at the man in the cage. "Have you still got no idea where the boy is?"

Micah was impressed. Pip would never have had the courage to speak like this when they'd first set out on this quest.

"He'll be in the mines!" The man got to his knees and clasped his hands. "With the Fossickers. They're all in the mines!"

"What's a Fossicker?" Micah stepped forward, wondering if Lily might also be in the mines.

"The children are Fossickers. They can get into tight places. All the children become Fossickers." The man said this like it was perfectly normal, not registering the shock on all their faces.

"What do they mine for?" asked Griffen.

"Crystals."

Now, this was interesting. The vision of Lily that Micah had shared with Raphael and Azrael had been of her underwater holding a purple crystal. She was now more certain than ever that they'd come to the right place to find her. But why had she been underwater instead of in a mine?

"What do you do with all the crystals?" asked Pip.

"They go to the palace. The King collects them. Takes them out to sea for his Queen."

"The sea?" asked Micah, trying to put the pieces together.

"She lives in a lighthouse," said the man. "I've never seen it though, so don't ask me where it is. Middle of nowhere somewhere."

"What's the Queen look like?" asked Micah, desperately hoping the King hadn't taken Lily as his young bride. It just seemed too coincidental that their vision of Lily had been under the water and now there was a Queen who lived in the middle of the sea.

"I've told you enough, I reckon."

"That's strange." Griffen brandished his knife at the man. "Because I don't reckon you have."

"Nobody's seen Her Majesty for years now. But last time I saw her. She... well, she looked like you."

He fixed his gaze on Micah and she flinched. This was a nightmare! Lily was too young to be a King's bride.

"How old is she?" asked Raphael.

The man shrugged. "Twice what you are."

Micah let out a deep breath. It couldn't possibly be Lily.

"Who lives there with her?" asked Raphael.

"Forget it, Raphael." Micah touched him gently on the arm. "It can't be her. She's too old."

"There's a girl out there with her," said the man. "I've never seen her, but I'm told she has the same red hair as the Queen."

Raphael raised his eyebrows at Micah.

"And how old's the girl?" he asked.

The man shrugged again. "Half what you are."

"Tell us where the lighthouse is." Micah paced in front of the cage, certain now he was talking about Lily.

"I told you, I don't know!" The man held out the palms of his hands. "You'd have to find one of the oarsmen and ask them. They're the only ones who've been out there."

"And where do we find them?" Micah's pacing came to a halt, in direct contrast to her mind, which was whirling with plans of how they might get themselves to a lighthouse in the middle of the sea.

The man rolled his eyes. "Well, they ain't out here, are they?"

"Nobody's out here," said Azrael, rubbing at the purple streaks on her neck.

"Point us in the right direction and we'll let you live," said Griffen.

"That way." He pointed to his left.

"And where are the mines?" asked Micah, wondering if they were better to go after Lily or Gabe first.

"Same, same," said the man, still pointing to his left.

"Do we trust him?" Micah looked at her companions one by one to see what they thought.

"Not sure we have a lot of choice," said Raphael, shrugging.

"If we find out you're lying to us." Griffen shook his knife at the man. "I'll come and find you."

"That way." The man pointed to his left again. "I swear it."

Micah walked immediately away from the cage in the direction the man pointed, despite being totally unsure if he was telling them the truth.

The others followed, and the man shouted after them. "You can't leave me here! It's not right!"

"Thanks for the chat," Griffen called over his shoulder.

"Should we let him out?" asked Azrael. "He's going to die if we leave him there."

"Someone will find him," said Griffen. "No great loss if they don't."

"This doesn't feel like the right direction." Raphael stopped and looked around.

"How can something *feel* like the right direction?" asked Pip, stopping by his side.

"Let's just keep going and see what's out here." Micah kept walking, pleased to see that Raphael and Pip followed. They couldn't afford to lose any time.

"Micah," said Azrael, placing her hand gently on her arm. "I really am very sorry about Gabe. He let go of my hand for only a moment. I feel terrible about it."

"I was the one who left him," said Micah. "It's my fault."

Pip shook her head and Micah sighed. The truth was that she couldn't help but blame Pip just a tiny bit, but she knew this was unfair. The only people truly to blame were the men who'd dragged them away. And they'd paid the price for that now.

"We'll get him back," said Micah, forcing a smile.

"We will," said Pip, falling back into step with Azrael and Griffen, leaving Micah to talk to Raphael.

"What would you do if you were that man?" she asked. "Would you have given us true directions?"

He shook his head. "I'd probably tell them the truth in the hope they thought I was lying."

"Clever," she smirked. "If only we had some way to know. We have to find Lily. And Gabe. This might sound strange, but finding Gabe felt just like coming home. Like I was meant to be his mother."

"Can I try something on you?" asked Raphael, his eyes twinkling in the way they did whenever he had an idea.

"Of course." She'd learned to trust this man completely. There was no way he'd ever hurt her.

Raphael reached for his bag of elixirs. "Hold up for a moment."

"She needs energy?" asked Azrael, coming to a stop behind them.

"No. This is an experimental elixir I was working on when Micah came looking for me in my apothecary. It's a homing elixir." He shuffled about in his bag until he found the bottle he was looking for.

"But I don't want to go home," said Micah. "I want to find Lily and Gabe."

Raphael nodded. "I got close with this elixir, but I could never quite get it to work. Something was wrong with it. This is just a theory, but I think I might have figured out what it was."

Micah let out a deep sigh. He wasn't listening to her. "But I don't want to go home," she said again.

"What did you just say to me?" he asked, dabbing some of the elixir onto a clean cloth. "About Gabe."

"I said… that finding Gabe was like coming home." She smiled, his enthusiasm infectious.

"That's right!" he said. "What if my elixir is already working perfectly? What if home isn't about the building you live in or the land it's set on? What if it's about the people in your heart? What if they're your home?"

"You think if I smell this elixir, I'll know what direction we should walk?"

Raphael nodded. "We already know what direction your home is in, so if you're drawn in that direction, we can dismiss that. But what if you're drawn somewhere else."

"I don't know about this," said Pip.

"I think we should try it," said Azrael. "Raphael's elixirs work. We know they do."

"Probably more chance of that elixir leading us to the Princess than that swine in the cage," said Griffen.

Pip nodded, realizing she was outvoted.

Micah stretched out her hand to take the cloth from Raphael. She held it to her nose and inhaled deeply.

"Bring them to your mind," said Raphael. "Both Lily and Gabe."

That made sense. Both of them were in her heart. Hopefully, if one of them was nearby, she'd be able to feel it. She pictured Lily's sad face under the ocean, and the trusting way Gabe looked up at her.

"Do you feel a pull?" asked Raphael.

She could, but wanting to be certain, she held up her hand and inhaled again.

"That way," she said, pointing south, almost the exact opposite direction to which they'd been walking.

"You sure?" asked Raphael.

"Positive."

LILY

THE NOW

*W*hen Lily had heard Father speak of 'the Terrace', she'd imagined a pretty walled garden with flowers and fountains and a woman sitting in the corner playing the harp.

But the Terrace wasn't like that.

The Terrace was more like a version of hell. Dark. Isolated. Hopeless. And… cold.

The guards had dragged her up some stairs, then through a door and up more stairs. They'd climbed and climbed and Lily had been genuinely surprised that so many stairs could exist within the one building. She'd have been able to climb the lighthouse three times over by the time they arrived at a large steel hatch at the top of the stairs.

The guards had opened the hatch and instructed her to climb a ladder. Once she reached the top, they'd slammed it closed again and she heard them turn the lock, leaving her alone and confused about where she was and what Father hoped to achieve by keeping her here.

Two days and two nights had passed since then and in that time, Lily had explored every inch of this so-called Terrace.

What it really was, was a roof. The roof of the palace to be more accurate. It was essentially a giant stone rectangle, painted white, without a single railing or barrier to stop her from walking straight off the edge if she were to get close enough.

And that was it. Nothing else. Not a seat. Not a plant. Not a table. Not a blanket. Just a white rectangle perched in the sky with an impenetrable hatch at one end and two wooden buckets beside it. One for water and one for waste. Not once since she'd been here had the water been replenished or the waste taken away. She was tempted to throw the contents at the next person who opened that door. Especially if it were the King.

She'd lain down on her stomach and wriggled over to the edge to see if there was anything she could use to climb down but there was nothing except sheer walls on all four sides. And the distance to the ground had made her stomach flip. The dirt below was hard and barren, not a single tree or moat to break her fall. Not that either of those things would help her from this height.

In the distance, she could see the ocean. It was a strange thought knowing that the lighthouse was somewhere out there. What was Mother doing without her? Polishing her own crystals? Telling herself bedtimes stories?

How long Father intended to keep her up here was a mystery. He'd said she needed time to remember who she was. Who she *really* was. Which meant who he wanted her to be. Because no amount of time spent in hell would make her forget who she was. What she needed to decide was whether or not she was better off pretending to be who Father wanted her to be, or if she'd die holding onto her name.

When she'd first been brought up here, she'd thought her name was the most important thing. But after two days without food or shelter, she was leaning toward survival. She'd already lived more than half her life pretending to be someone else. She could do that again until she figured out how she was going to get back home to Forte Cadence.

Worse still, her angels seemed to have all but abandoned her. She knew she should've tried harder to take the amethysts with her. Carved them out of the rock somehow. How naive she'd been to have believed that her visions belonged to her.

She lay down on her back and closed her eyes, trying to speak to her angels. Where was her golden Prince? Had something happened to him? Had he decided she wasn't worth rescuing after all? And what about Aunt Micah and the woman with the black hair? Had the woman in the shadows behind them decided to step out and join them or had she convinced them to turn around?

"Father!" she called, knowing he'd never hear her. Her voice was dry and cracked under the strain of being used for the first time since she'd left that room covered in diamonds. "Father!"

She closed her eyes once again and covered her face with her hands. She was so cold. But thankfully her daily plunge into the ocean had taught her how to withstand extreme temperatures like this.

A noise startled her and it took a moment to figure out it was the sound of the hatch opening.

Sitting up, then pulling her weak body into a stand she took some steps forward.

"Father!" she called again, her voice gaining strength now that she knew it could be heard.

The doors of the hatch opened and swung back to lay against the stone surface of the terrace.

Lily's shoulders slumped to see it was a guard and not Father.

The guard set down a fresh bucket of water and picked up her bucket of waste. If she weren't so hungry and cold, she'd have been humiliated by this.

When the guard turned around, ready to head back down the ladder, she ran to him.

"Stop!"

The guard put down the bucket and held out his hands, warning her to keep her distance.

"Please, tell the King I wish to see him," she said.

"Who wishes to see him?" He smirked at her.

"I do." She felt her brow furrow as she tried to make sense of his question.

"And who are you?" asked the guard.

"Oh." She understood now. Father had put this guard up to this. Testing her.

The guard tapped his foot as he waited. "You have no name?"

"I do have a name." Her stomach growled loudly at her, as if reminding her that she needed food.

"And what is this name, so I can pass on your message to the King?"

Lily bit down on her bottom lip. Did saying she was Angel, make her Angel?

"I'll return in two days to ask you this again," said the guard, picking up the bucket once more.

A large drop of rain landed directly in the middle of Lily's forehead and she winced. Could the universe be any clearer with her? She had to get off this Terrace. If a storm were to hit, she'd never survive.

"A-angel!" she stammered. "I'm Angel of the Lighthouse, daughter of King Sterling and Queen Eileena." She swallowed but the bitterness of her lie stung the back of her tongue.

"I'll tell His Majesty that his daughter, Princess Angel, wishes to speak with him." The guard passed the bucket down the ladder and took hold of the handles of the hatch.

"Please!" cried Lily. "Let me come with you. Don't leave me up here."

But the guard swung the hatch closed without giving her a second glance.

Lily crouched down on the cold doors and banged them with her fists. "Don't leave me up here!"

As if on cue, the rain started to fall in earnest and soon fat droplets were pounding the Terrace and soaking into Lily's dress, her hair, the very core of her soul. She let go of some tears she'd been holding onto and the salt of her teardrops mingled with the ferocity of the rain. Life couldn't get more miserable than it was right now. Was she being punished for letting go of her name so easily? All it'd taken was two days without food or warmth and she'd been prepared to completely disown her family.

"I'm Lily," she called to the clouds. "I'm Lily."

But the clouds only rained harder, sweeping her words away and dragging them down to the earth.

Then the lock in the hatch turned once more.

She scrambled off the metal surface and stood watching as the dark space opened up below.

A guard had opened half the hatch and was gesturing for her to follow him down. A different guard to the one who'd come before.

"Princess Angel?" he asked.

"Y-yes." She was shaking quite violently now, the lack of food paired with the freezing temperatures having taken its toll. "I'm Angel. Please, help me."

She was aware of the guard scrambling up the ladder and catching her just before she hit the hard surface of the door.

Her eyes closed and a feeling of warmth enveloped her.

Then, nothing.

RAPHAEL

THE NOW

*R*aphael stopped so abruptly that Azrael walked into the back of him.

"Did you feel that?" he asked.

"Yes, I feel a sore head after banging it on your shoulder blades," said Azrael, smirking.

"Not that." He didn't have time for jokes right now.

"I felt it," said Micah. "It was Lily. Something happened to her."

"Is she all right?" asked Pip, letting go of Griffen's hand.

Raphael shook his head. "I... I don't think so. I haven't had a vision of her for days but just then she flashed into my mind. She was..."

"She was what?" prompted Azrael.

"She was screaming." Micah finished the sentence he'd been unable to.

"Oh." Azrael's face filled with anguish. "What do you think that means?"

"It means she's still alive," said Pip. "That's good, isn't it?"

Raphael shrugged. Maybe it was good, but maybe it wasn't. Maybe a vision so short and sharp and clear meant something had happened to her. That maybe the worst had happened.

"We should take a rest here and look for some food," said Pip, glancing up at Griffen. Raphael had noticed she liked to feed him more than she liked to feed herself. It was no wonder she was so thin.

"We can't rest," said Micah. "We have to hurry, now more than ever."

"I agree." Raphael was glad someone felt the same way he did. There was no time to waste. "Let's keep moving before the sun sets. Lily needs us."

"And Gabe," added Micah.

"And all the children in the mines," said Raphael, refusing to call them Fossickers.

"What's our plan?" Raphael motioned for them to continue walking as they spoke.

"It's a bit hard to have a plan when we don't know what we're up against," said Pip, annoyingly correct as usual.

"We'll hide somewhere and observe for a while," said Griffen. "Figure out how many guards we need to take out to gain access to the mines."

"If there's a choice, I think we should get Lily first," said Raphael.

"I agree," said Micah.

Raphael's head turned sharply to look at her. He'd been certain she wasn't going to like that idea. She was so focused on finding Gabe.

"She's in more danger than Gabe," said Micah, stooping to pick up a fallen branch and using it as a walking stick. "Plus, releasing who knows how many children from a mine isn't going to be easy. Lily might be able to help us. She'll know how it works down there."

"But what if Raphael's magic potion is taking us to Gabe?" asked Pip.

"Elixir," Raphael corrected. "Not a magic potion."

"Elixir then," said Pip.

"There's one way to find out." Raphael reached into his bag and ferreted about for his bottle of homing elixir.

"Are you going to put some on?" asked Micah, noticing what he was doing.

He nodded, pausing his steps for a moment so he could apply the elixir without spilling any of it.

Lily had owned his heart ever since he'd first seen her in the vision he'd had in the apothecary. He'd walked away from his entire life to find her. If she wasn't the definition of *home* then he didn't know what was.

He placed several drops of the elixir onto his shirt collar and tightly secured the bottle. Walking on, he picked up his pace to fall into step beside Micah. The terrain had thinned out the further they'd walked. Dead trees had become scraggly living trees which had then become a sparse forest with bracken on the ground and the rare bird hopping between the shrubs.

"Do you love her?" Micah kept her voice low, her words only for his ears.

He nodded, knowing that Micah would sniff out a lie in a matter of moments. Nothing got past her.

"But I have no expectations of my feelings being returned," he said. "I want to save her because she deserves to be saved. Not for any selfish reasons."

"You're a good person," said Micah. "And believe me, I've met some really horrible people, so I know. I'm sure Lily will see that."

"There's an age difference," he said. "And a kingdom difference."

Micah laughed. "You're hardly an old man! It can't be more than a few years between you. Tallis is older than me."

Raphael nodded, aware that a flush was spreading to his cheeks. He wasn't used to having these conversations.

"I'm glad you love her," said Micah, nodding her head. "Because it means you're going to try harder to find her."

He smiled.

"And because you're a good person," she added.

His smile turned to a gentle laugh.

"So." Her voice turned serious and he knew this personal chat was finished. "We need to find some oarsmen and get them to tell us where this lighthouse is. We go there, rescue Lily, then we get back here and find Gabe and release the children from the mines. We then go home."

"Sounds so simple." He shook his head.

"I've executed far more complicated plans." She lowered her voice. "But do you know what worries me? This time I have so much to lose. There's Tallis back home, and little Gabe, and Jeremiah and Rose waiting for Lily. We can't fail."

"We're not going to f—"

"Raphael! Micah!" hissed Griffen, pointing ahead. "Hush!"

Raphael strained his eyes to see what Griffen had spotted. Whatever was in those tonics he'd been raised on had certainly helped his eyesight as Raphael could see nothing but a blur of shrubbery ahead. But his finely tuned sense of smell tipped him off as to what Griffen had been pointing at. There was the distinct smell of salt in the air. It was hard to tell if they'd walked in a circle or across a section of this strange kingdom, but whatever had happened, they'd managed to find themselves at the ocean again.

"Up there," said Griffen, pointing.

Raphael looked up to see a large rectangular column rising into the sky in the distance.

"Oh," said Raphael, realizing that Griffen hadn't been talking about the ocean. "What is that?"

Griffen shrugged. "Could it be the lighthouse?"

Was this where the homing elixir was leading them? Could Lily be in there somehow? But this column was most definitely located on the land, when they'd been told the lighthouse was surrounded by water.

"It's not the lighthouse," he said.

"Then what is it?" asked Pip.

Micah rubbed her hands together. "I guess we're about to find out."

AZRAEL

THE NOW

Keeping their voices low and their steps measured, Azrael followed her companions across the terrain, noticing how sand was starting to overtake bracken. A copse of trees near the waterline seemed the obvious place to head while they worked out their next best move.

"Can we dip our feet in the water?" asked Pip.

"Not just yet," said Griffen, forever protective of his Princess. "We need to make sure it's safe first."

Azrael put down her bag and leaned against a tree, slipping off her shoes and wiggling her toes as she sank to the sand.

"Don't get too comfortable," said Griffen, peering between the trees and scanning the sand for a sign of any activity.

"Is someone there?" asked Raphael, squinting.

Azrael held her breath.

"It's a woman." Griffen stepped back to better conceal himself. "Sitting on the sand, way down there on the beach."

Azrael breathed a sigh. Surely a woman alone on the beach was no threat to them.

"She might be able to tell us what that tower is," said Micah. "We should go and talk to her."

"What if it's a trap?" Pip's eyes were wide with concern. "A hundred men could jump out of the bushes when we approach her."

"I'll talk to her." Azrael hauled herself up, feeling her feet ache in protest. "On my own, in case it's a trap."

"No, I'll go," said Raphael.

"She'll be less threatened by a woman." Azrael smoothed down her hair, hoping she didn't look too much of a mess.

"I'll do it," said Micah. "I dragged you all out here on this quest. It should be me."

"None of us were dragged." Azrael wasn't going to take no for an answer. "And you have more to lose than me."

"You have a mother who loves you," said Micah. "I saw the sadness in her eyes when you left."

"She's strong." Azrael blinked back a rush of emotion at the thought of Freya. "And it'll be fine. One woman alone isn't a threat."

"Let Azrael go," said Raphael. "She's good with people."

"And I'm not?" Micah's jaw fell open and she raised her eyebrows at Raphael.

"You have... a different manner," said Griffen, stepping in. "It's a little more forceful. A gentle approach is sometimes better."

Micah huffed and Azrael saw her companions stifle smiles.

"Azrael can walk down the sand and I'll follow from the tree line," said Griffen. "I won't let anything happen to her."

"We'll all follow," said Raphael.

Sensing a losing argument, Griffen fell silent.

Azrael nodded, scooped up her shoes and walked down to the sand, enjoying the softness under her feet. The sand back home was coarse and burning hot. This was like another substance altogether. She should collect some of it to bring back home to show Rani.

As she walked down the sand toward the woman, she wondered what her friend was doing right now back home. Busy being Empress, she supposed. And mother to those beautiful twin girls. She and Aarow had a lot of work to do to unite their kingdom's two cities and establish a new rule of peace and respect. Azrael didn't envy them that task, but knew if anyone could achieve it, it was them.

Now that she was closer, she could see the woman was sitting on the sand staring out at the ocean. She was so still that Azrael wondered if perhaps she wasn't real. But then the woman picked up a handful of sand and threw it at the water, her movements filled with fury.

This complicated matters. Angry people didn't normally part with information in the same way as someone who was relaxed. She'd been right to volunteer for this job. If anyone could calm this woman and get the information they needed, it would be her. She was used to dealing with people who needed help. And there was something about this woman that screamed of being a person in need.

The woman was so wrapped up in her thoughts she didn't notice Azrael approach, so Azrael took her time, observing the woman, trying to gather as many clues about her as possible.

She was older than Azrael by maybe ten years, with the same dark hair, although she had streaks of gray running through it. She wore a brown vest made from some kind of heavy wool to keep out the cold, paired with a long skirt made from the same fabric and a white shirt underneath that was stained with years of wear. This woman didn't have wealth, and the deep lines on her face told Azrael that she wasn't free from worry either.

She could be very wrong, but something told Azrael that this was someone she could talk to. She just needed to find her way into her confidence.

Sitting down next to the woman, Azrael looked ahead to the ocean without saying a word.

The woman turned her head and Azrael drew in a breath and met her gaze to see that her eyes were bloodshot with heavy bags underneath. She'd been crying. Not today, but in recent days. And not a small amount, but a lot.

"Who are you?" asked the woman.

"My name's Azrael."

"Azrael's the angel of death. Are you here to kill me?" The woman said this without any concern in her voice. Was death something that appealed to her right now?

"Perhaps I'm here to bring you back from death," said Azrael.

"Pity." The woman picked up another handful of damp sand and threw it at the ocean.

"What's your name?" asked Azrael, treading carefully. There was more to this woman than anger. Azrael had seen it many times before in people. She was wrapped in a blanket of grief so overwhelming she had no concern for what happened to her.

The woman sighed. "Enid."

Azrael's hands itched to heal this woman. There was so much she could do to relieve her despair. Although, admittedly, there was nothing she could do to lift it altogether. Despair that sat on shoulders as heavily as this was difficult to shift.

"You're not from here." Enid scanned Azrael, as if seeing her for the first time. "You dress differently. Your skin's different. So are your eyes."

"I'm the same here." Azrael put her hand to her heart.

"I don't know where you came from, but they'll kill you when they see you." Again, her voice was impassive, like she was commenting on the weather, not about a potential risk to her life.

"Who'll kill me?" she asked.

"The King's guards." Enid shook her head. "They like killing. They killed Carson."

Azrael nodded, waiting to see if she'd elaborate on who Carson was and if he was the reason for her grief.

"He's out there somewhere," said Enid, pointing to the ocean. "Did you come from out there? Maybe you saw him."

"I did cross an ocean to get here," said Azrael, hearing the snap of a twig in the bushes behind her and hoping Enid hadn't. Her companions really needed to learn to be more quiet. "But I arrived from the west."

"Are you from The Bay of Laurel?" Enid studied her once more, taking in Azrael's long robes stained with dirt.

"No," said Azrael. "My kingdom's called The Sands of Naar. It's covered in sand, too, only our sand is red and the sun is hot."

Enid nodded, looking back out at the water, so Azrael decided to continue talking, hoping maybe Enid would join in and tell her something useful.

"There's also Forte Cadence, although that's made up from rocky mountains and rolling hills. And Wintergreen, which is green like its name and filled with plants and flowers. Then there's The Bay of Laurel where we left from. They grow crops of every type of food you can imagine."

"Then why would you come here?" she asked. "We don't grow food or flowers. We grow nothing except crystals and they're all for the Queen. They take our children from us, return them to us, then take them again. There's nothing you could want here."

Another twig broke behind them and Azrael held up her hand as subtly as she could to warn them to be quiet.

"What's that tower?" asked Azrael, pointing to the column stretching into the sky.

"That's the King's palace." Enid turned to glare at it.

"So it's not the lighthouse?" asked Azrael, just to be sure.

Enid shook her head and looked back to the ocean. "I blame the King for killing Carson."

"Who's Carson?" she asked gently.

"My son." Enid looked at Azrael and her eyes spilled over with tears. "They took him from me when he was three years old, just like I was taken when I was that age. Just like all the children. Do they do that in your kingdom?"

Azrael winced. "They used to. I was taken from my mother at birth and didn't see her again until I was grown. But that doesn't happen anymore. Not in any of the kingdoms."

Enid nodded. "I didn't see Carson for years, either. He was returned to me when he got too big for the mines. I was happy for a while. Then the palace claimed him as an oarsman and he had to leave again."

Azrael tried to hide her gasp of surprise. An oarsman! This was just too perfect. She needed to tread carefully or Enid was going to clamp her lips closed and she'd get no further.

"What did he do as an oarsman?" she asked.

"He took the King across the ocean to see his Queen. But last time he went, he fell off the boat. That's what they told me, anyway. Said they couldn't find him. The ocean ate him right up. So now I sit here waiting for the ocean to spit him out and return him to me. He was a good boy. An honest one. He made me proud."

"I'm sure he did," said Azrael, unsure what else to say.

"They said he fell just out there," said Enid, pointing. "I don't know why it's taking so long."

"How far is the lighthouse?" Azrael squinted but was unable to see any structures on the horizon.

Enid shrugged then turned her gaze back to the water. "What stopped your kingdom from taking away your children? You said they don't do that anymore."

"Lots of things happened," said Azrael, finding it hard to explain. "But mainly it was a revolution."

"Revolution." Enid turned the word over with her tongue. "What does that mean?"

"It means all the people got together to prove they were stronger than the people in charge. We have new people in charge now. People who don't take our children."

Enid's eyes lit up and Azrael saw the young woman she must have once been. A woman with a son she'd loved and a life she'd been happy to live. Not this woman who no longer cared if she lived or died.

"Do you have any other children?" asked Azrael.

Enid shook her head. "Hardly anybody has more than one child here."

"Why's that?"

"Hearts are all broken. Once we feel the pain of having one taken, we don't have more. They'd just take them, too. I was lucky, really. At least I got Carson back. Most of the children die down there when the tunnels fall in. Least I had him back for a little while. You come here looking for your child?"

Now it was Azrael's turn to look startled. "Why do you think that?"

"Because there's no other reason to come to a place like this. I know they've been taking little ones from other kingdoms. We're running out of children here and those treasures need mining."

There was an audible gasp from behind them and Azrael coughed, hoping Enid hadn't heard.

"You can tell your friends I don't bite," said Enid, not missing a beat. "Knew they were there the whole time."

Azrael nodded, realizing this woman was far sharper than she'd given her credit for.

"You can come out!" Azrael called to her friends. "She's a friend."

"Is that what I am?" asked Enid.

Azrael nodded without hesitation.

"You didn't answer my question," said Enid, as Micah and Raphael appeared out of the scrub. "Are you here to find your child?"

Azrael shook her head. "A child, yes. But not a child of mine."

"I'll help you find the child," said Enid. "But I need something in return."

Azrael's eyebrows shot up. "What do you need?"

Enid smiled for the first time in their conversation. "A revolution."

PIP

THE NOW

"Wait." Griffen grabbed Pip gently by the arm as she went to follow Raphael and Micah out from the scrub.

"What's the matter?" She searched his eyes for a sign of what was clearly troubling him.

"I just… need a moment. Alone. With you."

It was then that she saw the problem. It wasn't trouble in his eyes. It was longing.

"Oh, Griffen." She wrapped her arms around his waist. "Why do you love me so much?"

"Can't help it." He stooped to kiss the top of her head. "Always have. Always will."

She squeezed him tighter, wishing she were worthy of such devotion.

"Do you think the others like me?" she asked. "I'm not sure if Micah will ever forgive me for losing Gabe."

"Does it matter what they think?" he asked. "Or does it matter what I think?"

She smiled at the way he'd avoided her question.

"Pip, I've never liked anyone better than you."

"You like me?" She blinked innocently, aware she was digging for him to say more. "Is that all?"

"You know what I mean," he said without hesitation. "I love you, Pip."

And with those words, she felt a part of her heart heal. She looked up at this handsome, blond giant who'd wormed his way into her heart. She'd been a fool not to let him in far earlier. It wasn't right to have judged this man on the actions of another far less worthy man who'd hurt her.

"Are you going to kiss me?" She smiled in a way she was aware she'd never smiled at anyone else before.

"Here?" He looked around.

"I thought maybe here." She raised a finger to her lips and blinked twice, waiting for him to act.

He bent forward, gripping her tightly around her middle and urging her up to his face as his lips brushed over hers.

Pushing up onto her toes she pressed herself against the hardness of his chest and returned his kiss, resisting the overwhelming urge to cry. She may have spent the first half of her life thinking that she didn't deserve happiness, but she was determined to spend the rest of it wallowing in the fact that she absolutely did. And nobody could bring her happiness in the same way as Griffen.

She waited for him to break the kiss, knowing she didn't have the strength to pull away.

"We need to join the others." He kissed her lightly on her forehead.

"We do," she agreed. "In a moment."

Reaching for the back of his head, she pulled his lips to hers once more.

"Come on, lovebirds!"

They broke away to see Micah standing at the edge of the scrub with her hands on her hips.

"You'll make us all jealous." She shook her head and turned away.

Griffen brushed down his clothes and winked at Pip, before leading her out of the scrub. They joined the others on the sand, sitting in a circle with the sad strange woman the focus of their attention.

"This is Enid." Azrael went around the circle, making the introductions. "Enid's going to help us. And in return, we're going to help her."

Pip glanced around the circle to see if she was the only one surprised by this news.

"That tower definitely isn't the lighthouse," said Azrael, pointing to the column Griffen had spotted from the scrub. "It's the King's palace. Enid's going to organize a boat to take us to the lighthouse."

"And what are we doing for her?" asked Micah.

"We're going to... well..." Azrael rubbed at her chin and looked around at them.

"Well, what?" prodded Micah.

"We're going to have a revolution!" Azrael smiled, as if this were exciting news. "We're going to find a way to release the children from the mines."

Pip watched Micah nod furiously.

"We're going to stay in Feldspar until we find a way to make sure the children are safe," said Azrael. "All of them. That's the deal."

Griffen's eyes shot to Pip and she nodded slowly at him, knowing he was keen to get back to The Bay of Laurel, but also knowing she couldn't leave while so many children were in danger. She may not have been much use when her own kingdom needed a ruler, but there was a lot she could do to help this troubled island.

Griffen nodded. A subtle nod just for her, but she appreciated it all the same. He'd stay with her, or he'd leave with her. The decision was hers.

"First we get Lily back," said Micah. "Otherwise, the deal's off."

"Lily?" asked Enid, looking at Azrael. "I thought you said it was the Queen's daughter you were seeking."

"We are. Well, at least we think we are."

"Carson said her name's Angel," said Enid.

"It's just a name," said Pip, trying to calm the panicked look in Micah's eyes. "The Queen's hardly going to use her real name, is she?"

"True." Micah's shoulders relaxed. "So, why are you really helping us, Enid? Do you have a child in the mines?"

Enid grimaced. Pip felt for her, knowing what it was like to not want to talk about something.

"Her son was killed recently," said Azrael.

"I want his life to have meant something," added Enid. "You need to save the children. You need to save the parents from having their children taken. We need a revolution."

Enid smiled at Azrael, who smiled back. "That's right."

"It's not safe here," said Griffen, rising to his feet and looking around. "We're too exposed."

"We're okay, Griffen," said Pip, knowing it was her safety that was his paramount concern.

"No, he's right," said Enid. "This beach is deserted, but if you're seen out here, the consequences could be dire."

"How are you getting us to the lighthouse?" asked Raphael.

"Go back to your hiding place." Enid stood and brushed the sand from her skirt. "A boat will come for you tonight. And this time, don't make so much noise."

"Thank you," said Azrael.

Enid nodded, turned and walked away.

Pip followed her companions back into the scrub, glad they'd have some time to rest before nightfall. She'd find them something to eat while they waited.

"Do you think we can trust her?" Micah slid down a tree trunk and came to rest on the ground.

"Do we have any choice?" asked Raphael.

"She's trustworthy," said Azrael. "I spoke to her for longer than you did. She's a good person. I could tell straight away."

"Ariel can do that," said Pip. "Our herbalist back home. She can look at someone and know if they're good or bad. Is it like that for you?"

Azrael shook her head. "Not quite so clearly as that. But I can usually get a sense of someone."

"I wish I could do that," said Pip. "That would be a very handy talent."

"Speaking of talents." Micah patted her belly. "Any chance you could see if there's anything safe to eat around here, Pip?"

Pip straightened her back, pleased to be useful. "I think I spotted a coconut tree not far back."

"I'll come with you," said Griffen.

"No kissing out there!" said Micah.

Pip felt her face flush and was about to offer a terse reply but stopped herself. Micah was only joking. There was no harm in that. She'd grown very attached to her group of companions. It felt nice to have friends.

"I can't promise anything," she said over her shoulder, grinning.

Micah burst out laughing.

"You seem happy," said Griffen, catching up with her.

"I am," she said. "I shouldn't be, but I am."

"Are you homesick?" he asked.

She shook her head. "I think Raph is right. People are our homes. And I think my home is right here."

LILY

THE NOW

"*W*ho are you?"

Lily, blinked, then opened her eyes to see Father bending over her.

"Who are you?" he asked again.

"Angel," she said, her voice cracked and croaky. "Your daughter."

Her health may be compromised by starvation and cold, but her mind wasn't. She knew exactly who she was. Or rather, she knew exactly who the King wished for her to say she was.

She was lying down with a heavy blanket on top of her. Not in the room covered in diamonds, but another with blue quartz everywhere she looked. Mother's room. But... how could that be? Had she passed out for long enough that Father had been able to transport her back to the lighthouse? She could swear it hadn't been more than a few minutes.

"You need food," said Father, holding out a spoon.

She lifted her head and allowed him to tip some soup into her mouth.

It was hot, burning her tongue as she swallowed it down, but this didn't deter her and she opened her mouth for more.

"I'm sorry, Angel." Father continued to feed her. "I didn't want to leave you out there, really I didn't. It's just that… well, sometimes we have to be cruel to be kind."

Lily nodded, not caring what nonsense he spouted, just as long as he kept nourishing her with soup.

"You've been very unwell, lately," he said. "You really must start taking better care of yourself."

Lily cleared her throat, trying not to choke. How could she take better care of herself when people left her locked on Terraces in the sky or made her dive into freezing water to look for treasures? It was ludicrous!

"Yes, Father," she said, her mind already scrambling for more ideas as to how she could get off this island again. "Where's Mother?"

"Eat your soup." He lifted another spoonful of soup to her lips. "Don't worry about her for now."

"Why aren't I in my bedchamber?" She slurped in the soup, already starting to feel a little stronger.

Father's eyebrows shot up, then his face relaxed into a smile.

"How about I ask the questions first?" he suggested.

"I already told you who I am," she said. "I'm Angel."

The lie felt easier to say, the more times she said it.

"What did you do with the amethyst?" he asked.

This time she did choke on the soup, coughing madly as her body tried to stabilize itself and her mind attempted to come up with an answer to his question.

"I know you have it," he said. "I put it in your bed the last time you were sick."

"Mother must've taken it." This lie was harder to tell than the last one. She wasn't even sure why she was telling it. Was it because this information was the last bit of power she had left? "There was no amethyst in my bed."

"Oh, Angel." He shook his head and set down the spoon, placing the bowl beside her bed. "I really don't want to send you back up to the Terrace to think about this. I was hoping you might remember without that being necessary."

"It's in the ocean," she said without hesitation. She couldn't risk going back to the Terrace. Not today and not ever. He could take the amethyst from her. He could take both of them. Just as long as she never had to see that terrace again.

"You threw it in the ocean?" he asked.

She shook her head and sat up, reaching for the soup bowl herself now that he'd stopped feeding her. But Father put his hand on it, preventing her from picking it up.

"Questions first," he said.

"Where's Mother?" she asked again, not wanting to risk being overheard. She may have told Father a lie just now, but she'd been lying to Mother for years.

"My questions," he said. "Not yours. If you didn't throw the amethyst in the ocean, then how did it get there?"

"I put it there," she said. "To hide it from Mother."

"Interesting." He removed his hand from the bowl, although she didn't dare reach for it again. "The woman who loves you and raised you and you're hiding things from her."

"I thought... that you didn't want her to see it. That's why you gave it to me in secret."

"It's worth nothing on its own," he said.

She really didn't want to reveal she knew where the other amethyst was, but one thought of the Terrace had her talking again.

"It's not on its own," she said. "I put it next to its twin. They sit under the ocean together."

The King beamed at this news, wider than Lily had ever seen before. "I knew it hadn't gone far. I knew it!"

Daring to reach for the soup now, Lily stretched out her hand. Father had stood up and was pacing around the room, not seeming to care if she ate.

As quickly as she could, Lily spooned the soup into her mouth, wondering who cooked it. Mother never cooked. Lily prepared all the meals in the lighthouse. This wasn't a recipe she recognized, either.

She got to the bottom of the bowl then held it up to her lips and tipped it back, wanting to enjoy every last bit of the warm liquid. Now that her stomach was full and her body was warm, she looked around Mother's room. It looked different somehow, but perhaps that was just because she'd never been in this bed before so she'd never seen it from quite this perspective. Although why did it smell different? It sounded different, too. Perhaps her illness had affected her senses somehow.

"As soon as I'm well enough, I'll get the amethysts for you," said Lily, resigned now to the fact she was going to have to give them back.

Father nodded, thoughtfully.

"Angel," he said, returning to her side and sitting by the bed. "I gave you the amethyst for a reason."

"I don't understand." Lily shook her head. What possible reason could Father have for giving her his amethyst? He'd never paid her much attention in the past. Why would he give her what would have to be one of his most valuable possessions?

"Angel, I don't have any children, as you know. It's only you. The amethysts have magical properties. I knew it would help to heal you if I left one by your side."

"But what are they?" she asked, not understanding why he'd gone to so much trouble to heal her only to almost kill her on the Terrace.

"They're a pair of love stones," he said. "Handed down for generations to ensure the right people are ruling the kingdom, and that they're doing it with their soulmate by their side so they can rule with true happiness in their heart."

Lily had to work hard not to grimace. Feldspar was many things, but definitely not a kingdom that seemed to have been built by rulers with happiness in their hearts.

"I used the amethysts to find your Mother. My intention was always to pass them onto you one day, but the Queen's actions made that impossible. She should never have thrown her amethyst into the ocean."

"But... why me?" she asked.

"Because one day you'll rule Feldspar, of course."

Lily lay back down and shook her head as she tried to absorb this news.

"Who else did you think would rule it?" he asked.

"I guess I thought you might have a brother or a cousin or someone who'd take over." The truth was that she'd never really given it much thought at all.

"You're my daughter, Angel." He crouched down beside the bed, reaching for her hand. "That's why I sent you to the Terrace. I needed you to remember who you are. I've been a terrible father to you and I'm sorry for that. I'd like to start again. Can you ever forgive me?"

Lily blinked at this man, who was both familiar to her and a stranger at the same time, resisting the urge to pull away from his clammy grasp on her hand. She could never forgive him. Not for the Terrace and not for taking her from her family and locking her in a lighthouse. She didn't want to rule Feldspar. She was the future ruler of Forte Cadence. Although, really, she didn't want to rule that kingdom, either. All she wanted was to be free.

"There's a story that I tell Mother to help her sleep," said Lily, avoiding his question. "It's about a girl who lives with her stepmother and dreams of meeting her Prince and living in a castle. I feel like that girl sometimes."

"You can be that girl," said the King. "We can use the amethysts to find you a Prince and you can live in the palace."

"What about Mother?"

"It's time she left the lighthouse," he said. "You can help her with that. You see her in a way that nobody else does. Nobody knows her like you do."

Now it finally made sense to Lily. Father didn't want her to find her Prince and live with him because it was what was best for her. He wanted to use her to lure Mother away from this wretched lighthouse.

"I can try," she said, honestly. The palace would be easier to escape from than the lighthouse. And if she were Queen of the kingdom, then nobody could stop her. Could they?

The King rubbed his hands together. "I'll get you some more soup, shall I?"

"That would be lovely," said Lily.

"We need you nice and strong." He smiled as he opened the door.

"Oh, Father," she said, smiling as sweetly as she could. "I forgive you."

She saw his shoulders relax as he slipped out the door.

As soon as she was alone, she brought her hand to her mouth and quite literally wiped the smile from her face. She didn't forgive him! Not even close. But he didn't deserve the truth from her. She was going to tell him whatever she needed to in order to get what she wanted.

Freedom.

MICAH

THE NOW

*D*arkness fell and with it came a sense of trepidation.

Micah wasn't used to trusting strangers like this. Although, she reminded herself that she'd trusted Rose back when she'd been trapped in the palace as a Whisperer. And Rose was the last person she should've trusted. But that had worked out for the best.

Meeting Enid on the beach had just seemed too convenient. Perhaps Jeremiah and Rose were whispering for their safety and that had influenced things. Or perhaps sometimes good luck just happened in the same way that bad luck sometimes did. Or maybe they were walking into a trap?

She wrapped her shirt around her body a little tighter to keep out the cold and paced the shrubs that were keeping them hidden.

"Should we wait somewhere else?" she asked, directing her question at Griffen. "In case it's an ambush."

"Good idea," he said, always happy to take the lowest risk option to keep Pip safe.

"It's not an ambush," insisted Azrael. "You can go, but I'm staying here. We need to show Enid a sign of good faith. Getting us to the lighthouse won't be without risk for her."

Micah sighed. "Okay. We stick together. We've seen what happens when we don't."

"We'll get Gabe back," said Pip. "We won't give up on him."

"Thank you." Micah was starting to see what Griffen liked so much about Pip. She did have a kind heart.

"How long do you think we have to wait?" asked Pip, sounding more like her old self.

"It's only just gotten dark," said Raphael.

"Can I take a moment to say something?" Micah cleared her throat, wondering if this might be the last chance she had to talk to them as a group. "I want to thank you for coming on this crazy quest with me."

"You didn't tell us it was crazy when you asked us to come." Raphael's voice was laced with amusement.

"I'm trying to be serious," she said, smiling. "I'm really grateful you listened to me. I'd never have gotten this far on my own. All the attempts to find Lily in the past have failed and it's got to be because the kingdoms weren't working together. But we've had Azrael to heal us, Raphael to keep us safe with his elixirs, Pip to keep us strong and well-fed, and Griffen to protect us."

"And your whispers," added Pip. "We'd never have found that boat without you. And who knows what other luck your whispers have brought about."

Micah smiled again. "I wonder if Feldspar has a power?"

"Maybe they look through the crystals they mine?" suggested Azrael.

"I think it's our visions," said Raphael.

Micah nodded in agreement. "I think you might be right."

"Well, I'm having a vision of a boat right now," said Griffen.

Micah could just make out his large frame in the moonlight. He was peering out to the water through the trees.

"How close is it?" asked Raphael.

"Still a little while off."

"Have we got time for a quick whisper?" asked Azrael.

Micah breathed a sigh. They needed all the good luck they could get.

They stood in a circle and grasped hands.

"Focus on our safe arrival at the lighthouse," said Micah. "Bring it to the front of your mind."

Following her own instructions, she imagined them on a boat, arriving safely at a lighthouse.

"The Whisperers are whispering," she said.

"The Whisperers are whispering," they all repeated. "The Whisperers are whispering. The Whisperers are whispering."

"We have arrived safely at the lighthouse," said Micah, keeping her voice low.

"We have arrived safely at the lighthouse," her companions repeated in a hush. "We have arrived safely at the lighthouse. We have arrived safely at the lighthouse…"

They chanted quickly, knowing they didn't have much time, sending their wish into the sky, over and over.

"That's enough," said Micah, dropping Raphael and Azrael's hands. "The universe has heard us. It's out of our hands now."

"Do we step out of the bushes?" asked Pip.

"Enid said to wait here," Azrael reminded them.

They watched as the shadow of a boat beached itself on the sand and a man climbed out. Another man remained on board.

"I don't know if we can trust them," said Griffen.

Micah nodded, a similar feeling of unease building in the pit of her stomach.

"We can trust them," said Azrael.

"Friends of Enid!" the man called. "Please show yourselves."

"Here we go." Micah was the first to step from the safety of the scrub, holding up her hands as she approached to make no mistake she was unarmed.

Her companions did the same, although they all knew that Griffen still had that knife tucked in the back of his trousers. Hopefully, he didn't need to use it.

"Who are you?" asked Micah as she approached.

"I'm Enid's husband, Robb," the man said. "Carson's father. I'm helping you in his name, even though I don't believe you can save the children. But Enid says it's worth a shot."

"We're going to do our best," said Raphael, positioning himself between the man and Micah.

Micah huffed. Hadn't Raphael realized by now that she didn't need a man to protect her?

"Who's the other man?" asked Griffen.

"Me brother." Robb waded back to the boat. "Someone had to help me row here."

Micah eyed the two men in the darkness, hoping Azrael had made the right decision.

"Quickly and quietly on board." Robb held the boat steady. "I need to return this boat before it's noticed missing."

Micah was first on board and the others quickly followed, same order as last time with Griffen and Pip on one side, and Micah, Raphael, and Azrael on the other with Robb's brother who sat silently avoiding eye contact.

Robb pushed the boat free of the sand and climbed in. He was a big man and the boat tipped dangerously to one side. Micah leaned over, trying to help balance the weight.

"This ain't going to work." Robb pointed to Pip. "Move to the other side, girl."

Griffen shifted in his seat, clearly not happy to be separated from the woman he was here to protect.

"You're a big bastard, aren't you?" said Robb. "Don't worry, I'll sit on this side with you. I ain't gonna touch your girlfriend."

"She's—"

"It doesn't matter, Griffen!" Pip hushed. "Let's get going."

Micah shuffled over to make room for Pip. There weren't enough oars for her to row on this side, but from what Micah had seen last time, there wasn't a lot of point in Pip rowing anyway.

"We can take turns," said Pip.

"Okay," said Micah, not intending to hold her to that.

They hauled the boat over the waves, toward the darkness of the ocean.

"Just to be clear, I'm not getting off the boat when we arrive," Robb called out to them. "And we're not hanging around to wait for you, either."

"You're going to leave us out there?" Pip's voice was laced with panic.

"That's right. If you're not happy with that, we can turn around now."

"That'll be fine," said Micah, nudging Pip to keep her quiet. It was a miracle they'd found a way over to the lighthouse. It would be foolish to ruin that now.

Besides, it was likely the man they'd left in the cage would've been discovered by now and raised the alarm. Being out here in the middle of the ocean was the safest place they could be right now.

Micah's arms burned, her muscles still sore from the last time they'd been used like this. Ignoring the pain, she rowed on.

"Can you feel her?" she leaned forward and asked Raphael. "Is your elixir working?"

"No," he said, avoiding turning his face. "I keep thinking of that tower back there..."

"That wasn't a lighthouse," she said. "We saw her under the water and we know a girl with red hair lives there with the Queen. This has to be right."

Going to the lighthouse was the right plan. It had to be. At any rate, they'd come too far now to turn around.

"Would you like me to row?" asked Pip.

Micah shook her head. "It can't be much further. Save your strength. We don't know what we'll face out there."

"Hush!" The whites of Robb's eyes flashed at them in the moonlight and he pointed to a tall shadow looming in the distance.

The lighthouse. A strange name for a building with no light. It was just a tall dark shape sitting in the water with waves crashing at its sides. Could Lily really be trapped inside?

They got close and just as Micah was wondering where they might be able to dock, Robb threw a large anchor into the water.

"I go no further," he said, in a coarse whisper.

"You have to get us closer!" said Griffen.

"Please!" said Micah, looking at Robb's silent brother, who still seemed not to want to have anything to do with them.

"I don't need a hole in the boat from those rocks." Robb pointed to the rocky outcrop the lighthouse was perched on. "Out! Now! Or you return to Feldspar with me."

Micah removed her shoes and put them in her small bag of belongings, which she tied around her waist.

"I'm gonna count to ten," said Robb. "Then I pull anchor and head back."

Micah considered for a moment if they should kill this man and take control of the boat but dismissed it straight away, ashamed she'd become so desensitized about the idea of taking a life.

"Ten!" Robb pointed to the water.

"Come back for us tomorrow night," pleaded Pip.

"Nine!"

"We can't start a revolution if we're stuck out here," Raphael pointed out.

"Eight!"

"We'll meet you right here," said Pip.

"Seven!"

Micah plunged into the water, gasping as the cold swallowed her up and salt leeched into the back of her throat. She bobbed to the surface and looked back at the boat.

"Six!"

Raphael was next, followed shortly by Azrael.

"Five!"

Pip jumped in, her skirt billowing in the air before being swallowed by the ocean. Griffen didn't wait for any further numbers to be called before following her, his eyes never leaving Pip.

Not bothering with the rest of his countdown, Robb hauled the anchor from the water and he and his brother took hold of two oars in the middle of the boat and maneuvered themselves away.

Feeling herself sinking, Micah kicked and dug at the water trying to propel herself toward the rocks. It wasn't all that far, but in these freezing and rough conditions, it seemed like the other end of the world.

She kicked out again. It was no use. Her bag was weighing her down. She was going to need to untie it and hoped it washed up on shore.

Her friends were struggling as much as she was, their heads disappearing then reappearing as the water grabbed at them with icy fingers.

"Dump your belongings!" shouted Micah. "They're weighing us down. Take off your shoes."

Trying to tread water, she got to work on the rope of the bag around her waist. But just as she felt it begin to pull loose, a huge wave swallowed her up and dragged her under. She tumbled, holding onto her breath as she waved her hands and waited for the ocean to decide if it was going to keep her or spit her back out.

Enid's son crossed her mind. Had he drowned like this out here? Surely many people had. It'd be a miracle if all five of them made it to the shore alive.

She moved through the water, not by any choice of her own, relieved when finally the tumbling stopped and she was able to break through the surface and take in a breath of sweet air.

"Lily!" she cried, no longer caring if they arrived by stealth or in a riot. If there was anybody in that lighthouse, they'd surely have heard or seen them by now.

Then a sharp pain grazed her shins and forearms and she cried out, taking a few moments to realize she'd been tossed onto the rocks. She crawled forward, ignoring the pain until she was free from the water, and lay down on the freezing rocks, powerless to check if any of her friends had made it or if they were still in the water.

For the first time since they'd set out on this journey, she let tears roll down her cheeks, saltwater merging with saltwater in a giant puddle of terror and relief.

LILY

THE NOW

*A*s soon as Father left the room to fetch her some more soup, Lily scrambled from Mother's bed and headed for the balcony. She was desperate for some fresh air in her lungs after being cooped up in Mother's bedchamber. Desperate to clear her head from all the lies she'd just told him and just as desperate to see if there was any sign of her Prince coming to rescue her.

She'd had more dreams of the lighthouse crashing into the water, certain that something or someone was trying to warn her. Now that she'd been brought back here, she wasn't sure she'd be able to escape again in time. Father would make sure of that. It seemed she had no choice but to do what he'd asked and somehow achieve the impossible by convincing Mother to leave the lighthouse and come with them to the palace.

Opening the balcony doors, she stepped out and gasped. Gripping the railings, she drew in deep breaths, trying to steady herself from the shock of what lay before her.

Instead of seeing the raging sea below, all she could see was... dirt. For miles and miles, brown dirt where there should have been crashing waves and swooping gulls. Straining her eyes, she saw the ocean in the distance. This was a view she'd become familiar with from the Terrace and the realization that she was still in the palace hit her hard, making her question if she was losing her mind.

Reminding herself that this was a good thing, she went back into Mother's room, immediately noticing differences that would be impossible for someone unfamiliar with the room to pick. But to her, they were glaring now that she was looking for them. The blue agates that lined the foot of Mother's bed were smaller than the ones in the lighthouse, and the large one that always dug into her thigh when she sat in the chair beside her bed was absent. Instead, flat agates lined the chair. The curtains at the balcony door were a slightly darker blue and the quilt on the bed had a softer feel to it.

She now also understood why the room smelled different. Instead of the salty tang of the ocean air, it was dry and dusty. And the sound of the waves and gulls had been replaced with silence.

The walls were still curved though, leaving her thinking that the room must be located in some kind of turret. Why would Father have such a close replica of Mother's bedchamber right here in the palace? Or was it the other way around? Had he replicated her bedchamber in the lighthouse when she'd moved there to make her feel more at home? Somehow, that seemed more likely.

Lily's immediate instinct was to run and she had to stop her feet from taking her immediately from this strange room and out the front door of the palace. She'd learned her lesson the last time she'd acted in haste and remembering that kept her feet glued to the floor.

She needed to be clever about this. She had to bide her time so that the next time she made a run for it, she could truly be free.

Climbing back into bed, she pulled up the covers and waited for Father to return. There was no doubt in her mind the lighthouse was going to crumble into the ocean, and it was going to happen soon.

As much as discovering she was still in the palace had been a shock, it was also a relief. Because when that lighthouse came down, anybody near it was going down, too.

RAPHAEL

THE NOW

*R*aphael heaved for breath, his hands and knees bleeding as
he crawled along the sharp rocks, trying to find dry
ground.

He could hear Micah calling for Lily. So much for sneaking up on
this lighthouse. Although, he supposed if there was anybody in there,
they'd already have heard them. Could Lily really be somewhere
inside that giant shadow? He'd been certain she was in that tower near
the beach. It seemed his homing elixir still needed some work.

He hadn't had a single vision of Lily since he'd seen her scream
and that'd been ages ago. Why would they suddenly go blank now?

The stars were even brighter out here, lighting a shadowy path
ahead of him. He strained his eyes and realized there was no sand on
this beach. Just a large pile of rocks with a lighthouse looming in the
middle. He blinked up at the tall structure, certain for a moment that
it was swaying. Rubbing his eyes, he decided it was just the moving of

the clouds making it look like the lighthouse was losing its grip on the rocks.

"Lily!" he heard Micah call again.

He lay down on his stomach and concentrated on slowing his breath. He was alive and that was all that mattered. Micah had made it, too. But how had Azrael, Pip, and Griffen fared? That sea had been merciless.

Now that he'd caught his breath, the world around him was becoming clearer and he rolled onto his back and tried to assess the extent of his injuries. It didn't feel like any bones were broken and the cuts on his hands and knees were only superficial.

Something wasn't right, though. Something was missing.

His elixirs!

He felt around his body and inside his sodden jacket, but the elixirs were missing.

This was a real blow. Unlike his companions, his powers didn't come from within. He couldn't lead a whisper like Micah or heal a person with his hands like Azrael. And he couldn't find more of what he needed along the way, like Pip could. His elixirs were distilled from carefully grown ingredients in his apothecary. Without them he was… just an ordinary man.

He'd never been an ordinary man before. Always the son of the Alchemist or brother of the Queen, and then finally the Alchemist himself. But it seemed he was destined to meet Lily as Raphael alone. That was if he was going to meet her at all. This lighthouse seemed deserted. Had this been some kind of elaborate trick to trap them here?

"Raphael!" He turned his head and saw Azrael on the rocks, not far away.

Scrambling until he found himself upright, he went to her.

"Are you okay?" he asked.

She nodded. "I'm okay." Her dark hair was plastered to her pale face. Even in the dim light, he could see that her lips had turned blue.

"Let me help you up." He reached out his hands and Azrael took them, hauling herself to her feet.

Her dress was soaking and water pooled on the rocks at her feet. It was amazing all that fabric hadn't pulled her under the water. She was even luckier than he'd been to have survived.

"I heard Micah," she said. "But I haven't heard Griffen or Pip yet."

A strange animal made a sound in the distance and Raphael felt Azrael tighten her grip on his hands.

"It's okay," he said, letting go of her hands to put an arm around her shoulder. To his surprise, she leaned into him. "We're okay."

"What animal could survive out here?" she asked.

"I don't know." He really didn't. He'd never heard an animal make a sound like that before.

A shadow came stumbling across the rocks toward them and Raphael released his grip on Azrael to position his body in front of her. Whatever that was, it was going to need to get past him first.

"It's just me!" hissed Micah as she stepped into the moonlight and her face illuminated. She looked even more of a mess than Azrael, with a large cut on her forehead and her shirt torn to shreds.

"Are you okay?" asked Raphael, rushing forward.

"I've been worse." She pressed her palm to her forehead and winced. "You both okay?"

They nodded their responses.

"Where are Pip and Griffen?"

"We don't know," said Azrael. "But I hope they're nowhere near whatever creature is making that awful noise."

"We need to look for them." Micah's hand fell to her side as a familiar look of determination crossed her face. This wasn't a woman who gave up easily, no matter how dire the odds. "They might need our help."

"You're right," he said. They'd come here together and they needed to stick together.

They clambered over the rocks, making their way closer to the noise, scanning the shoreline for any sign of their friends.

"Griffen!" called Micah. "Pip!"

"Don't you think we should be quiet?" asked Raphael.

"If we were going to be attacked, don't you think it would've happened by now?" said Micah.

"Over there." Azrael pointed to a moving shadow in the shallows of the water.

Waves were crashing into whatever it was, but in the darkness, it was hard to make out what they were dealing with until they could get closer.

"Is that a bear?" asked Micah. "I've never seen a bear before."

"It's not a bear." Azrael's voice had a strange tone that Raphael hadn't heard her use before.

"A dragon?" asked Micah.

"They're not real." Raphael winced as he stepped on a particularly sharp rock.

"They might be," said Micah.

"It's Pip," said Azrael. "Pip's making the noise."

The clouds moved across the sky, sending moonbeams pouring to the rocks and Raphael's heart sank to see that Azrael was right. Pip was standing in the shallows bent over a dark shape in the water, which was unmistakably Griffen.

Ignoring the pain in his feet, Raphael ran forward, splashing through the water with Azrael and Micah beside him until they reached their friends.

"Help me!" Pip was trying to drag Griffen's enormous frame from the water. "Please, help me."

Raphael glanced at Micah and saw she'd reached the same conclusion as he had. They were too late. But that didn't mean they could leave Griffen there. If the roles were reversed, he wouldn't leave them.

"Micah, you take one arm and I'll take the other," he said. "Pip, Azrael, you take one of his legs each. We'll carry him in."

Griffen was even heavier than Raphael had expected it was possible for a person to be. He could only hope they were strong enough. But if motivation counted as strength, then they had that in abundance.

Pip's howling had ceased and now she was sobbing, begging Azrael to tell her if she was going to be able to save him.

"I'll try," said Azrael.

"You have to save him," said Pip. "You have to!"

"If it's possible to save him, then I will," said Azrael.

Raphael corrected his grip on Griffen's arm to support him under his shoulder, impressed that Micah was able to keep up on her side.

"He saved me," howled Pip. "I went under the water and couldn't get back up. My dress was heavy and it was dragging me down. But then I felt Griffen there, bringing me back up to the surface. I grabbed onto him. I couldn't breathe. And he held me up, so my face was out of the water. Then. Then. Then..."

"It's okay, Pip," soothed Azrael. "You don't need to tell us now."

"Then he went under!" sobbed Pip. "And a big wave swept me in to shore. I tried to get back out to him, but the waves were so strong. And then. Then. Then..."

"Oh, Pip," said Azrael, as they got to a rock that was flatter than the rest, and laid Griffen down.

Pip knelt down next to Griffen and planted kisses on his cheeks. "Come back to me, Griffen. Please, come back."

"Can you save him?" Raphael asked Azrael in a hushed voice.

The fear in her face gave him the answer without the need for the slight shrug of her shoulders and she knelt down beside Pip.

"Pip, I don't know if I can save him," she said, checking his neck for a pulse and shaking her head as she moved her fingers around.

"But you saved Micah!" wailed Pip.

"Micah was still breathing," said Azrael, bending forward and holding her ear to Griffen's mouth.

"Let her work." Raphael reached for Pip, but she shrugged him away, too distressed to receive any comfort.

"He's too far gone." Azrael looked up at Pip, her face crumpling. "I'm so sorry."

"You have to try!" Pip clutched at the front of Azrael's sodden dress. "Please, we've all seen you work your magic. You can do it."

"Pip, it's too late." Azrael covered Pip's hands with her own and held them. "His body's cold. He's gone."

"He can't be gone," said Pip.

Raphael looked away, her grief too raw and deep for him to witness. He knew what it felt like to lose someone. Not a lover, perhaps. But he knew what it felt like to lose a parent. How would he feel if the reason for his visions of Lily going blank was because the worst had happened to her?

Just the thought of that sent arrows of pain into his heart and he'd never even had the chance to meet her. Poor, Pip.

"Do you see that?" asked Micah, tugging at his sleeve and pointing to the ocean.

He followed the direction he was pointing. "Just water. Why? What are you looking at?"

"You can't see... that." Micah's face was contorted and she clutched his sleeve as if asking for his protection for the first time since they'd set out on this quest.

He looked again. "Micah, I really can't see anything. What is it?"

"Never mind." She shook her head, her eyes still glued to something he couldn't see.

"Can you at least try to bring him back?" Pip begged Azrael, clearly not able to let Griffen go.

Azrael nodded, letting go of Pip, so she could place her hands on Griffen's chest.

"Micah, can you whisper?" asked Pip.

Even in the moonlight, Raphael could see the tears flood Micah's eyes as she dragged her gaze from the ocean to look at Pip.

"I can whisper," she said.

Then Pip directed her gaze at Raphael.

"I lost my elixirs in the ocean," he said, before she could ask. "But I can whisper with Micah."

Pip nodded. "Thank you."

Micah slipped her cold hand into Raphael's and together they whispered into the night, their words rising to the sky and Raphael imagined them finding Griffen's soul and dragging it back down to them.

Azrael worked on Griffen, her hands shaking from cold and the futility of the task they'd been set to achieve.

How long they spent trying, Raphael didn't know, but after some time, Azrael's hands came to a stop and Micah and Raphael fell silent.

"He's at peace," said Azrael.

And that was when Pip's howling began once more. For Griffen may be at peace, but it was obvious that never again would the woman who loved him be able to find peace again.

AZRAEL

THE NOW

*I*t was with a heavy heart that Azrael removed her hands from Griffen. Pip's wailing didn't help. But how could she explain to her that healing didn't work like that? Not everyone could be healed, just because you wanted them to be. Especially people who'd crossed so far over into death.

If death could be cheated so easily, then it had no meaning. And if death had no meaning, then life itself was also meaningless. And that, Azrael knew was untrue.

Life was full of meaning, even if sometimes it wasn't obvious. She only had to look at her own life to see the truth in that. Terrible things had happened to her. And she'd not only survived it, but those experiences had made her who she was—a person who was able to help others. A healer.

And although she couldn't help Griffen, in time she'd be able to help Pip. If she let her, of course. And judging by the way Pip's pale irises were flashing at her in the moonlight, it seemed that it was going to take a while before Azrael was allowed anywhere near her.

Pip was going to want to blame someone to avoid having to shoulder all the responsibility herself. And there was no doubt that someone was going to be Azrael. The Angel of death, as Enid had pointed out to her not so long ago. But if it helped Pip to blame her, then she was willing to accept that for now.

Azrael went to Micah and Raphael, who stood shivering on a nearby rock.

"We need to get warm," said Azrael, knowing she had no strength to heal anybody who fell prey to the cold. She barely had enough strength left for herself. "Do you think there's anybody in the lighthouse?"

"There's a woman on the balcony," said Micah. "She's been watching us."

Azrael tilted her face toward the night sky but couldn't see who Micah was talking about.

"I can't see her," said Raphael, squinting.

"She's right there," said Micah.

Azrael blinked. Her eyes must be too tired to see what Micah could see.

"Please help us!" called Micah, waving her arms frantically at the lighthouse.

"If she was going to help us, she'd have come down by now," said Raphael.

"Then let's try to get inside to talk to her," said Micah.

"What about Pip?" asked Azrael. Pip had draped herself over Griffen's body and didn't look like she was going to move any time soon. "We can't leave her here."

"Can you stay with her for the moment?" asked Micah. "Raphael and I will walk around the lighthouse and see if we can find a way in."

"I'm not sure I'm the best person to stay with her," said Azrael.

"You're the very best person to stay with her," said Raphael.

Azrael nodded. "Find a way in and call out to me when you do. I'll try to convince her to leave Griffen and come inside."

She sat down and watched them climb over the rocks toward the lighthouse, drawing her knees up to her chest to try to get warm, but it was impossible in these wet clothes. Her gaze was pulled upward again to the balcony, trying to see the woman Micah had been pointing at, deciding it was either a shadow or the woman was no longer there. Whichever way, she didn't have a good feeling about this.

"Pip," she called out. "Say your goodbyes, then we need to find shelter."

"Azrael." Pip's voice had risen to an excited pitch. "Come here."

"I'm cold, Pip." Azrael sighed. "And tired. I'm sad that he's gone, but there's nothing more I can do for him."

"He moved, Azrael. His chest. It moved." Pip was on her knees now, leaning over Griffen, her ear pressed to his mouth. "I think he's breathing."

"He's not breathing, Pip."

"Azrael, come here right now!"

Azrael's eyebrows shot up, surprised to see the bossy side of Pip having returned so soon. She must really believe Griffen had come back to her.

She got to her feet, wincing at the sharpness of the rocks, wondering if she'd ever see her soft leather shoes again, and clambered over to Pip.

"Put your hand here." Pip placed Azrael's palm on Griffen's cold chest. "He's breathing. I can feel it."

As soon as Azrael made contact with Griffen, his eyes sprang open and he drew in an enormous gasp of air.

Azrael had to steady herself as her heart rate spiked and she drew in a gasp of her own. Pip hadn't imagined it. Griffen was alive!

"You did it, Azrael!" Pip held her hands to her mouth. "You really did it!"

"Help me turn him to his side," said Azrael, trying to lift and roll this huge man over.

With some effort and a little help from Griffen himself, they managed to turn him and he coughed, expelling saltwater from deep in his lungs.

"Griffen!" said Pip. "I knew you wouldn't leave me. I knew it."

Griffen rolled onto his back once more and blinked up at Pip. His face was gray, his lips blue, but still he held love in his eyes.

"It was you who didn't leave me," he said.

"This isn't possible," said Azrael, more to herself than to anyone else. He'd been too far gone. But clearly, she'd been wrong. Because here he was, breathing, and coughing and talking to the woman he loved.

"Azrael did it," said Pip. "She brought you back. And Micah and Raphael whispered for you. It's a miracle!"

Pip reached out for Azrael and wrapped her arms around her. Azrael resisted her reflex to pull away and instead accepted Pip's embrace, which was so much warmer than the blame she'd thought she was going to wear.

It seemed Griffen wasn't meant to die just yet. Perhaps the universe had bigger things planned for him.

A rumbling sound caught her attention and she let go of Pip to look up at the lighthouse, which had unmistakably started to sway.

MICAH

THE NOW

"*D*id you hear that?" asked Micah. "A rumbling sound."

"It's just the waves," said Raphael, although she noticed he looked up at the lighthouse rather than out to the ocean.

"Is it moving?" She put her hand on the cold stone exterior.

"I thought that earlier," he said. "But if feels steady enough."

Micah nodded. Maybe it was normal for it to sway? It wasn't like they had anywhere to take cover if this thing did decide to come down. Better to press on with trying to find a way in. She was sure they'd walked almost the full way around the lighthouse already.

"We should've gone the other way around," said Raphael.

"There!" Micah pointed as a door came into view.

They ran to the large steel door built to withstand the harshness of the elements, Micah's heart beating wildly. Was it possible Lily was behind this door? They'd traveled so far to find her. It'd be heartbreaking to discover that a strange woman on the balcony was the only person here.

"How are we going to get this open?" She studied the lock, wondering what she could use to pick it.

Raphael reached out and turned the handle.

"Like this," he said, swinging open the door.

"Very clever." She was certain they'd have grinned at each other if it weren't for the harrowing scene they'd just witnessed out there on the rocks.

It seemed she'd also witnessed something in the water that nobody else had. Unless she'd imagined it. She was going to need to think about this before she shared it with anyone. Not that she had time right now to ask Raphael whether or not he thought she was going mad.

"I don't suppose there's a lot of point locking your door when you live out here," said Raphael, stepping through the door.

"I guess not." She was quick to follow him inside, blinking in the darkness.

"Do you think Lily's here?" asked Raphael, bumping into her.

"I want her to be." It was hard to speak over the chattering of her teeth. "But... I don't know."

"I don't feel her here." Raphael's voice was full of despair.

Micah blinked in the darkness as her eyes found their focus. Moonlight was pouring in through the windows, lighting up a circular staircase that'd been lined with bright crystals of every color imaginable. Such a contrast to the dull exterior. They'd definitely been brought to the right lighthouse. Only a Queen could possibly live here.

"We should go back for Azrael and Pip," said Micah. "It's warmer in here without the wind."

"Let's just check that it's safe first," said Raphael.

"Hello," Micah called up the stairs. "Anybody home?"

"We're unarmed," added Raphael. "We just want to talk to you."

Micah reached for the handrail, running her palms over the smooth bumps of the crystals. She'd like to see them in the daylight, although she doubted they'd be beautiful. These crystals were stained with the blood of children who'd been taken from their families and forced into the mines.

She began the climb with Raphael close behind her.

"I should go first," he said.

"Why? Because I'm a helpless female?" she asked.

"There's nothing helpless about you, Micah," he said. "It's just... okay, you go first."

She smiled in the darkness at Raphael's attempt to be a gentleman. Tallis had given up on that act years ago, accepting she wasn't like other women. It seemed Raphael was learning fast. It was nice that he'd wanted to protect her, though. The world could use more men like Raphael and Tallis.

They climbed the stairs, each step feeling like a hundred, until they got to a landing.

"The woman was on the balcony, right at the top," said Micah, ignoring the small groan Raphael made at the thought of more stairs.

"Is it worth searching this floor first?" He tilted his head toward a door on the landing.

"Why don't you have a look and I'll continue up?" she said, keen to reach the top to see if the woman was indeed the Queen.

"I'm not sure we should split up." He crossed his arms.

"Well, it's up to you, but I'm going to continue up." She couldn't see the harm in separating for a few moments. If they were going to be attacked, surely it would've happened by now.

"I'll just have a very quick look then," he said. "It's safer if we clear each floor as we go."

Micah had barely paused her steps in her eagerness to get to the woman on the balcony. If Lily wasn't here—and she was starting to doubt that she was—then at the very least the woman should know where she was and what'd happened to her.

She climbed past another landing and went up further. The exertion was increasing her heart rate, but her clothes remained damp, clinging to her skin and keeping her bones cold.

Finally reaching the very top landing, she walked cautiously toward a door covered in blue crystals. It was closed, although if the front door hadn't been locked, then she doubted any of the interior doors were locked either. She grasped the handle and turned it slowly.

Moonlight flooded the room and Micah saw that every surface was covered with the same blue crystals as the door. They were everywhere. On the floor, the bedposts, the chairs, the window frames, and table. A set of blue curtains were billowing at an open doorway that Micah guessed led to the balcony.

"Your Highness?" called Micah, heading for the door. "I saw you from below. I know you're here."

Moving one of the curtains to the side, Micah stepped out onto the balcony, wincing as the cold air nipped at her face.

There was a woman, huddled in a corner of the balcony, her knees pulled up to her chest and her face buried in her hands. She reminded Micah of a child thinking they can't be seen, because they can't see anybody else.

"I'm not going to hurt you," said Micah. "I just want to talk to you."

The woman huddled down further and Micah noticed the color of her hair was red. This had to be the Queen. It couldn't be Lily. There was no way her niece would try to hide from her like this.

"My name's Micah." She stepped forward, aware of the racing of her heart. If the Queen attacked her then she needed to be ready. "I've come a long way to talk to you."

Very slowly, the woman lifted her face and looked at Micah.

"You can see me?" she asked, in a voice little more than a whisper.

Micah nodded. "Are you the Queen? I was told that a beautiful Queen lives in this lighthouse."

A little flattery wouldn't go astray.

Very slowly, the Queen nodded, seeming to gain a little confidence. Micah hoped Raphael took his time, or at least didn't approach too quickly and scare her back into her shell.

"You look like her," said the Queen.

Micah's heart soared. She had to be talking about Lily. They hadn't come here for nothing.

"I'm Lily's aunt," she said. "I've come to... talk to her."

Best not to reveal her true motivation just yet.

"Where is she?" asked Micah.

"Her name's Angel now," said the Queen, slowly pulling herself to a stand.

"Where's Angel?" Micah remained where she was, doing her best not to look too intimidating.

"He took her," said the Queen, visibly shaking. "He left me all alone."

"Who took her?" Micah dared to take a small step forward.

"The King. He hid her in his boat and took her away. He thought I didn't know he did it, but I saw. He took my Angel."

"Where did he take her?"

She shook her head. "I've been waiting for her to come back. I thought maybe your boat was my Angel, but it wasn't."

"I saw you watching us," said Micah.

"I thought you were my Angel at first."

There was a noise behind Micah and she spun around to see Raphael stepping out onto the balcony. She winced and held up her hand to warn him to be quiet.

"All clear downstairs!" He'd spoken far too loudly. Had he not seen her warning? "Seems we're the only ones here."

"No, we're not." Micah pointed to the darkened corner of the balcony where the Queen had taken a step back into the shadows.

"What do you mean?" asked Raphael.

"She's right there," said Micah, pointing again. "The Queen."

"Micah. There's nobody there."

"But..."

Micah looked at the Queen who was coming toward her now.

"He can't see me," said the Queen. "Just like he couldn't see your friend's soul rising from the ocean out there. Nobody can see me. Except for Angel. And now you."

"I don't understand." Micah was the one to step back now and she put her hand to her heart trying to still its rapid beat.

"What don't you understand?" asked Raphael. "It's pretty simple. We've come to an empty lighthouse. Lily's not here."

"You really can't see her? Please don't joke with me, Raph." Micah shook her head, unable to remove her eyes from the woman that only she could see. How was this possible?

"Micah, you're starting to scare me," he said. "There's nobody out here."

"There is." Her voice dropped to a whisper and she studied the Queen more closely now, unable to tell the difference between this apparition and a regular flesh and blood human. Griffen had also looked real when his soul had detached itself from his body and hovered over the water, still reluctant to leave his Princess's side. And Raphael hadn't been able to see him either.

"I need your help," said the Queen. "I need you to find my amethyst. Please, will you help me?"

"Where is it?" asked Micah, glancing around.

The Queen pointed to the ocean. "I threw it out there. I shouldn't have thrown it. Now I'm trapped here. I can't leave this lighthouse until the amethysts fall into new rightful hands. You have to help me! Please! Angel left me and can't help me now."

"I don't even know what an amethyst is," said Micah. "And going back out there into the water is certain death. I'm sorry, but—"

"What's going on?" Raphael grabbed her by the arm. "Who are you talking to?"

"You swear you can't see her?" asked Micah. "The woman standing right there in front of me."

"I really can't," he said. "Micah, I think you need to come inside and warm up."

"Give me a moment."

Raphael stepped back and sighed. But she didn't have time to explain to him right now. She reached out her hand toward the Queen. If she really was an apparition then surely, she wouldn't be able to touch her.

The Queen held steady, blinking at her in the moonlight as Micah's hand passed right through her body.

"You understand now, don't you?" asked the Queen.

"This is... I can't..." Micah's heart thumped and she wondered if she might pass out. How was this possible? She stumbled back and clutched at her chest, trying to draw air into her lungs.

"Micah!" Raphael rushed to her and wrapped an arm around her shoulders. "Come inside."

"She's coming back!" The Queen went to the railings and pointed out at the sea. "This time it's really my Angel. I can feel her. Can you feel her, Micah?"

Micah looked out across the water and saw what the Queen was pointing at. A boat was fighting the waves and heading directly for them. The sun was rising behind them casting orange streaks across the sky, reminding Micah of her brother Jeremiah whose color blindness would prevent him from seeing this spectacular sight. But he wouldn't need to see the colors to appreciate it—for Lily was a far more welcome sight than any sunrise could ever be.

"Look, Raphael," said Micah. "It's Lily."

Raphael let go of her to go to the railings to look out.

"Please, tell me you can see that boat." A new fear bubbled inside Micah's chest.

"I can see it," he said.

Now all she had to do was hope that he could see Lily, too. She hadn't come this far to chase after some kind of ghost.

LILY

THE NOW

*L*ily was being forced back to the one place she'd hoped never to return. To see the one person she never wanted to see again.

She'd begged Father to let her stay in the palace but he'd refused and she knew he'd never let her out of his sight again if she didn't have his trust. And the best way to get trust was to earn it.

She was going to get Father his precious love stones from under the ocean and convince Mother to leave the lighthouse. That was assuming it didn't fall down on their heads first. If that didn't earn Father's trust, then she didn't know what would. Once she was safely back at the palace again, she'd wait for the right opportunity to flee.

As the boat crashed over the waves, thoughts of the children in the mines nagged at her. If she were to stay in Feldspar and take over from Father, she could set the children free. But was this her responsibility? She hadn't taken them from their mothers' arms.

"If something were to happen to me, who'd rule in my place?" she asked Father from the stern of the boat.

"Nothing will happen to you?" He shook his head and pursed his lips, clearly unimpressed with her question.

"But what if something did?"

"Nothing will." He shot her a look that told her it was time to be silent. Something had very nearly happened to her. Twice. She'd almost died of cold in the ocean, then again on the Terrace. Both times, Father had been the one to bring her back from the brink of death. Was this why he'd saved her? Because he didn't know what he'd do to fill her place if she died. Maybe she shouldn't have fought so hard to live if that was the destiny he had mapped out for her.

As they drew closer to the lighthouse, Lily could see Mother on the balcony watching them approach, despite the earliness of the hour. So, the lighthouse was still standing. She'd half expected to find nothing but water in its place. Please, let it hold steady just long enough that she could do what they'd come here for and then get far away to safety.

"She's been waiting for us," said Lily, pointing.

"You know my eyesight is terrible." Father squinted at the balcony. "But I'm not surprised."

There was a shadow behind Mother and for a moment Lily was certain that she wasn't alone? She blinked, deciding she'd imagined it. Who would possibly be out here with Mother?

"You won't leave me there, will you?" begged Lily, suddenly fearful of the power held in this man's hands. "We're just going to get the amethysts, then we go back to the palace, right?"

"That's right," said the King. "Your time out here has come to an end."

Not believing him for a moment, Lily attempted to smile at this man who had the power to decide if she lived or died.

"What happened to Norris?" she asked, remembering the man she'd promised to make rich with a ruby.

"What do you think happened to him?"

"I honestly have no idea."

"He's no longer rowing," said the King. "Let's leave it at that."

"Oh." So, that was another death Lily had on her hands, along with that poor oarsman who'd been thrown overboard for refusing to be bribed.

There was only one place a boat could safely dock at the lighthouse, and it was hidden between the rocks. Just another measure to ensure unwanted visitors were kept away. The oarsmen directed the boat between those rocks now, bringing the boat to rest at the only patch of sand on the entire rock-filled island.

Lily stepped from the boat and removed her hood, letting her hair fly free in the breeze, as she undid the buttons of her cloak.

"What are you doing?" asked Father.

"I'm going to go and get the amethysts," she said.

"First, you talk to your mother." He put a firm hand on her shoulder and her busy fingers stilled.

"Don't you mean *we*?" she asked.

"You talk to her," he said, a weight seeming heavy on his shoulders.

Letting out a sigh, she marched toward the lighthouse, her ears already feeling the pain of Mother's shrieking anger that would no doubt be unleashed. She couldn't blame Father for not wanting to be a witness to that.

She climbed the familiar staircase, running her hands along the fluorite stones, wishing she wasn't comforted by their familiarity. She stepped lightly and carefully, not wanting to push her luck in a structure that she was certain was about to fall.

Reaching the first landing, she went to the kitchen to find Mother standing at the table wringing her hands in front of her.

"Hello, Mother," she said.

"Angel." Mother's voice was soft and warm, not at all what Lily had been expecting. Something must have happened while she'd been gone. But would it help or hinder her cause?

Lily kept her distance, aware of Mother's intense dislike of being touched.

"You left me," she said.

"I'm sorry, Mother. Father brought me back, though. We want you to leave the lighthouse."

"I can't leave here," spat Mother. "The King knows that."

"You can!" said Lily. "We want you to come home with us to the palace so we can be together properly as a family."

This was the only argument Lily had been able to come up with on the boat ride here. Mother loved family time, even if Lily didn't intend to stick around to experience too much of it.

"The King didn't say that." Mother crossed her arms. "He may have said that he wants me to leave here, but he'd never have said I should return to the palace."

"Where else would you go?" asked Lily, unsure what she meant. Father hadn't needed to say she should return to the palace for her to know that's what he'd meant.

"It doesn't matter," said Mother with a sigh. "Without my amethyst, I can't go anywhere. That was why I shouldn't have thrown it away. Why I wanted you so desperately to find it."

"If I find it, will you come with us?" Lily took a step toward Mother, only for her to step back.

"No. I told you I can't." She shook her head. "But if you find it, I'll leave the lighthouse. Don't you know that's why I've always wanted you to find it? I want us both to be free of this place."

"Mother, I think you need to lie down. You're not... making any sense. Why don't you hop into bed and I'll tell you a story?"

"There are people in my bedchamber," she said. "Two of them."

"Who?" Lily remembered the shadow she'd thought she saw.

"There's a man and a woman. They're the ones you've been waiting for."

Lily reached out for the back of a chair to steady herself.

"The man has golden hair," said Mother. "The woman looks like you."

Lily left the room and ran up the stairs, this time with no concern for taking the steps lightly. Warmth radiated through her body, her feet flying even faster than the rate of her heart. Her angels were here! Aunt Micah and her Prince! It had to be them.

She got to the top landing and saw Aunt Micah standing at the door to Mother's bedchamber.

Lily ground to a halt, standing in front of her aunt, panting, puffing, crying, and trying not to fall down.

"Aunt Micah?"

"Oh, Lily."

It'd been so long since anybody had called her by her name. The sound of it was like listening to all of heaven's angels singing at once.

"It's really you." Aunt Micah reached out to embrace Lily, but let her arms fall to her side as if she'd thought again.

Just like it'd been years since she'd heard her name, nobody had hugged her either. Not since she'd been taken from the desert and she yearned to feel her aunt's arms around her.

Aunt Micah was pale and shaking, but there was no mistake it was her. She looked a little older and a little thinner but there was fire in her eyes and the familiar way she tapped one foot on the ground, as if it had a mind of its own and was ready to take off.

"You're afraid of me?" Lily had never imagined a situation where she'd see her brave aunt afraid.

"I'm scared you're not real," she said, holding out a shaking hand. "I can't bear to have found you only for you not to be real."

"Why wouldn't I be real?" she asked. "You can see me, can't you? I'm right here."

Lily stepped forward and slid her arms around her aunt's waist. Her clothing was damp and Lily realized she must be shivering not just from fear, but from cold.

Then she felt the warmth of Aunt Micah's embrace as love overpowered the cold and her arms wrapped tightly around her shoulders.

"It's really you," said Aunt Micah. "We've been looking for you all this time. Nobody ever gave up on you."

"I saw you," said Lily. "I knew you were coming. I saw you in my mind."

"I saw you, too." Aunt Micah pulled back so she could look at her once more.

"You do look like me," laughed Lily.

"I'm sorry, but you look like me," she corrected.

Lily smiled, then braced herself to ask the question that most needed asking.

"My parents," she said. "Are they okay? Are they here?"

Aunt Micah nodded. "They're not here, but they're okay. They're going to be more than okay when I bring you home with me. They've missed you so much. It broke their hearts when you disappeared."

"The men took me," said Lily. "I had no choice."

"I know you didn't, my sweet girl. I know."

There was a noise behind Aunt Micah in Mother's room and Lily remembered what Mother had said.

"Who's with you?" she asked.

"Someone who's been waiting a long time to meet you." Aunt Micah moved aside to reveal Lily's Prince, standing a few steps behind her.

"Lily," he said. "I can see you."

This wasn't quite what she'd expected his first words to be when he saw her, but it didn't matter. All that mattered was that he was here. She hadn't imagined him. She hadn't made him up.

Aunt Micah put a gentle hand on her back to urge her forward and stepped out of the room and closed the door behind her.

"What's your name?" asked Lily, feeling suddenly shy.

"Raphael," he said.

"Raphael," she repeated, loving the feel of his name on her lips.

"I'm from Wintergreen," he said.

"Are you a Prince?" she asked.

He shook his head. "I'm afraid I'm just an ordinary man."

She smiled. There was nothing ordinary about this man. He had an aura about him that was reeling her in.

"Micah convinced me to come with her to look for you," he said.

Lily nodded. "She's the bravest person I ever met."

"I used to think the same," he said, biting down on his lip. "But now... well, I suspect now that I've met you that she might have to be the second bravest. How did you survive for so long out here?"

Lily smiled, enjoying the feeling of his eyes on her. They were even bluer than she'd seen in her vision. He was taller than she expected, too. And stronger looking.

"I never lost hope that one day I'd go home," she said.

He took a few steps toward her, until he was so close, she could almost hear his heart beat.

"This might sound strange, but... can I touch you? Just to make sure you're real."

She tilted her head, remembering that Aunt Micah had said something equally as perplexing. Then a surge of the bravery that Raphael seemed to believe she possessed raced through her body and she drew in a breath.

"Go ahead."

He reached up for her, placing his hands on each of her arms and she stepped closer until there was only the smallest gap between them.

"I saw you," he said. "You were under the water holding a purple stone. You were calling to me."

"I saw you, too," she said, her eyes firmly on his lips. "You were reaching out to me, trying to help me."

"I thought you were beautiful," he said.

"I knew you were beautiful," she replied.

Instead of kissing her, as she'd hoped, he leaned down and pressed his forehead to hers, his hands slipping from her arms to her back until she was pressed up against his chest.

There was a gentle knock at the door and they stepped away, their eyes remaining locked on each other.

"I'm sorry to interrupt," said Aunt Micah. "It seems the King has found Azrael, Pip, and Griffen."

"Who are they?" asked Lily.

"Your new friends," said Aunt Micah. "And they need your help."

"I can talk to the King," said Lily. "I know what to say to him."

Lily nodded at Raphael, knowing that something special had passed between them, but anything more would have to wait.

Right now she had friends to help. Father may be the King of Feldspar, but it was time he found out that he wasn't her King. Nor was he her Father. Someone else was going to have to rule this kingdom of misery.

Because it was time that Princess Lily of Forte Cadence went home.

PIP

THE AFTER

"Get your hands off him!" Pip snarled at the two men holding Griffen by the arms. "Can't you see he's unwell."

Her euphoria at Griffen's miraculous recovery of only moments ago had been ruined. He was standing limply between these two men who were half his size like he was some kind of puppet.

Pip and Azrael had only just managed to get Griffen to a stand and help him to the doorway of the lighthouse when a man who told them he was the King of Feldspar had approached them.

He wouldn't have been so much a threat on his own, but the six men he had standing behind him were an issue.

Pip had seen a flash of Micah in the stairwell behind the King and could only hope that she'd gone back inside to get Raphael to help them. Thankfully, neither the King nor his men had noticed her.

"Can we talk inside?" asked Pip. "He needs somewhere warm and dry to lie down."

She winced as the King burst out laughing. "You're trespassing on royal land. You're caught by the King, and now you want somewhere warm and dry to lie down?"

Pip pulled back her shoulders and looked the King squarely in the eyes. "My name is Princess Philippa, sister of the King of The Bay of Laurel. We have not come here to hurt you. We've come here to talk to you."

This only made the King laugh harder. "And who here is this with you?" He pointed at Azrael. "You going to tell me it's the Queen of the desert?"

"Close," said Pip. "She's the best friend and advisor of the Empress of The Sands of Naar."

"Well, it's a whole royal party then, isn't it?" The King looked across at his men, who joined in with the laughter. "Who's this big guy then? The King of Wintergreen?"

"I'm a Guardian," said Griffen, lifting his head. "Protector of the Princess."

"Yes, well I can see you're doing a fine job of that." The King shook his head.

"He saved my life," said Pip. "And…"

Griffen was shaking his head, urging her to be quiet.

"And how do we know you are who you say you are?" asked Azrael, stepping forward.

"This is my land, girl. I don't need to prove myself to you. I'm the King because I say I am."

"And who's in the lighthouse?" asked Pip. "Why don't you want us to go in there?"

The King flinched for a moment long enough to tell Pip that she'd hit a nerve.

"I'm afraid your timing is terrible," said the King. "I'm here on urgent family business and you're wasting my time. Where's your boat?"

"We don't have one," said Pip.

"You swam here, did you?" The King laughed once again in such a way that Pip was starting to think he was unhinged, rather than amused. "Perhaps I should make you swim back. I'd like to see that."

"No!" Azrael put her hands on her hips. "We've come here in peace. You cannot send us to a certain death out there."

"You're right," he said. "I'd like to hear more of your amusing stories later when I have more time. Luckily for you, I have some excellent accommodation known as the Terrace where I'd be happy to put you up for a time."

The King's men sniggered at this suggestion.

"Father! What are you doing?"

Their eyes collectively swung to the girl who'd appeared behind the King. A younger version of Micah. There was no doubt this was the girl they'd been searching for. They'd found Lily at last.

"Angel, get back inside." The King stepped in front of Lily.

"I want to help you, Father," said Lily.

Pip couldn't help but groan. This was what she'd been afraid of. That when they eventually found Lily, she'd be so brainwashed she wouldn't want to come with them.

"Angel, I don't need your help," said the King.

It was at this moment that Raphael came down the stairs, positioning himself beside Lily.

"And who are you?" asked the King.

"Raphael, brother of Queen Jasmine of Wintergreen."

"Oh, this is just too much," said the King, his smirk returning once more.

Then Micah came forward to stand on Lily's other side and the smile fell from the King's face. Seeing them side-by-side like this was remarkable. The King was going to have to believe them now.

"I'm Micah, sister of Prince Jeremiah of Forte Cadence. Aunt to Princess Lily, who stands beside me now."

"This isn't funny!" said the King, despite him having been the only one who'd been previously amused. "Angel, come here. My men can take these trespassers to the Terrace so we can get on with what we came here to do."

As Lily went to stand beside the King, Pip did a quick count. Six men plus the King on one side. And four of them plus an injured Guardian on the other. Five if she counted Lily, although she seemed to be on the King's side for now. If Griffen hadn't been so unwell then she wouldn't have hesitated. But could they take on this many men alone? It was doubtful.

"Did they hurt you?" the King asked Lily.

"No," said Lily. "They said they just want to talk to you."

"They didn't need to come all the way out here to talk to me," he said, narrowing his eyes on Pip, who he seemed to have decided was their leader. "They came here to talk to you."

"There are too many of us to return to the palace in your boat," said Lily. "Why don't we do what we came here to do and leave them here? They won't survive out here for long on their own."

Pip bit down on her tongue, not wanting to say the wrong thing as she tried to decide what to make of this. She had a feeling that being left out here would be preferable to this Terrace the King spoke of. But what if Robb never returned for them? He hadn't seemed to care for their welfare too much when he'd insisted they jump from his boat into the freezing water. Were they better off being kept prisoner with no guards in the middle of the ocean, or surrounded by guards on the mainland? Neither option sounded appealing.

"No," said the King. "We can make two trips in the boat. What we have to do might take a while, anyway."

The King's men nodded.

"How many passengers can you take?" he asked.

"Four at the most," said the tallest of the men.

"You must take all five," said the King.

The man shook his head. "I'm sorry, Your Highness, but not with the size of this one."

All eyes turned to Griffen.

"What if you left this skinny one behind?" suggested the King, pointing at Pip. "She doesn't look like much of a threat."

Panic surged through Pip's veins. She couldn't be split up from Griffen. They'd fought so hard to stay together.

"She's more dangerous than she looks," said Micah, who surely knew how distressed she was right now. "Are you sure that's wise?"

"Take them all to the boat," said the King. "Remain on shore for now. Another boat will come when we don't return. We'll just have to wait."

"Perhaps we could wait inside," said Pip, still concerned about the state of Griffen's health. He needed warmth and shelter.

"You'll wait in the boat," said the King, sneering. "Where we can keep an eye on you. Apparently, you're dangerous."

Pip winced. Micah had saved her from being separated from Griffen, but at what cost?

The men took hold of their arms, preparing to lead them to the boat.

"Please!" begged Pip. "Can we wait inside?"

"You're better off on the boat," said Lily, locking eyes with her and seeming to want to tell her something more. Was it possible she wasn't as brainwashed as she seemed?

"He'll freeze out here!" Pip couldn't let it go. They couldn't possibly be better off on the boat than out of the cold.

"Enough!" The King held up his hand. "Take them to the boat. Now!"

The men dragged them a few steps away, Pip struggling as much as her weak body would allow her to.

"Wait, Father," said Lily. "I need someone strong to help me shift a rock. And the large man doesn't look much use to me right now. Leave the other man behind for now."

Pip turned to see the King narrow his eyes at Lily. "One of my men can help you,"

"And risk leveling out the numbers with our prisoners?" said Lily. "What if the large man regains his strength?"

"His name's Griffen," said Pip. Couldn't these people see that he was so much more than just a large man?

"Unless you think you might be good at holding your breath, Father," said Lily.

A look flashed across Lily's face, fast enough that the King missed it, but just long enough for Pip to catch hold.

Contempt.

Lily hated the man she called Father. Pip was certain of it. She'd seen that look before. The girl they'd come to rescue was on their side. Not only that, but it was clear she was up to something. Whatever it was, Pip just hoped she'd hurry. Griffen needed to get warm or she'd lose him all over again.

"Fine then." The King dug his finger into Raphael's chest. "But don't you try anything, or you won't be sent to the Terrace on our return, you'll be sent to the gallows."

Pip had never heard that word before but didn't think it sounded very promising. Raphael seemed to have heard it, though, as his eyes darkened and he swallowed hard.

"I'd never hurt your daughter," said Raphael.

Pip suppressed a smile. No, he'd never hurt Lily.

As for the King, no promises could be made about that.

RAPHAEL

THE NOW

*W*ith his companions secured on the boat, Raphael followed Lily and the King around to the other side of the lighthouse. Raphael studied the King closely, trying to get the measure of him. This was the man responsible for causing so much misery by taking Lily and countless other children from their homes. Yet, he seemed to have genuine affection for Lily, despite his otherwise somewhat heartless demeanor.

No wonder Feldspar had never responded to invitations from the other kingdoms reaching out to talk about finding peace. Not when he had so many of their children locked inside his mines. They were the only kingdom not willing to work with the others.

"It's out there." Lily pointed out to the ocean.

"What are we looking for?" asked Raphael, wishing the King would disappear into the sea so he could take this beautiful girl into his arms again. They had so much to talk about. But once again, patience was going to be required. The way she'd greeted him in the lighthouse had already been so much more than he'd dared to hope for. He couldn't blow it now.

"Love stones," said Lily. "There are two of them out there. One belongs to the King, the other to the Queen."

"He doesn't need to know what they're for, Angel," said the King.

Lily nodded.

"Am I allowed to know what they're doing out in the ocean?" asked Raphael.

"Definitely not," said the King. "Your job is to help Angel retrieve them. Now, off you go."

"Why don't you wait in the lighthouse?" Lily asked the King. "Mother would love to see you. She was acting very strangely just now."

"And I'd love to see her, too," said the King. "If only I could."

"But, why can't you?" Lily seemed confused, in the same way Micah had been when Raphael had been unable to see the Queen on the balcony. Was it possible that Lily didn't realize the woman she'd lived with, out here in the middle of the ocean, was little more than an apparition? Micah wouldn't have known if he hadn't been there to tell her.

"Never mind," said the King.

Taking off her cloak, Lily revealed that she was wearing the pale blue dress Raphael had seen on her in his vision.

When she undid her top button, the King put out his hand to stop her.

"Today, you swim in your dress." He glanced at Raphael as he spoke.

Raphael's cheeks reddened. Had she really been about to swim in her undergarments?

Having no coat to remove and with his shirt and trousers already wet, Raphael waded into the water.

"So we're looking for two stones?" he asked Lily.

"I know where they are," she said, wading into the water behind him. "I just need your help to remove one of them. It's stuck between two rocks. I put the other one in front of it, so that should be easy enough to move."

"You're being watched!" called out the King. "And if anything happens to her, you'll wish you were never born."

"He's very protective of you." Raphael kept his voice low so the King couldn't hear.

She nodded sadly. "He is."

"I notice you call him Father," he said.

"That's just a name. I never call him *my father*. Not ever. I already had a father when he took me."

He nodded, thoughts of the handsome Prince Jeremiah coming to mind.

"We need a plan," he said. "For after we find these magic stones."

She nodded again. "It's going to be okay. Father wants me to use the amethysts to find my true love."

His eyebrows shot up. The grim idea of her true love being anyone other than him gripped him around the spine. He wasn't so sure he wanted to find the stones anymore with that at risk.

"How do the stones work?" he asked. The water was lapping at their thighs now. It was just as cold as before, although the bright morning sun made it a little more tolerable. Or was it because Lily was with him?

"When the amethysts are close to each other, they're warm," she said. "When someone touches them, they get a vision of their true love. And if their true love touches one of the stones at the same time, the stones will glow. And if the lovers touching the stones are the true rulers of the kingdom, then something else happens, although I'm not sure what. I'm still trying to piece it all together."

"And why are you so sure everything's going to be okay?" he prompted, desperate for her to say more.

"Because I saw you when I touched them," she said. "It has to be you. When we find the amethysts and bring them to the surface, Father will see who you are to me. He can't send you to the Terrace if you're the true ruler of Feldspar. Nor can he send the others."

Raphael's eyes widened at this. The true ruler of Feldspar? He wanted no such thing. But there was no denying that he wanted Lily. Especially now that he'd met her and his feelings were even stronger than they'd been in his visions. Would he stay and rule over a kingdom for a woman he loved? That decision would be far easier to make if it were her true home of Forte Cadence—a kingdom filled with light. Not this dark place.

"You don't want to be the ruler of Feldspar, do you?" she asked, tapping into his thoughts.

"Not especially," he said, wincing as the cold water reached the base of his spine. "But I'd like to be your true love."

She smiled at this. A shy smile, averting her eyes.

"Hurry up then!" called the King from the shore.

"Then let's find out what happens," she said. "Are you ready? Can you swim?"

"A little." He wondered if it was his imagination or if the water had gotten warmer, the further out they'd waded. "I do know how to hold my breath."

"It might take a few tries," she said. "We'll go down first and I'll show you where the amethysts are, then we can come back up for breath. On the second attempt, I'll remove the amethyst I placed there. Third attempt, I'm going to need you to remove the stone that sits behind it. Does that sound okay?"

He nodded. "I can do that."

"Can you feel the warmth of the amethysts?" she asked.

"Is that what it is?" He touched the water with his hands, almost looking forward to diving into its warmth now.

"I can't wait to see the amethysts glow." She smiled and dread punched him in the gut. What would happen if the stones failed to glow? Lily clearly believed in their powers. If the stones didn't think they were destined to be together, then it looked like he'd be spending the rest of his life alone. Because now that he'd met Lily there was nobody else he ever wanted to be with. That was never going to change.

"Hold my hand," she said.

Her hand was warm and he took hold of her, hoping that there never came a time when he'd have to let go.

"On the count of three," she said. "One… two…"

Raphael drew in a deep breath.

"Three."

They ducked under the water, pulling themselves down. Raphael blinked, the salt of the water stinging his eyes, but found that although it was blurry, he could see.

Lily led him to some rocks, not all that far under the surface and she pointed to a dark space between two of the larger ones. The water was warm here, just like she'd said it would be. If only they could bring some of that warmth back up to the surface for Griffen.

Already feeling his lungs protesting at the lack of oxygen, it was a relief to head back up for a large gulp of cold air.

"You saw where I pointed," she said, wiping water from her eyes.

"Yes. The space between the two largest rocks."

She let go of his hand now, and he felt the separation like a loss. "I'm going to get the first amethyst now. You watch how I do it, so you can get the next one."

He nodded, trying to suppress a laugh. She was more like Micah than in just looks alone. This was a girl who knew how to focus on a task.

"Did I say something funny?" she asked.

"No," he said, still grinning. "You're perfect."

She smiled then shook away the compliment seeming to remember they were here to do a task.

"Ready to go again?" she asked.

He nodded.

There was no countdown this time. She plunged under the water and he followed, using both hands this time to swim down to the rocks. She reached into the dark space and he worried there might be something more there than the amethyst. A fish with a sharp set of teeth came to mind.

He watched as Lily pulled a large purple gemstone out from between the rocks and she held it out for him to look at.

But it wasn't the beauty of the stone that made him almost gasp and draw in a mouthful of water. It wasn't even Lily's beauty. It was because she looked exactly like she had in his vision. Pale blue dress, red hair fanning out like a halo and a purple amethyst in her hands. The only thing missing was the desperation in her eyes. Because the unmistakable look on Lily's face right now was one of hope.

If it weren't for the lack of air in his lungs, he'd stay right there under the water, staring at Lily. The King had certainly named her appropriately when he'd called her Angel. She shot straight back up to the surface, clutching the amethyst in her hand. He followed without hesitation.

"I got one!" she called to the King, who waved back at her.

"May I see it?" Raphael stretched out his hand as he shook the water off his face. "So I know what I'm looking for."

Lily passed him the amethyst and he winced at the heat it was producing. It was deep purple in color, with the sun's rays glinting off the surface, but producing no light of its own.

"What do you think?" she asked.

"It's magical," he said. "But what if—"

"No what-ifs," she said. "They're going to glow. I know they are."

"What's the Terrace?" he asked as he passed back the amethyst. He may as well come to terms with what the alternative was if the amethysts refused to glow.

"You'll never find out," she said. "Come on. I've waited so long for this moment."

"You didn't really need me to move any rocks, did you?" He was certain she'd used that as an excuse to bring him out here.

"Actually I do need you," she said. "I've tried to dislodge the amethyst myself but never could. You're stronger and that amethyst is meant for you. I'm hoping it comes out easily in your hands."

"Let's see then." He took in a deep breath, pushed down his fear and dove under the water, aware that Lily was right behind him.

Without wasting a moment, he went to the gap in the rocks and plunged his hand into the darkness, feeling for the warmth of the amethyst. His fingertips brushed the smooth surface and he wrapped his hand around the stone and pulled. It was stuck tight and he pulled harder. If only he could see what he was doing, this may be easier.

As he tugged at the amethyst, a soft purple glow poured from between the rocks. It was happening. It was really happening. Just as Lily had said it would. They were meant for each other. True love. He'd known it in his heart but now he was seeing it with his eyes.

With the purple glow lighting the crevice, he could now see the stone wedged behind a small but jagged piece of rock. Using the strength of his thumb, he pressed down on it until it broke away. Then taking hold of the now burning hot amethyst, he yanked it free and pushed off the ocean floor to drive himself back up to the surface.

Lily was already standing in the waist-deep water, holding the first amethyst, turning it over in her hands as she studied the tendrils of light that were pouring from it, gaining strength the more time that passed.

Raphael looked to the shoreline and saw the King shake his head, his mouth gaping to witness the glowing of the love stones. He turned his back on them immediately and ran toward the lighthouse.

Lily smiled as she waded across to Raphael and they held their amethysts out in front of them, her dark eyes locking on him. She was so beautiful it made his chest ache. He really had found his way home.

"I knew it was you," she said. "I knew you were my Prince."

"I hoped it was you," he said. "I was so afraid it wasn't."

"Even Father knows it." She pointed at the lighthouse just as the King disappeared inside. "No doubt he's gone to tell Mother."

"Lily," he said, wondering how he was going to tell her the truth about the woman she called Mother. Now just didn't seem the right time.

"Are you going to kiss me now?" she asked, sending thoughts of the Queen flying out of his mind.

"If you..." Now wasn't the time to hesitate. He kicked himself. "Yes, Lily, I am."

Still clutching the amethyst in front of him he leaned down and pressed his lips against hers. She was soft and warm and her lips parted to welcome his kiss.

He'd never kissed a woman before. He'd never wanted to. But now he never wanted to stop and as he took in the taste of her, he felt her pressing her amethyst against his heart, sending warm waves through his tired body and bringing him back to life.

This was a kiss of discovery and celebration. A kiss of freedom and victory. But most of all, this was a kiss of true love.

They broke away and looked back down at the magical love stones that had bonded them. It was hard to tell if it was the magic of the kiss or the magic of the stones, but he felt better than he had since he'd set out on this quest to bring Lily home.

"I thought something else was supposed to happen," said Lily.

"I'm pretty sure something else just did," he said, running his thumb across her bottom lip.

"Maybe it doesn't happen straight away," she said.

He nodded. "Maybe."

"Or maybe I had it all wrong?"

"Maybe," he said again.

"Raphael, are you listening to me?" She tapped on the side of his head.

"Maybe," he said, leaning down to kiss her once again.

He knew they had plenty to talk about and he didn't want to dismiss any of her concerns, but right now, right in this moment, all he wanted to do was be as near to her as he possibly could.

"I love you, Raphael," she murmured against his lips.

Without stopping to wonder if it was possible to love someone he'd only just met, he drew back just a fraction so he could reply.

"I love you, too."

LILY

THE NOW

"*L*ily! We need your help!"

Lily reluctantly broke away from the warmth of Raphael's kiss to see Aunt Micah scampering over the rocks on the shoreline. Two of the oarsmen were chasing after her waving their arms. Clearly, she'd managed to get away. But what could be so urgent?

Raphael took her hand and they waded back to shore as quickly as they could.

"It's Griffen," Aunt Micah called to them, as they clambered back up onto the rocks. "We're losing him again. He needs warmth. Please, can you see if the King will allow him a blanket?"

The oarsmen grabbed Aunt Micah roughly by the arms.

"Do *not* hurt her." Lily glared at them. "She'll go with you willingly."

The men kept their tight hold on her, so Lily held up the glowing amethyst for them to see.

"Do you know what this is?" she asked them.

Their eyes widened as they took it in. Of course, they knew. Everyone in Feldspar knew about the love stones. The Fossickers had whispered stories of their existence to Lily long before she ever laid eyes on one of them.

"That's right," said Lily. "These stones are held by the ruler of Feldspar and the King has given them to me. What do you think that means?"

The men loosened their grip on Aunt Micah.

"It means the King plans to hand the throne to me and do you really think I'm going to look favorably on men who mistreated my aunt like this?"

"His Majesty is still the King," one of the men said. "He told us to keep these intruders captive."

"But you can still treat them nicely," said Lily. "Because I have a great memory for faces."

She locked her eyes with him, daring him to argue.

"Griffen needs a warm blanket." Aunt Micah glared at the men. "And he needs it now."

"I have something better than a blanket," said Lily, passing the amethyst to her aunt, who looked like she could use a blanket herself.

As the stone left her hands, the light faded, but given its close proximity to the amethyst still in Raphael's hands, the warmth continued to radiate.

Aunt Micah brought the amethyst close to her chest and drew in the comfort. "What is this?"

"We need to get it to Griffen," said Lily. There was no time to explain the magical properties of the amethysts now.

"We have two of them," said Raphael, holding up his amethyst. "He'll be warm in no time. Come on."

They picked their way quickly and carefully around the light-house, Aunt Micah warming herself with the amethyst as they went.

"I can feel my fingers again!" she said, as they reached the boat.

Lily could see Griffen lying down in the boat. The dark-haired woman whose name Lily had forgotten was doing something with her hands above him and the thin woman called Pip was raking her fingers through her blonde hair, her face filled with anguish. The King's men were standing in the water, not looking in the least concerned. It was no wonder Aunt Micah had been able to escape so easily.

Aunt Micah climbed into the boat and held out the amethyst to the dark-haired woman.

"Azrael," she said.

That was her name! Azrael. Lily stood beside the boat wondering what was taking Raphael so long. He seemed preoccupied with something and had lagged behind.

"Use the stone to warm him," said Aunt Micah.

Azrael's face lit up the moment she took hold of the amethyst. She placed it on Griffen's chest and moved his hands so they were cupping the warmth of the stone.

"I can feel the heat from here," said Pip, renewed hope spreading across her face as the amethyst worked its magic on more than just Griffen. "That's amazing."

Raphael reached them now holding a brown sack he'd slung across his shoulders.

"You found them!" said Azrael, smiling at him.

He patted the bag and Lily heard the clinking of glass. Small bottles of something perhaps.

"Give Griffen this, too." Raphael held out his amethyst to Pip. "He needs all the warmth he can get."

Pip took it from him and immediately the amethyst started to glow.

"What's happening?" asked Pip, holding the stone out in front of her.

Lily broke into a smile.

"He's your true love," she said, pointing to Griffen, his eyes flickering open as the warmth of the amethyst in his hands worked its magic. His stone was glowing too, casting a purple light across his face.

Then the stones did something Lily could never have predicted.

The purple light they were emitting grew stronger and brighter with streaks of yellow and blue and orange flickering to life and shooting into the sky, higher and higher.

Lily gasped to watch these two spectacular beams light the sky. Sparks flew off them in every direction like some kind of meteor shower.

Then the beams bent toward the lighthouse, casting all the colors of the rainbow across the drab exterior until it looked like a giant crystal rising from the sea, sparkling and shining, its brilliance reflecting off both the water and sky, which twinkled in response.

The two beams of light continued to curve until the one coming from the amethyst Pip was holding found Mother standing on the highest balcony. Mother held out her hands and caught the light. Father did the same with the beam coming from the amethyst Griffen was holding, and the two rulers of Feldspar lit up, glowing like angels.

"I can see her!" gasped Raphael. "I can see the Queen standing right beside the King!"

Lily slipped her hand into his, not understanding what he meant. Of course, he could see them. They all could.

Father was looking at Mother in a way Lily had never seen him do before. She watched as they drew up their hands and pressed them together, joining the two columns of light, which shone even more brightly, sending sparks shooting from the balcony, raining down on the rocks below like a waterfall made from dazzling light.

Lily squinted as she followed the bright ray of light down to where it broke into two beams, one connecting to Pip and the other to Griffen, who was sitting up now, holding the amethyst in front of him with an expression of awe. He seemed to have been completely healed.

Then, Griffen held out his amethyst to Pip and they touched the love stones together. As they made contact, their beams of light joined so it was now one giant column connecting Pip and Griffen to Mother and Father on the balcony.

Then, without warning, the column shattered, beginning at the top and misting down, sending snowflakes of light floating to the rocks below.

It was, without doubt, the most beautiful sight Lily had ever seen and she gripped Raphael's hand tighter. Back in Forte Cadence, people had talked about their Evernow and Lily had listened with wide eyes wondering if she'd ever experience a moment when she was happy for time to stand still. There was no doubt that for her this time was now. Not only had she found her true love, but finally, she'd broken free of the life she'd been trapped in. It didn't matter what happened in her future. Right now, at this very moment, she was blissfully happy.

A rumbling sound shook her from her thoughts and as the last flakes of light settled on the ground, the lighthouse began to quiver.

It was actually happening. Her vision of the lighthouse falling *had* been a warning and they had to act fast or not only would her Evernow come to an end, but so would the lives of everyone on this tiny island.

"Get in the boat!" she called, letting go of Raphael's hand. "It's coming down!"

Everyone who wasn't already in the boat, clambered in. It was dangerously over capacity, barely managing to stay afloat as one of the men pushed them out into the water. There was some confusion and scurrying and tilting of the boat as the oarsmen heaved them further out into the water, but Lily's eyes were glued to the lighthouse as the trembling picked up.

"Hurry," said Lily. "We have to get as far away as possible."

The oarsmen powered through the water as sections of the lighthouse's roof broke away and plummeted into the water below, the ripple effect causing the boat to rock, coming dangerously close to tipping them out. But these men had been trained to row fast, and row fast they did. The boat slid through the water with what felt like was incredible ease.

Mother and Father were still visible, standing on the balcony, only instead of holding out their hands, Lily could see their tiny figures embracing. They were both going to die and Lily winced as she realized she didn't feel in the least bit sad about this. These two people might love each other, but they'd caused nothing but misery to everyone around them. They deserved no better than to go down with this tower of misery.

When the foundations could withstand the trembling no longer, the lighthouse collapsed into itself, taking Mother and Father with it. Lily held her hands to her ears to block out the terrible roar of the crashing of stone upon stone, rock upon rock, and Raphael wrapped an arm tightly around her shoulders. She buried her face in his chest, feeling safe when she knew she was anything but.

The noise was soon replaced with a giant cloud of dust that rose from the rocks and swirled in the currents of the sea air. And still, the oarsmen continued to row, only just managing not to capsize in their determination to get everyone a safe distance away.

And just like that, it was gone. The ocean swallowed up the lighthouse, the breeze swept away the dust and the waves lost their power, leaving them bobbing on a calm sea wondering if they'd imagined the whole awe-inspiring thing.

Pip and Griffen were sitting with stunned expressions on their faces, still holding the amethysts together, which were now emitting a gentle purple light.

"Did we do that?" asked Pip, looking around at all the faces staring at her.

The oarsmen shuffled off their seats and dropped awkwardly to their knees in the boat.

"Long live the King and Queen of Feldspar," said one of the men, bowing his head to Pip and Griffen.

"Long live the King and Queen of Feldspar," said the others.

Pip and Griffen looked at each other, their brows furrowed, then looked at Lily as if she'd be able to explain what had just happened.

"It's true," said Lily. "Father told me that the amethysts can be used to find your true love, but when the true ruler of Feldspar finds their love then something spectacular happens."

"Well, that was definitely spectacular," said Aunt Micah, shaking her head.

"You're the true rulers of Feldspar," said Lily, overjoyed to have been released from a duty she never wanted. "We all saw it."

"But..." Griffen had found his voice at last. "Surely that's you."

"Father thought it was," said Lily, smiling. "But it seems he was wrong. Just like he was about so many things."

"But how can we be the true rulers?" asked Pip. "We're not even from Feldspar."

"The crystals know," said one of the older oarsmen who'd been particularly quiet this whole time. "They always know and their decision is final. You've been chosen. Our future is in your hands."

Pip pulled back her shoulders. "So you mean, we can change how things are around here?"

"This is your kingdom to rule," said the oarsman.

"You can let the children go free." Aunt Micah smiled so widely, Lily almost wondered if she had a child inside those mines herself.

"It's a revolution." Azrael clapped her hands together. "It's actually happening!"

Pip nodded and looked at Griffen in stunned silence.

"Please, give us our orders," said the oarsman.

"Take us back to Feldspar," said Griffen. "We'll decide what to do from there."

The oarsman nodded. "Yes, Your Majesty. But if I may point out that the love stones have already decided. All the people from Feldspar will have seen the lights and will be awaiting their new rulers. I'm afraid we'll be arriving back to quite the scene."

Griffen wrapped an arm around Pip and they whispered to each other, no doubt trying to come to terms with the wild turn their lives had just taken.

Lily snuggled into Raphael, glad the ocean had fallen so still. With the boat so overloaded, at least they had a chance of making it back in one piece now. She'd had enough of swimming in the ocean for one day. Actually, she'd had enough for a lifetime. Now that the amethysts had been recovered and the lighthouse was no more, with any luck, she'd never need to swim again.

"Are you okay?" asked Raphael, placing a gentle kiss on her forehead as the oarsmen settled into a rhythm to take them back to the mainland.

"I'm better than okay," she said. "I never wanted to rule Feldspar. And I know you didn't want to either."

He smiled at her as his answer.

"How do you think they feel about it?" she asked. "Will they be good rulers?"

"They'll be wonderful," he said. "Once they get used to the idea. They have strengths that balance each other out. And there's no doubt they love each other."

"I was certain it was going to be us," she said.

"Are you upset to give the amethysts away?"

"They were never mine to keep." She reached up and touched him on the cheek. "And I don't need a vision of you anymore. You're right here."

"And not going anywhere, in case you wondered." He took hold of her hand and brought her fingers to his lips, kissing them softly.

"Besides, the amethysts told me everything I needed to know," she said.

"And what's that?" he asked, even though surely, he must know.

"That we're meant to be together."

"Just wanted to hear you say it." He tightened his grip on her and she heard the clinking of glass from inside the bag he carried.

"What's in the bag?"

"My elixirs," he said proudly. "Plenty of time to tell you about them later."

She let out a sigh of absolute contentment. Not at the thought of having to wait to find out more about Raphael, but just because now she had the opportunity to do just that. They had the rest of their lives stretching out before them. And now that the responsibility for the kingdom of Feldspar had come to rest on Pip and Griffen's shoulders, she was free to return home to Forte Cadence.

Lily looked back out at the flat expanse of ocean they were leaving behind them, finding it impossible to imagine that beneath that innocent calm surface lay not only thousands of crystals but the bodies of

Mother and Father. Those two people had taken her from her family and held her captive. She'd dreamed that this lighthouse would fall. And she'd wanted them to fall with it. But now that it had actually happened, it felt different somehow. They'd loved her. And they'd loved each other. Were evil people capable of love?

"Why didn't they try to get out?" she asked Raphael, not really expecting him to have an answer.

"He wouldn't leave her," said Raphael. "It really was true love."

"She could've left with him." Lily shook her head as she tried to figure it out. "They'd seemed so calm standing there in each other's arms, not fighting what they must've known was to come."

"She couldn't leave," said Raphael.

"That's what she kept saying. But why?" How was it that everyone seemed to know what was happening here, except her? Raphael hadn't even known Mother and Father.

"Lily, nobody could see her except for you," he said, lowering his voice. "And Micah, as it turns out."

"That can't be true." She clamped her hand over her mouth, searching his face for the hint of a smile but coming up empty.

"Lily, it's true. Micah tried to touch her and her hand passed right through her body."

Lily shook her head, pushing back thoughts that suddenly seemed to make sense. Not once in all those years had Mother ever touched her. Not once had she seen her eat. And often when Mother had talked to Father, it was like he couldn't hear. Was the family time they'd insisted upon a way for them to use her to communicate with each other? If Father couldn't see or hear Mother, then that would make some kind of sense.

No. This was impossible to believe. Surely, she'd have realized. It couldn't be... She turned to the oldest of the oarsmen.

"Excuse me," she said. "But who lived in that lighthouse?"

"You," he said, confused as he continued to pull his oar through the water.

"And who else?" she asked.

"Well, the King visited you every day, so it wasn't like you were alone. Bad timing though, really."

"What do you mean by that?"

"I was there the day the King brought you to the lighthouse as a gift for his Queen. He hoped once she had you, he'd be able to lure her back home. Horrible business it was."

"Tell me," she said. "What was horrible?"

"Her Majesty was so lonely out there, isolating herself as she pined for a daughter. Then the day the King finally brings her one, we arrive to find her floating face down in the water."

"But I don't understand." Lily felt Raphael's hand slide down her back as he tried to take the sting out of the oarsman's words

The oarsman shook his head. "We were late the day we brought you over. Seas were rough. The Queen must've thought we weren't coming. Threw herself off the balcony before we could get to her. Like I said, horrible business. Had to cover your eyes, we did. Being such a young one. The King made us swear not to tell anyone. Wanted everyone to believe she was still alive. The way he spoke about her, sometimes we thought she still was."

Memories of her arrival at the lighthouse flooded back to Lily. She'd been so traumatized that she hadn't paid all that much attention to how everyone else around her was feeling. But now she remembered the hand clamped over her eyes and the sound of Father's cries. Being carried into the lighthouse, her eyes still covered, and deposited into a kitchen where finally she was allowed to see again.

It was there that she'd come face to face with Mother, while Father and his men had been busy outside.

Mother had stood on the other side of the table and told her she was sorry she hadn't waited for her. Lily had remembered thinking she was quite mad as clearly, she had waited for her. Had she really been some kind of ghost, even back then?

She remembered Father coming up to the kitchen after what had felt like a very long time. His face was pale and tears were streaking white lines of salt across his face. He'd also said he was sorry Mother hadn't waited and Lily had found her voice and said she didn't understand how someone who was right there hadn't waited.

Father had cried loudly at this. He'd cried all night long, sitting at that table and Mother had had to guide Lily out of the room and show her the bedroom she'd set up for her, telling her to get into bed and laying out the rules she was to abide by. Father had followed them and watched from the doorway. He'd stayed for days and days before he eventually left, and then returned every day to ask Lily questions about Mother.

Without knowing it, she'd become his connection to his true love. He'd kept her in the lighthouse as his only link to the woman he'd loved.

"They're together again now," she said to Raphael, realizing it was going to take her an awfully long time to fully process all of this.

"They are," he said.

"That was all he ever wanted."

She could never forgive what Father had done. Not ever. But now that she'd found her own true love, she could understand it a little more. She'd do almost anything to keep Raphael happy. *Almost.* Because she knew deep in her heart that there was no way she could take away someone else's happiness in order to nurture her own. Father had destroyed not just her life, but all the lives of those children in the mines. And their parents.

But now that could be set right. Raphael had said that Pip and Griffen had kind hearts. Which meant there was hope not just for her own future, but there was hope for Feldspar.

MICAH

THE AFTER

Micah sat behind Lily and Raphael in the boat, watching them talk, enjoying the gentle romance that was blossoming between them. It hadn't been like that with Tallis, but that might have been because she'd known him her whole life, so her feelings for him had snuck up and surprised her.

Her heart ached for him now, but there was no way she could return to him until she'd found Gabe. She'd promised to look after that small boy and that was exactly what she intended to do. Once she got him out of the mines, of course. This job should be a whole lot easier now that Pip and Griffen were the somewhat shocked new rulers of Feldspar.

She hoped Gabe knew she was coming for him. He must be so frightened. First to have been taken from his home like that, and then ripped from Micah's arms when he thought he'd finally found safety.

They were approaching the mainland from somewhere completely different to the secluded beach where they'd left. She could see boats and ships docked at long jetties and a line of buildings along the coastline. But it wasn't the sight of civilization that startled her, it was the noise. Shouts and cheers echoed across the calm water. It seemed the oarsmen hadn't been exaggerating when they'd said there'd be excitement about the new rulers.

"Hold on a moment," said Pip.

The oarsmen stilled their oars and waited for their new Queen to speak.

"I'm not sure what you're taking us into," she said. "But I suspect there won't be a lot of time for questions when we arrive."

"Yes, Your Majesty," said the oarsmen in unison.

Micah smiled to see Pip taking charge like this. Good for her! Griffen seemed to have fully recovered ever since the amethyst had been in his possession, and was sitting proudly by her side, nodding at her every word.

"A boy was taken from us when we arrived in Feldspar," said Pip. "We were told we could find him in the mines. Where exactly are they?"

One of the oarsmen pointed to what looked like some low lying mountains. "Not far from the docks, Your Majesty. We can take you there. The royal carriage will be at your disposal."

"And will they release the boy to us?" asked Griffen.

"You're our King and Queen. The Masters will release every boy to you if you ask. And girl for that matter."

"Then, let's do this." Pip nodded her head at Micah, aware of how much this meant to her.

The oarsmen resumed their rowing, continuing to pull them toward the docks, the noise of the crowd of people getting louder with each stroke.

As they got close to the shore, Micah could make out individual people in the blur of color. When they'd seen the sky fill with light, they'd known their King was dead and the crown had been passed on. Keen to see their new rulers, they'd waded into the shallows to greet them. Micah was glad it wasn't Lily who'd be the center of all this attention. Although she seemed wise beyond her years, her life had been too sheltered for her to have to deal with something like this. Had the amethysts somehow known this when they'd chosen Pip and Griffen to rule the kingdom? Or had the magical stones sensed that Lily was already destined to rule another kingdom?

They passed the first of the people in the water and Micah saw their drawn faces and hopeful eyes. This was a kingdom that had seen much suffering. A new ruler was a chance for change. Perhaps all these people willing for this to happen had somehow brought this event to pass like some kind of silent whisper.

Micah resisted the urge to stand up in the boat and call to the people, telling them that everything was going to be all right. Pip and Griffen had good hearts and once they got used to the idea of exactly where their destiny had taken them, they were going to be wonderful rulers.

"Show them who you are," said one of the oarsmen, noticing the way the people were scanning the faces of the strangers on board.

Pip and Griffen looked at each other, then Pip held the glowing amethyst above her head, sending a colorful beam of light reflecting off the surface of the water. Griffen did the same.

A roar erupted from the shoreline and more people were running into the water to catch a glimpse of their new rulers.

"Release the children!" a woman shouted as the boat continued to make its way to the shore. "Set our children free!"

Micah tried to catch the woman's eye to send her reassurance but the ripple of excitement crashing over the crowd was too much and she quickly lost sight of her.

"Stand back," shouted the oarsmen.

They reached the dock and one of the oarsmen clambered out of the boat and tied it to the dock.

A circle of guards cleared space for them, pushing the crowd back by waving long-bladed knives at them, until the dock was clear.

"Please! No violence," shouted Pip, her words drowned out by the noise of the crowd.

"Ready the royal carriages," said the oarsman, sending one of the guards rushing off down the dock.

Griffen was the first to disembark, refusing any offers of help, before reaching out for Pip, gently pulling her up to the dock. He stood next to the guards, towering over them with his impressive height.

"Your Majesty," said the guards, bowing deeply.

Micah climbed out of the boat next, followed by Raphael, then Lily then Azrael.

They took their time walking down the dock, following behind the shell-shocked new leaders who waved at the people, trying to send them their reassurance of a better life through their nervous smiles.

When they got to the end of the dock, the crowd hushed and the people stood staring at them with open mouths as if waiting for something.

"They want you to speak, Your Majesties," said one of the guards, leaning toward Griffen and Pip.

Micah saw Griffen look to Pip to see if she wanted to speak. These two had a lot to figure out that went far beyond deciding how they were going to rule this kingdom, if indeed they accepted this role that was being thrust at them. Griffen had always been Pip's protector, ready to serve her in any way required. If he were to be her husband, and indeed the King of Feldspar, their relationship was going to need to settle into a new and more equal kind of partnership, much like the one that existed between Jeremiah and Rose.

Pip stepped forward, threw back her shoulders and cleared her throat.

"This change in leadership has come as a surprise, as much to us as it has to you," she said.

"Free the children!" someone called from the crowd.

Micah was pleased to see that this was the issue that troubled the people of Feldspar most. They needed as little resistance as possible to set the children free.

Pip held up her hand to silence the murmur of agreement rippling through the crowd.

"My name is Princess Philippa of The Bay of Laurel," she said, projecting her voice. "Beside me here is Griffen, a Guardian and sworn protector of the crown. But it seems that now we're King Griffen and Queen Philippa of Feldspar."

"How do we know you're loyal to Feldspar?" shouted someone from the crowd.

"We're not loyal to Feldspar," said Griffen, much to Micah's surprise. A collective gasp sounded from the sea of people. "We've had no reason so far to be loyal to this kingdom. You stole our children and when we came to bring them home, you locked us in a cage and threatened our lives. We did not choose to be your rulers. We were chosen. But if you give us a chance, we can see if we can make this work. Together, we can build a kingdom that's worthy of your loyalty. One that's worthy of all our loyalty."

A cheer erupted across the crowd. Griffen had said exactly the right thing, leaving Micah wondering if he was the reason behind the love stones' choice.

"I know what it's like to grow up without my mother beside me," said Pip, holding up her hand to settle the crowd. "We don't want that for your children. We want this to be a kingdom where your children can grow up in safety, surrounded by love."

Unexpected tears filled Micah's eyes as someone who knew what it was like to grow up without a mother or father. No child should have to experience that. This was part of the reason Gabe meant so much to her. She wanted to give him everything she'd missed out on herself as a child.

"Who here has a child in the mines?" asked Griffen.

A sea of hands rose into the air.

"Then follow us now as we return them to you," he said.

"It's a revolution!" called a familiar voice, and Micah turned to see Enid, with Robb standing next to her, an unmistakable look of pride on their faces. This wouldn't have been possible without their help. They'd honored their son's memory in the best kind of way.

Azrael rushed to Enid's side and Micah smiled to see them embrace.

Cries of joy and triumph echoed across the crowd as people hugged and slapped each other on the back. Some collapsed to their knees and others looked to the sky. This was the news they'd wanted. These were the rulers they'd hoped for. It made Micah wonder if her visions had really been about saving Lily. Perhaps the visions had led them all here, not just to save Lily, but to save everyone else.

Two horse-drawn carriages pulled up at the end of the dock and the guards motioned for Pip and Griffen to climb aboard the first one, while the rest of them took the carriage at the rear, after Azrael had said her goodbyes to Enid.

"Are you okay not being up front?" Micah asked Lily as she slid into the seat beside her.

"Better than okay." Lily took her hand and squeezed it. "I'm not ready for any of that."

Micah nodded, not convinced Pip felt she was ready for it either, but there was nothing to be done about that. Like Griffen had said only moments ago, she hadn't chosen the job. It had chosen her.

The carriages wound their way through the streets, a line of people on either side of them walking in the same direction, raising their hands and cheering as the carriages passed them by as they strained their necks trying to get a better look at their new King and Queen.

It was such different terrain here to what Micah was used to back in Forte Cadence. She'd thought her kingdom was relatively barren, but Feldspar redefined that word. There wasn't a tree in sight. How did they grow food? What did their livestock graze on? Did the whole kingdom look like this? She supposed these were going to be questions Griffen and Pip were going to need to ask. She didn't plan to stick around long enough to find out the answers to any of them.

But as foreign as the terrain was, there was something hauntingly familiar about the people. For a moment Micah wondered if it was because some of them had been taken from Forte Cadence as children and perhaps once she'd know them, but it wasn't that. They reminded her of the faces she'd seen in the crowds of people who'd welcomed Queen Rose and Jeremiah when they'd taken control of the kingdom. Micah had been with them the day they'd walked into the Valley of the Blessed on Giving Day bearing gifts for the people. It hadn't been the soap or loaves of bread that'd won the people over. It had been the hope.

It was no different with the people of Feldspar. Clearly, they'd suffered under their King's rule and were clinging to the hope that these two new rulers were going to make things better. The promise of their children being returned to them was enough to win them over.

The carriages passed the last of the people walking toward the mines as they began to climb a steep incline, the strong horses that pulled them slowing with the extra strain. Micah turned to look at the empty road behind them, knowing it would soon be filled with people on their way to reclaim their lost children.

"You have a child in the mines, don't you?" asked Lily.

"I do," said Micah. "Although, he wasn't taken from me in Forte Cadence. I found him as we were preparing to cross the sea to Feldspar. He needed someone to look after him. And I guess I need someone to look after, too.

It was only right to acknowledge her own needs in this. Loving Gabe would fill an aching hole in her heart left by the babies she'd carried who hadn't lived long enough to draw breath.

"What happened to him?" Lily's eyes filled with tears.

"We got attacked on the shores of Feldspar and they took him. I let him down."

"You didn't let him down," said Lily. "We'll get him back. What's his name?"

"Gabe. He's only small." Micah smiled at the memory of him. "He has these big brown eyes that just melted my heart."

"I can't wait to meet him," said Lily.

"What's it like down there in the mines?" asked Micah, wanting to know but afraid of what Lily might tell her.

A look of horror crossed Lily's eyes, before she seemed to consciously push it away.

"It's not the best," she said. "Lots of dark tunnels. We were forced down there with only a lantern and a small pick. The more gems we could find, the more we'd be fed at dinner. That's how they knew we wouldn't keep the gems for ourselves. A potato to fill our stomachs was a far greater prize than a heavy stone in our pockets."

"How long were you down there?" Micah shook her head, unable to believe anyone would treat a child like that.

Lily shrugged. "I honestly have no idea. Too long, but not nearly as long as most children. I admit that I was relieved at first when the King chose me as his gift for the Queen. Anything was better than the mines."

Micah cleared her throat, wondering if Raphael had told Lily about the Queen yet.

"Was she really a ghost?" Lily asked. "Raphael said you could see her, too."

Micah nodded, treading carefully, not wanting Lily to feel foolish. "I didn't realize either when I met her. It wasn't until Raphael couldn't see her that it became obvious. I can understand why you didn't know."

"Thanks for saying that," said Lily. "Still, it's going to take me a while to believe it."

The carriage hit a particularly bumpy stretch of the road and the opening to the mines came into sight. There was a flat clearing in front of one of the rocky mountains, with a large gaping mouth carved into the side. The opening was framed in timber with nothing but blackness beyond. Several guards were standing in the clearing, dressed in black like the men they'd first encountered when they'd arrived at Feldspar. Micah scanned their faces to see if the man they'd left in the cage was amongst them, but with their beards and dirty faces, they all looked much the same. The guards called these men the Masters, although Micah could think of a few far more appropriate names.

The carriages came to a stop and the Masters bowed. Had they seen the lights in the sky all the way from up here?

"I present to you the King and Queen of Feldspar," said one of the guards in the first carriage, gesturing to Pip and Griffen.

"How may we be of service, Your Grace?" asked one of the

Masters, directing his question to Griffen. "We've uncovered a large ruby and several impressive diamonds today."

The man gestured to a table behind him where hundreds of gemstones were laid out on a black cloth. Micah had no idea of any of their names but could see green stones and red and purple and blue. They were extraordinarily pretty and despite Micah not generally being attracted to anything especially feminine, she could see the appeal of these crystals. They were a gift from nature. But all she had to do was remind herself of the misery these stones had caused and they no longer looked beautiful at all. These were stones of blood and separation and pain, better off left covered in a mountain of dirt than unearthed at the expense of the lives of so many innocent children.

"We're not interested in your gemstones," said Pip. "We're interested in the children."

"Bring them out," said Griffen. "Every single one of them. We'd like to see them."

The men glanced at one another, then seeming to decide they had no other option, they disappeared inside the dark mouth of the cave and shouting could be heard.

Pip went to Micah and reached out for her hands, gripping them tightly.

"We're getting him back for you," she said. "We're getting all of them back."

"You're going to make a wonderful Queen," said Micah. "Really you are."

"I never wanted to be Queen," said Pip. "I was pleased not to be Queen in The Bay of Laurel. But now…"

"Now you see the opportunity to do so much good," finished Micah.

"That's right," said Pip. "We're needed here. And not only can we do good for this kingdom, but we can do good for all the kingdoms. Feldspar really is the last piece of the puzzle."

"Why do you think you were chosen?" asked Micah.

"I don't think I was," said Pip.

Micah's brows shot up and she gave Pip a questioning look.

"I think it was Griffen," said Pip. "He was chosen. You know how loyal and brave he is. Plus, he has an army of Guardians he can bring here to help with the task. They haven't had a lot to do since peace spread across our kingdom. It seems they have an important job once more."

Micah nodded, seeing the sense in what Pip said. "I'm sure he wouldn't have been chosen if his true love didn't have strengths of her own."

This made Pip smile. "I hope so."

"Have you ever found it strange how one by one each of the kingdoms has been finding peace?" asked Micah, scanning the entrance to the mine where all remained quiet for now.

"It's more than that," said Pip. "Each kingdom has unlocked the secret power of one of our senses."

Micah thought about this for a moment.

"Whispering"—Micah touched her ears—"elixirs"—she put her finger on the tip of her nose— "healing"—she held out her hands—"tonics"—she pressed her finger to her lips.

"And now sight," said Pip, pointing to her eyes. "These crystals have the power of light and I suspect their true power has only just started to be unlocked."

"Do you think there's another sense we've never really thought about?" asked Micah, chewing on her bottom lip.

Pip raised her eyebrows and waited for Micah to continue.

Micah pointed to the top of her head. "The sixth sense. The sense we can't explain. The one when we just know something without understanding how or why we know it."

"Like the visions you had of Lily under the water?" Pip nodded her head slowly.

"Exactly like that."

"Maybe," said Pip, grinning. "I like that idea."

Micah opened her mouth to reply but her words fell silent when a stream of children emerged from the mouth of the mountain and poured into the clearing.

"Gabe!" called Micah, leaving Pip's side to go to the children, checking each of their faces for the one she was seeking. "Gabe!"

But there were more children than Micah could ever have imagined. Dozens became hundreds and hundreds soon became what must be a thousand. How had so many children fit inside that mountain? There must be more tunnels than the Colony in The Sands of Naar.

The children looked around, blinking in the light and shuffling on their skinny legs as they waited to see why they'd been called upon. But none of them was the one Micah was looking for. There were some who looked little more than toddlers and others who were ready to burst into adolescence. Tall children, short children, male, female, dark hair and blonde. But the thing they all had in common was that they were covered in dirt. Layers of it stuck to their faces, their hands and their hair. The whites of their eyes were flashing out from behind the filth as they crowded together, some of them holding hands, the older children caring for the younger ones.

Realizing that she was never going to find Gabe in this crowd, Micah returned to the carriage and climbed aboard, standing up and scanning the crowd, hoping that Gabe would see her and come forward.

Griffen and Pip climbed aboard the other carriage and stood, holding out their hands as a quiet fell upon the crowd.

"My name is Griffen, and this is Phillipa." Griffen looked like a giant, towering over the children as his voice bounced toward the mountain face and back. "We are your new King and Queen."

The children looked up at them with stunned faces, not daring to talk but no doubt their minds were racing. What would this change in ruler mean for them?

"I want my mama!" cried a young girl at the front of the crowd.

An older boy next to her clamped his hand over her mouth, his eyes filling with fear. Micah felt sick at the thought of what must've happened to that poor boy for him to be so afraid for a young girl who'd committed the crime of asking for her mother.

"You're all free to go home," said Pip. "Never will you have to step inside those mines again."

The children looked at each other, as if wondering what the trick was.

"What are you waiting for?" asked Griffen. "You're free! Go home to your mothers and fathers."

The children at the front took a tentative step forward. Then seeing that nothing bad was going to happen to them, they increased their pace to a walk, then a run. Soon, children were streaming away from the mines, skipping and hollering, and now Micah could see the flash of teeth joining the whites of their eyes as they broke into smiles.

"We're going home!" they called to each other.

Micah continued to scan the faces, looking for Gabe. Climbing down from the carriage, she stopped a boy by taking hold of his arm.

"Did you see a young boy arrive in the last couple of days?" she asked.

"Yes!" He pulled away from her and took a step away, not wanting to be delayed by her questions. "New boys arrive every day."

With that, he took off and Micah's shoulders slumped at the hopeless task before her. She'd never find Gabe in this sea of youth.

"Gabe!" she called, despite the hopelessness of the situation. "Gabe!"

It seemed to only take a few minutes, but soon the clearing in front of the mines was empty of children as they'd made their way onto the road, heading to the town below.

Micah imagined the reunion that was going to take place on that road when the children met up with their parents making their way up the steep incline, eager to find their sons and daughters. Sadly, this wasn't going to be a happy day for all of them and Micah's heart ached to think of all the parents who'd fail to find their loved one in the sea of hopeful faces running down that hill. It seemed she was one of them. Surely, Gabe would have seen her if he'd been here.

She looked back to the mouth of the cave and saw a shadow lurking just inside the entrance.

"Look, Micah." Azrael put her hand on her arm and pointed. "I think it's—"

"Gabe!" Micah ran toward the shadow just as a small boy stepped into the light, holding up his hands to shield his eyes.

It was him! She'd found him just when she'd thought she lost him.

He seemed to find his focus as his hand dropped and he saw Micah running to him.

Just as keen to close the gap between them, Gabe ran to her, flying into her arms when they met and allowing her to swing him around in a circle before setting him down on the ground so she could look at him.

"You came for me," he said, not ready yet to smile but unable to help the joy from seeping into his eyes.

"I promised to look after you," she said. "I'm so sorry they took you from me."

"That's okay," he said. "I shouldn't have let go of the nice lady's hand. It was my fault."

"Oh, Gabe." She buried her face in his filthy hair, planting kisses on his head. "It wasn't your fault. None of this was your fault."

"Will things get to be happy now?" he asked, wrapping his little arms around her neck.

"They will," she said, blinking through her tears. "Things will be so happy now."

JEREMIAH

THE AFTER

*J*eremiah ran his hands through his thick hair, forever grateful he was no longer a bald Whisperer trapped in the King's palace. But he'd give up every single one of his freedoms if only it meant he could have his daughter back.

Lily's disappearance had been the worst thing to ever happen to him. Worse than being tricked by the King into giving up his life to serve him. Worse than have his name, his hair, and his voice taken from him. Worse than seeing Micah trapped in the same nightmare. Worse than finding out his parents were both dead. Worse than having to fight his way to freedom by taking the lives of the people standing in his way.

Losing Lily was worse than every single one of those things put together. It ate away at him every minute of every day. Part of his grief was not knowing what'd happened to her. But most of it was from knowing she was gone. The result was the same, no matter what had brought it about. It would feel no better if he knew she was dead.

Because although that would bring him closure, it would also extinguish his hope. And hope was what kept him alive. It was what had *always* kept him alive.

As he walked through the palace grounds, his eyes scanned the open land in front of him. It was habit now. His eyes were always searching for his daughter in the hope that one day he'd see her running toward him with her arms open wide.

It wasn't just Lily he'd lost that day in the desert. He'd lost his wife, too. Rose hadn't been the same since. She'd withdrawn, not just from him, but the whole kingdom. Not in physical presence, as she still had a job to do ruling the kingdom, but there was a part of her that she no longer let anybody see, including him. It was the vulnerable part that trusted without limits. The same part of her that he'd fallen in love with.

Seeing her in the garden now, he went to her, the pull between them just as strong as ever, despite their grief.

She looked up from where she was sitting under a large willow tree and smiled—not with her eyes for they'd lost their ability to show any joy, but she smiled with her heart. She still loved him.

"My Queen," he said, sitting beside her and reaching for her hand.

"My Prince." She stroked his hand with her thumb.

"What are you thinking about?"

"She's been gone such a long time," she said.

"She has. She'd be all grown up by now."

"No, not Lily," she said. "Although she's been gone a long time, too. I was talking about Micah."

"Oh." He nodded. "She said she wasn't going to return without Lily."

"What if she never finds her?" Rose plucked at a blade of grass. "I don't want you losing your sister as well."

Jeremiah wasn't sure what to say. He didn't want to lose his sister either, but he was still glad she'd gone. If anyone could bring Lily home, it was Micah.

"I joined in with the whispering this morning," he said. "It felt different somehow. Like the words were really working their magic. I feel like Micah will return soon."

"Let's hope she's not alone."

He reached out and tucked a long strand of blonde hair behind her ear. She was still the most beautiful woman he'd ever seen. "I'm going to go down to the Valley today to see how Tallis is doing."

He didn't ask if she'd like to come with him, as she rarely left the palace. She didn't like him leaving either, always worried something would happen to him.

"Would you like some company?" she asked.

"You mean… you?"

"Of course, I mean me," she said and just for a moment, he thought he saw a flash of the old Rose in her face and his soul lit with hope.

"Do you think that…" He grimaced. Finding the right words wasn't easy. "Do you think that if Micah comes back alone—or not at all—that we can… find a way to be at peace with all of this?"

Rose shook her head. "Never can I be at peace with it. But maybe we can find a new kind of peace. Find a way to say goodbye to our sweet child, while we make space in our hearts to welcome another."

Jeremiah's eyebrows shot up. Was she saying what he thought she was? They hadn't been able to have any more children after Lily. It was like Rose's body refused to put itself at risk of such heartache again. They could have whispered for it, but Rose hadn't wanted to, saying that if it was meant to be, then it would happen.

Rose moved his hand to her stomach. "We're having a baby, Jeremiah."

Never one to usually express his feelings too openly, Jeremiah was surprised to find tears flowing down his cheeks. He was going to be a father again.

"Are you happy?" he asked her, pressing his lips lightly to hers.

She nodded as she broke away. "Of course. Although, no child will ever replace our girl."

"You don't need to say that." He kissed her lightly once more again. "I know."

"So you're pleased?" she asked.

He nodded. "I can't remember being this happy for such a long time."

"Let's go and share the news with Tallis," she said. "Then he can tell Micah as soon as she returns home."

Jeremiah got to his feet and held out his hands to help Rose up. "Shall I organize a carriage."

She shook her head as she took his hands and stood. "No, I want to walk. We can always use one to get home later if we're tired."

He wrapped his arm around Rose's shoulders as they made their way toward the palace gates. Several guards would need to accompany them, but they'd keep their distance. As much as he liked his privacy, he'd prefer his wife was kept safe.

As they got nearer to the gates, they could see the guards allowing some people to pass while they stopped to talk to Tallis. It seemed they wouldn't need to go to the Valley after all.

He looked more closely at the group of people. There was one man with white-blonde hair, a woman with dark hair, a child, and two females, both with distinctive red hair.

Rose stopped very still and Jeremiah turned to look at her, not daring to believe what he was seeing.

"Jeremiah." Rose had tears rushing down her cheeks and she blinked, not taking her eyes away from the palace gates. "Jeremiah."

He looked back at the group of people, his eyes drawn to the two red-headed women, one of whom was unquestionably Micah. And the other... so much like Micah but slightly taller and quite a bit younger.

"Jeremiah," said Rose again. "It's her."

He'd imagined this moment a billion times before and in his mind's eye, he'd run to his daughter, his feet tripping over themselves to get to her. But now that it was finally happening, he couldn't move. Instead of tripping over themselves, his feet were glued to the spot, his arm still draped around Rose as he gripped her tighter each time she said his name.

Micah looked over and saw them, pointing them out to her companions, her grin clearly visible, even from a distance.

The four of them stilled their steps, until Lily did what Jeremiah and Rose were unable to do.

She ran for them, her feet moving swiftly and her hair blowing back behind her as it caught in the wind.

Rose broke out of her trance first, taking a step toward their daughter and Jeremiah followed, his heart beating faster than he ever knew it to pump before.

Their daughter was home. Sweet Lily. Their beautiful girl. Micah had actually done it. She'd brought their daughter back to them.

With one arm still wrapped around each other, Rose and Jeremiah both reached out with their free arm and Lily flew into them. As they enclosed her in a circle of love, Jeremiah pressed his cheek to the top of Lily's head, just as he used to do when she was small, drawing in the sweet scent of his daughter, hardly able to believe he had the chance to do it again.

Fighting the urge between wanting to hold her and wanting to drink her in with his eyes, he found his arms making the decision for him as they refused to let go.

They stood there like this, their small family of three that was soon to become four.

Eventually, Lily broke the embrace, her dark eyes scanning their faces and it occurred to Jeremiah that she was just as eager to look at them. They both looked older, the stress of their situation visible in the lines on their faces, but hopefully they were still the parents she remembered.

"You're so beautiful," said Rose, reaching out to touch their daughter's face.

Lily shrugged away the compliment. "I missed you so much."

Jeremiah bit down on his tongue to stop himself from asking where she'd been all these years. There'd be plenty of time for questions later. Now was the time for reveling in the reunion, not lamenting their lost years.

"I can't believe you still wear it!" said Lily, reaching for the lucky walnut shell Jeremiah wore around his neck. "I remember this."

"It seems it's still lucky." He smiled. "It brought you home."

"Aunt Micah has one now, too," said Lily. "Only she keeps it in her pocket."

"Who's that with you?" he asked, hardly daring to believe this was really happening.

"Obviously, that's Aunt Micah," she said. "And the woman in the red cloak is Azrael. She's from The Sands of Naar. She helped Micah find me. The child is Gabe. I'll let Micah explain to you who he is. And then there's... Raphael."

There was something about the way Lily said Raphael's name, that made Jeremiah stop and pay attention. Had his little girl fallen in love? It didn't seem possible. But looking at her now, he knew that it was. She was no longer his little girl. She was undoubtedly a young woman.

"Is Raphael from wherever you've been?" asked Rose, who'd clearly picked up on the same thing he did.

"No." Lily shook her head and her cheeks went a pink color. "He's the Alchemist from Wintergreen. He also helped find me."

"Queen Jasmine's younger brother?" asked Rose. "Oh, I thought I'd seen him somewhere before."

Jeremiah supposed there could be worse matches for his daughter than the brother of a Queen, even if he was from a neighboring kingdom. And if he'd helped bring Lily home, then he already had Jeremiah's approval.

"I've been in Feldspar." Lily's voice broke with emotion. "I tried to get back to you. But I couldn't. I was in a lighthouse and—"

"Lily," said Jeremiah reaching out for her and bringing her to his chest. "We don't need to know everything right away."

Not missing the opportunity, Rose stepped closer and Jeremiah opened his arms wider to include her. He had plenty of room in his arms for both his girls. And once the baby was born, he'd have plenty of room to include one more. His heart was limitless, especially now that finally it would have the chance to heal.

THE EVERNOW

$\mathcal{G}$abrielle smiled down on the Evernow, her eyes that were once blind could now see, and what she saw lit every part of her weightless soul.

When she'd had a human body, she'd had a vision of a King's army whispering to the universe. She'd been locked away for her visions, but that hadn't stopped them from coming to her. She'd seen peace across the Evernow. She'd seen the Whisperers. She'd seen an Alchemist mixing elixirs to cure the people. She'd seen healers balancing the body's energy patterns. She'd seen tonics feeding the people with strength, and she'd seen crystals lighting the path ahead.

One by one, each kingdom had discovered its strength, just as she'd known they would. Each weak or vicious ruler had fallen, making way for the new generation who ruled with peace and kindness in their hearts.

She went now to Queen Rose in Forte Cadence, who stood with Jeremiah by her side and their newborn son cradled in her arms. A son who'd one day lead the kingdom when his older sister refused. He'd grow to be loyal like his father, wise like his mother, and brave like his Aunt Micah. A King who'd whisper for the good of all, ensuring the Valley of the Blessed remained exactly that. Blessed.

Gabrielle looked down on the Valley now and saw Micah sitting beside Tallis, with a horde of children who'd lost their parents at their feet. It'd started with Gabe, then another small boy came to live with them, then they'd been sent more children who'd run from the mines only to find their parents were no longer alive, and soon they had a home filled with children just as desperate to be loved as Micah and Tallis were to love them.

Gabrielle went to Wintergreen now, and saw Raphael in his apothecary, surrounded by tiny bottles of oils, a determined look on his face as he experimented with different combinations. The people of his kingdom depended on him, and increasingly people in other kingdoms, too. But no one more than his sister, Jasmine, and her husband, King Ari, who'd been pleased to have their brother home safely. They no longer hovered over their sons quite so much, focusing once more on their kingdom and each other. As Gabrielle looked at them now, she saw a bond that would last far beyond this lifetime.

But not everyone in the Evernow needed a mate bound to their soul. Some could find joy in other ways. There was one such soul like this in The Sands of Naar and Gabrielle went to her now. Azrael was one of the few people in the Evernow who understood the power of all the senses. One day, she'd find her joy in traveling between the kingdoms and teaching people how to unlock the power that existed in the world around them. She'd learn to trust, allow herself to be touched, and the joyful child that she'd once been would find her way out again.

The desert was a safe place to grow up now with Empress Rani and Colonel Aarow working tirelessly to implement a new way of life that made sure respect was at the core of every decision that was made, while raising their young daughters to believe the same. The population was flourishing once more and laughter could frequently be heard floating across the lawns in the Round as the timekeepers turned over the giant Orbs of Time.

Now, Gabrielle went to The Bay of Laurel, to look in on the eldest daughter of King Tate and Queen River, a girl who was eagerly learning from her grandmother, Ariel, how to make tonics. With an understanding and passion for food that had been running through her veins for generations, she'd one day step up and be a powerful herbalist, while her older brother Jacob would be crowned King, continuing to ensure that everyone had access to tonics that would keep them well.

Next, Gabrielle went east to Feldspar to look in on Queen Philippa, a woman of surprising strength who'd discovered her true destiny had been to rule a faraway kingdom. She'd set the children free, married the Guardian who'd almost lost his life saving hers, and slowly the kingdom was healing as they established a new way to live. Even the trees were coming back to life, as if having hope in the air was what they'd needed to help them grow.

Having visited all five kingdoms, there was one last soul that Gabrielle wanted to check in on. Never quite sure where to look for her, she found her standing on top of a hill with her arms outstretched as she looked to the sky. Her red hair caught the sunlight and shimmered as it flowed down her back.

If Gabrielle could talk, she'd call out Lily's name and tell her how proud she was of her. Here was a soul who'd been ripped from her home and been sent deep underground, only to be pulled back up to the surface and kept in a lighthouse, like a bird in a cage. But she was free now, a freedom that had only been possible due to a group of souls banding together and using all their powers so she could stretch her wings and fly away. That was why Lily could never rule a kingdom. Her spirit needed to be free for her soul to be happy. Instead, she'd learn to share her time between her old home of Forte Cadence and her new home of Wintergreen, where she'd immerse herself in her love for a man who'd promised to never clip her wings.

Lily turned her head and looked directly at Gabrielle, smiling broadly.

Gabrielle rained down light, watching as Lily caught it with her hands and spun around in a circle. This soul was Gabrielle's favorite soul of all, because she was the one who'd brought everyone together in just the way it was meant to be.

The Evernow was here at last. For everyone. And it was beautiful.

THE END

Ready to discover another series by Heidi Catherine?
Check out The Soulweaver now!
http://mybook.to/hcsoulweaver

THE SOULWEAVER

TWO GIRLS. TWO LIVES. ONE SOUL.

Long before her time was supposed to be up, Hannah finds herself in the Loom, the place where souls are woven into the life they must live next. Except Hannah wasn't ready to leave her old life. Nor was she ready to leave Matthew…

As the weaving takes place, Hannah fights to hold onto a part of herself, knowing it's the only way to solve the mystery of her death. Her memories are her link to the boy who tried to save her. Her last hope of ever finding him again.

In a faraway city, Lin is born. As she grows, her dreams become haunted by faces of people she's never met. Of a boy her soul aches to be with again. But she also has a life of her own. And when a stranger called Reinier seeks her out, her heart is torn in two.

Lin must decide if she follows the thread that's tugging her toward the life she shouldn't remember, or if she weaves herself a new life.

Winner of RWA's Emerald Pro Award, lovers of Outlander and The Time Traveler's Wife will be spellbound by this story of love through the ages.

Grab your copy now! http://mybook.to/hcsoulweaver

ALSO BY HEIDI CATHERINE

The Kingdoms of Evernow

Five kingdoms. Five senses.

One secret that will change them all.

The Kingdoms of Evernow (Prequel)

The Whisperers of Evernow

The Alchemists of Evernow

The Empress of Evernow

The Guardians of Evernow

The Angels of Evernow

The Soulweaver series

Two girls. Two lives. One soul.

The Soulweaver

The Truthseeker

The Shadowmaker

The Sovereign Code

Humans saved bees from extinction...

and created the deadliest threat we've seen yet

Harvest Day

Hive Mind

Queen Hunt

Venom Rising

Sting Wars

Elemental Games

Elemental powers. Deadly games. No escape.

Elemental Games

Elemental Uprising

Elemental Wars

Elemental Solution

The Thaw Chronicles

Four tests. Seven days. Nine teens.

Only the chosen shall breed.

Burning (Prequel)

Rising

Breaking

Falling

Reckoning

Extant

Exist

Exile

Expose

Tournaments of Thaw

Conquer the Thaw

The Oasis Trials

The Oasis Deception

The Last Oasis

WANT TO STAY IN TOUCH?

Heidi loves to connect with readers, so please say hello on social media, leave a review on Amazon or Goodreads, or visit her at www.heidicatherine.com

facebook.com/HeidiCatherineAuthor
instagram.com/HeidiCatherine
tiktok.com/@heidicatherineauthor
amazon.com/author/heidicatherine

ABOUT THE AUTHOR

Heidi writes fantasy and dystopian novels, which gives her a chance to escape into worlds vastly different to her own life in the burbs. While she quite enjoys killing her characters (especially the awful ones), she promises she's far better behaved in real life. Other than writing and reading, Heidi's current obsessions include watching far too much reality TV with the excuse that it's research for her books.

www.ingramcontent.com/pod-product-compliance
Lightning Source LLC
Chambersburg PA
CBHW031552240626
47153CB00002B/479